PRAISE FOR *I AM YOU*

'A stunning accomplishment'
Michael Cunningham, Pulitzer Prize-winning
author of *Day* and *The Hours*

'Victoria Redel masterfully evokes the rich period of Golden Age
Amsterdam and the centrality of its artists ... It is spellbinding,
wonderfully atmospheric, and impossible to forget'
Sarah Jessica Parker, SJP Lit

'Unforgettable picture of the erotic, entangled,
tragic nature of art itself'
Benjamin Moser, Pulitzer Prize-winning author of
The Upside-Down World: Meetings with the Dutch Masters

'[This] lush, sexy, absorbing novel ... brings to life two artists
who are inextricably linked in passion and competition'
Melissa Febos, bestselling author of *Girlhood*

'*I Am You* is earthy and fleshy and pulsates with suppressed
emotions of rage, envy and desire. A wonder of a novel'
Elizabeth Fremantle, bestselling author of *Firebrand*

'Exquisitely drawn ... a love story full of colour and light'
Stacey Halls, bestselling author of *The Familiars*

ALSO BY VICTORIA REDEL

Novels

Before Everything

The Border of Truth

Loverboy

Short Fiction

Make Me Do Things

Where the Road Bottoms Out

Poetry

Paradise

Woman Without Umbrella

Swoon

Already the World

I AM
YOU

Victoria Redel has written four books of poetry, most recently *Paradise*; her last novel, *Before Everything*, was published in 2017. Her short stories, poetry and essays have appeared in *Granta*, *The New York Times*, *Los Angeles Times*, *BOMB*, *One Story*, *Salmagundi*, *O*, and *NOON* among many others.

She has received fellowships from the Guggenheim Foundation, The National Endowment for the Arts and the Fine Arts Work Center. She is a professor in the graduate and undergraduate creative writing programs at Sarah Lawrence College and lives in New York City.

I AM YOU

A NOVEL

Victoria Redel

FIREFINCH

First published in the UK by Firefinch Publishing Ltd
21 Lombard Street
London, EC3V 9AH
England

First published in Hardback in 2026

Hardback ISBN 978-1-9181-0700-5
Trade paperback ISBN: 978-1-9181-0707-4
Paperback ISBN: 978-1-9181-0714-2

Also available as an ebook and an audiobook

All rights reserved. No part of this publication may be reproduced, stored in a retrieval system, or transmitted in any form or by any means, without the prior permission in writing of the publisher, nor be otherwise circulated in any form of binding or cover other than that in which it is published and without a similar condition including this condition being imposed on the subsequent purchaser.

British Library Cataloguing-in-Publication Data:

A catalogue record for this book is available from the British Library.

Design by Neuwirth & Associates, Inc. this edition by Envy Design Ltd
Printed in the UK by CPI Group (UK) Ltd, Croydon CR0 4YY

1 3 5 7 9 10 8 6 4 2

© Text copyright Victoria Redel 2025

The right of Victoria Redel to be identified as the author of this work has been asserted by her in accordance with the Copyright, Designs and Patents Act 1988.

Extract from *Amsterdam* on page 9 © Russell Shorto, 2013. Reproduced with permission of the Licensor through PLSclear

This is a work of fiction. Names, places, events and incidents are either the products of the author's imagination or used fictitiously. Any resemblance to actual persons, living or dead, or actual events is purely coincidental.

Every reasonable effort has been made to trace copyright-holders of material reproduced in this book, but if any have been inadvertently overlooked the publishers would be glad to hear from them.

Our authorised representative in the EU for product safety is Easy Access Systems Europe, Mustamäe tee 50, 10621 Tallinn, Estonia gpsr.requests@easproject.com

www.firefinchpublishing.com

This book is dedicated to the memory of my mother, Natalie Soltanitzky Redel, who brought art and dance into my life.

And for B. V. D., who walked me up the Prinsengracht.

In 2019, reading Russell Shorto's wonderful book *Amsterdam*, I came upon the following: "Maria van Oosterwijk was that rare thing: a highly successful woman artist. . . . The frustration is that so little is known about her life, other than that she started her career in Delft and ended it in Amsterdam. The lack of information may have to do with her sex: as a woman, she was not allowed to join the painters' guild." I was intrigued and began poking around for what could be found. Indeed, as I learned about Maria van Oosterwijck and her servant/assistant Geertje Pieters Wyntges, I found that even the scant supposed facts of their lives are contradicted—down to alternative spellings of their names. As a fiction writer, this allowed me enormous freedom imagining the lives of two women painters in the seventeenth-century Dutch Golden Age. This is a novel and not a work of nonfiction, and among the many liberties taken in the course of shaping the narrative, I've bent and compressed time, most notably pushing both women's births forward by more than ten years.

Tis that she, yet a maiden bore a maiden, to wit a maid,

And cast work-cloth, broom, and heart aside.

The Oosterwijck maid was nurtured so quick and so well

That 'tis Oosterwijck's brush alone her can quell,

Think ye, my witty friend it is a great mistake,

To call Geertje Pieters Geertruyd van Oosterwijck?

Oosterwijck's teaching has guided her fate,

She is her own print;

Or clearer to state,

She is Oosterwijck's moon; so give her such shine,

Think what light must be in the Sun to give off a glare so fine.

CONSTANTIJN HUYGENS
1679 poem to Willem van Heemskerck

BOOK I

ONE
1653, Voorburg

I WAS SHY OF EIGHT WHEN I was put out to work. The family that took me in was in need of a boy and so it was a boy I became. Hair sheared, last name twisted to my first, I was known as Pieter. Pieter Wyntges. My two family names stacked as one.

It was a long time before I was once again Gerta.

I was happy to be Pieter. I fetched and carried, split wood, and rubbed dirty, splintered hands along my woolen pants. I scurried up to the roof to repair tiles. I did my share of slaughter. From the other workers, I learned a fast mouth and was unafraid to use a boy's bristled tongue.

Given a bed I didn't have to share with two sisters, my own yellow coverlet embroidered with lilies, sweet and savory cakes, bowls of stewed meat—second helpings without even asking—already my life was much better. Hunger makes a selfish grabber of the sweetest child. And the promise of a child's belly full will make it easy to turn a daughter to a boy and a rampant liar of even the kindest parent.

A full belly is no small thing. I didn't for a moment miss the girl I'd been or imagine the woman I might become.

I didn't cry once for my mother.

NO DOUBT YOU'VE HEARD about the glorious time we lived in, where every day some porcine gentleman trumpeted great new wealth. But it's not only the men of wealth. The fishmonger, the boatman, the tile maker, even a family servant like myself, we may not have been the owners of the East India Company, still we laced our wine with cinnamon and nutmeg. We learned to talk with a slick merchant's tongue and a philosopher's loft. We were all bestowed with the blessing of those fat years. No doubt the pigs and cattle that roamed the fetid canal streets also heard that they were fatter and luckier pigs and cattle than any before.

Everything wonderful came through our Dutch ports. A crowded harbor of ships arrived with new goods every day. Silk and lace finer than any slipped through our fingers. We'd not known what we'd lacked till we touched gold and purple threads or wiped the sticky juice of a pineapple from our lips. Then it became our standard. Of course, we've all of us seen the rare tulips. Even the butcher, the street sweeper felt feverish watching the auctions. A golden age, we were. We, in this rare moment of peace and health, didn't feel shame to be announced lucky. We remembered war. We remembered plague marks on our doors. And knew they would return.

AT FOURTEEN Maria hardly noticed me. Why would she? I was seven, half her years. My days were outside, my nights bunked in a side shed close to the animals, though like the other servant, Anke,

I ate meals at the family table. Unlike bossy Anke, who, slowed by a lame hip, busied through the day with more opinion than work, I kept to tasks and had little to say. I mostly spoke with the chickens and the rabbits. I knew to coo and talk a rabbit quiet in my hands. Or, hearing a hen's roost cackle, knew where to find a warm egg and, before she pecked my fingers sore, knew to give her my own broody growl. People were the mystery, so it was the people I watched.

Maria was the one to notice. Her particular words. The varieties of her laughter. The concentration of her fingers as she skimmed or flicked the board with a paintbrush. The slight purse of her lips while she painted. The hairs that laced her forehead. The determined *swiff* of her dress as she entered a room. Her fingers lifting a pale green egg—one I had collected!—from the bowl, turning it slowly, and, with precision, letting it roll on the wood table until it balanced half in, half out of a slice of sunlight. More than once, when she believed herself alone, I watched her waste a fresh egg, cracking it in her hands, pulling the runny yolk like taffy.

"Beautiful," she said to no one, as it seeped through her fingers and glazed her narrow wrist.

I HELD THE RABBIT TIGHT. Its nose twitched in the crook of my arm. I petted and scratched the bony skull, pulled the long ears till they relaxed down its back.

"Oh, pretty young friend," I said, "what a warm day." It wasn't a lie. Though we'd suffered a first frost, I stood in the open doors of the hutch and tipped my face into the early winter sun. Heat prickled my neck. I'd never lie to a rabbit. Especially one I've known since it was a furless kit. I've watched others pin a rabbit under a broomstick and, in a single movement, lift it by the hind legs to snap the neck. It's certain and fast. But I've only to imagine my neck trapped under a stick to know I could never do that. Instead, I eased my right hand to my trousers. "Pretty little lady, you'll feed us pretty stew," I sang, keeping the wood mallet loose at my side. I continued singing, "Pretty, pretty, stew," and the third or fourth time, I yielded a sharp blow to its skull. It's important that death be swift and easy, or the meat goes stringy. Then, after hanging the rabbit by its hind legs on two nails, with a quick blade I gutted it, saved the head to feed the yard pup, and let the rest bleed out into the bucket. I kept up a chatter. "The pup loves your head, the garden your blood, and we all thank you for the supper stew," I chanted. Then I flipped the rabbit and, with few cuts, slipped free the skin and sang, "And so will the neck warmed by your fur."

"Well, Pieter, that's quite a song."

I spun, blade and fur in my bloody hands. There was Maria leaning in the door with paper and a stick of charcoal.

"Turn back," she insisted. "Please, Pieter, turn."

For a second time, my name! I turned.

"Keep at it. Yes, keep singing, too. But step to the side of the bucket so I can render the bloodstream." *Boy skinning rabbit. Boy sharpening knife. Boy carrying wood.* Like that, sketch by sketch, Maria began to claim me.

No longer could I watch her; now she watched me. She sat in the upstairs window, charcoal in hand while I kept at my chores. She set up in the courtyard as I raked and tended the herb garden. Once I woke in the shed and found her squatting close to my pallet. "You were dreaming, Pieter," she announced. I quickly pulled the coverlet tight, careful to keep the girl-child of me unseen.

I couldn't imagine why she drew me. I was hardly anyone. When she left her sketchbook open on the table, I snuck over to look. It seemed impossible, how, with a piece of charcoal not much different from what remained in the fireplace, she'd conjured the dense velvety layers of a rose whose scent seemed to rise from the paper. I put my finger to the drawing and was surprised when it came away sooty. I turned the pages. And there, among precise drawings of grapes and vines and flowers, was page after page she'd sketched of my form.

My first inclination was to slam shut the book. Or better still, shear from the sketchbook every drawing of me. To be so ruthlessly observed. With each drawing, she'd come closer to discovering my deceit. I had everything to lose. Day to day, I never gave it a bother. In muggy heat, my ribby chest was bare, same as other boys. What was there to hide? Just the slim cut between my legs. And it had been easy enough to learn to do my business standing. At first I'd fashioned a tin cup and poke spout, but that was bothersome, and soon enough I'd mastered pulling my lips apart and pressing the bit of me so its stream had an arc. I'd learned to taper without a single lingering drip.

My fear aside, what shook me most looking at her drawings was to see my face. How, on a thin piece of vellum, she'd captured the feelings that passed like weather through me. Feelings I recognized only by looking at her sketchbook. The knit scowl of concentration as I rolled out dough. The frustration as my tooth caught and chewed my lip. Or standing before neat rows of stacked split wood, the wind of satisfaction that lifted one corner of my mouth into a crooked smile. And more clearly in her drawing than I could make out in the front room's mirror was the slight scar on my chin where I'd slipped and cut myself on a roof tile. I ran my finger against the jagged pucker of skin. She'd seen that. She'd looked at my face as closely as I looked for signs of bugs or black spots on leaves or cankers on the stems of climbing roses. I was not any working boy in these drawings. I was myself, Pieter.

Yet, despite my fear, despite not wanting to be closely watched, I craved her attention. That I was frightened and excited all at once unsettled me. That I wanted at the same moment to be invisible and to have her see me unsettled me. Who wouldn't want to be noticed by Maria? Even if I didn't believe myself worthy of her notice.

One morning I looked up from paddling the butter churn and said, "Why?"

She was seated on a stool, her book filled with quick drawings of hands, the curve of a neck and shoulders, the weighted stance of feet, all mine. I hadn't planned on asking the question. I hardly had the right. But it felt crucial somehow and that made me bold. "Why draw me," I repeated, "when there's your father, sister, everyone else?"

The scratch of charcoal stopped. The room quiet except for the steady rhythm of my butter paddle. "I don't know." She sounded as tentative as me, which made me even more frightened that I'd overstepped. "You're always in motion. I like that," she continued. And after more silence added, "I don't know. You're so diligent and skilled. I like to look at you." I felt her gathering to say something more, but Anke waddled into the kitchen scolding that butter shouldn't take a whole lazy day and I'd best hurry the paddle or I'd find myself scouring floors when the moon rose.

The next day, splitting wood, I tried to hold off from looking up to see if Maria was nearby, but as I hefted the axe I snuck a glance, and seeing her drawing at the garden table, I gave an extra arch to my back. And, at the height of the axe's swing, I confess, I paused like a statue before stepping in to slam the blade through the log.

BOY FEEDING PIGS or, worse, *Boy tossing the family's waste* was strange business for a woman artist, though that claim—woman artist—was strange enough alone. The rendering of botanicals was permissible woman's art and, to be certain, Maria was far along in the study of still-life flower painting that she'd begun years before. But what she loved most of all was what was never allowed for a woman. To draw the human body in motion. Why Maria filled sketchbooks with drawings of me was simpler than I understood at that time. In the courtyard, in the kitchen, at the washbasin, on the floor scrubbing, I was the body most available.

IT WAS EARLY EVENING. I was clearing the supper table. Maria's father, the minister, held my narrow shoulders. "She's been relieved," he said. I must have looked confused because he added, "Your mother. She's gone forward. There'll be no mourning." Lifting a hand, he gestured for me to finish stacking the dishes.

Later, I hid in the stalls, straw sheeted over me like a cape. I turned to the back wall; my forehead rasped against raw wood. Insistent sounds ushered from me as if from a trapped animal. It had been brief; that was what the minister said of the fever that had wrestled through her. *A good thing, that* were the final words the minister offered. But to me that brevity said something difficult I didn't quite understand. That maybe her will was too slight. Or that if I'd been there, I might have wrestled death's stern hold from her. I cried for that, and then I cried for how little I could remember. In my memory, I saw her fingers dusted with flour. And remembered an extra scallop of butter she'd spooned into my mouth. I remembered a blue bowl on the table and her ragged breaths as she'd gathered shards into her apron after the bowl shattered on the floor. I cried because I couldn't remember if she'd mended it. Or if there had ever been a new bowl on the table. I tried to recall her face lifted when, after days of damp spitting rain, the sun had finally broken through the steely clouds. Then I cried because though I remembered her dark hair pulled back into a low knot and the angular outline of her face, I couldn't fill in the rest. I remembered her only in pieces. Hands. The slope of her shoulders. Like the fragments of the broken bowl—I couldn't fit her together.

And finally, I cried because at best I'd have her as a ribbon of memory. These years later I know that a ribbon of memory, even a tendril, is no small thing. But that day, when at last I'd rubbed away the final smear of tears, I brushed off what bits of straw clung to my shirt, and resolved to toughen like a tree sealing at the site of a severed limb. As I stood and turned, there was Maria in the doorway with her tablet. When I slid past her, I saw a drawing of my boots poking out from a shaggy bulk of straw. The heap she'd sketched was alive with the motion of my grief.

When I learned of my father's and my little sisters' deaths just a month later, I felt the ready pounce of Maria all day. With delight she'd no doubt written below a new drawing: *Study of an Orphan Boy*. I refused to give Maria any of my tears. When sadness rose in my throat, I repeated the minister's instruction: *There'll be no mourning*. I kept about my work and, even if I had little hunger, gladly took a second helping at the family meal.

"HE SAYS ALL HIS FINEST pigment comes from Aleppo," Maria announced, rushing home breathless, setting stoppered ink on the table by the open window, positioning the bottle as if it alone were a work of art. Without bothering to take off her cloak, she propped against her knee a drawing board with a paper clipped to it. She dipped her pen as if the apothecary had presented her with a vial of liquid gold.

Some weeks it was the apothecary, some weeks the grocer, but whoever claimed a new shipment of pigment, Maria was a twist of skirt, off to that shop, impatient to be the first to buy that which had arrived from a distant shore.

"The consistency of ink from Aleppo is the smoothest he's ever received," she called out the window, as if I'd time in my day to care about what the apothecary claimed. I pretended not to notice her as she followed me about the garden with her sketchbook.

"Pieter, not so fast," she ordered as I hung the freshly washed bedsheets up in the yard.

I tucked myself behind the damp sheets. I didn't know where Aleppo was, but I hated the happiness the shopkeeper gave Maria with his refined pigments. I hated Aleppo. Hated how she rolled her tongue over the *l* of it, then slowed to push air over the final *po*. When she called for me to come to one side of the laundry line so that she might catch a leg or arm in motion, I pretended I hadn't heard.

That night I dreamed of my mother. I'd barely thought of her in the year since her death. Here she was, fixing willow bark tea as she had done to keep our chests clear in the damp winter months or when we were fidgety and couldn't sleep. In the dream we weren't in our home, rather in a low boat on an unknown canal. My mother touched my head as I drank the tea. Her touch was gentler and less hurried than any I remembered from those first years. Her voice tenderer too, saying, "Look around. Right here, Gerta. Be her Aleppo."

I WOKE EARLY AND BEGAN. Like any servant, I was no stranger to the making of dyes for cloth. Just look at the nut-brown of my work shirt and breeches, and you'd see I didn't have to go around the world to find rich saturated dyes. I pulverized the rotting hulls of black walnuts, cutting out the nutmeat and soaking the husks in a bucket of water. For two days the bucket heated in the sun. Then I boiled them for three hours, reducing the liquid to a sooty sludge. Straining the liquid through cloth and cooking it a second time, I added a rusty nail yanked from a beam in the shed. Then, I filtered the second boil through a tuft of matted lamb's wool into a bottle, adding a final drop of thyme oil. Surely she'd recognize that my deep brown rivaled any she'd bought.

I left a neat bottle of walnut ink on her drawing table. Maria said nothing. Did not so much as acknowledge the bottle I'd carefully finished by wrapping a strand of fresh thyme at its throat. I too stayed quiet. And busy. With the added winter preparations, there was no shortage of chores. Still every time I looked up, her pen steadily dipped into my walnut ink. A cart full of apples. The sheep in their stall. The neighbor threshing wheat. Her sister pickling vegetables. And, of course, me.

Soon I left on her desk an ink from alder cones cooked with willow bark and chimney soot. And then one from oak galls soaked and boiled in vinegar. Lampblack, mahogany, pewter—in time I gave Maria darks of every range. I gave her inks of the deepest black and ones as pale as the coat of a newborn fawn. I made purple ink from lichen, and a buttery yellow steeped from marigolds. Each ink was finished with a drop of thyme oil, and around the neck of each small bottle was wrapped a strand of fresh thyme. With each new ink, I shaped a reed pen whose mark had a different thickness. When word arrived of great shipments, Maria no longer bothered to rush to town.

I was polishing copper one morning, all the pitchers and pots arranged on the table, when Maria broke the silence. "In your next preparation of ink, I'd prefer more depth in the darkest hue," she said from her worktable.

I nodded but didn't look up and bit at the inside of my mouth to keep from smiling.

I labored to sharpen my recipes, to give her consistency in hues. However, let me say, if it's certainty you desire, the business of ink will make you crazy. Best to learn to make do with what you have and accept error. Once I didn't have horse piss and used my own, though I knew the acid didn't have an equal bite. Still, I mixed it with alum and tartar, then added the leaves of buckthorn I'd strained, a pinch of turmeric, and three ounces of realgar, boiled it all twice then twice again hoping for a good rich brown and got at best a sour yellow. It made me remember old stories I'd heard about the dyer's art, how it relied on the magic of women, and how the presence of even a single boy could make it go afoul. You can imagine I had a good laugh tossing out that weak ink.

It made me proud when artists visited the house—as they frequently did—and I heard their comments. Such brilliance! Such luminosity! Lifting the various bottles to the light, shifting the glass to gauge viscosity, they implored Maria to divulge the name of her remarkable ink maker.

"Beg all you want, but aren't the best recipes secret?" Maria said as they tried to guess each ink's exotic origin. Then Maria beckoned me to refill the guests' tumblers. "Thank you so much, Pieter," she said with a wink.

MANY ARTISTS VISITED her father's house, but they couldn't disguise that their interest in Maria was ultimately more domestic than artistic. Each praised her skilled hand, her confident and expressive management of ink and paint, then quickly slanted the conversation to the few notable artists who were wives of painters. Pay attention, the men lectured Maria, the good fortune and success these women achieve is bound to their esteemed husbands. Each man gently counseled Maria, as though he had no personal stake in her future and was simply reminding her that without a father or husband in the Guild of Saint Luke, there was meager chance Maria would do much more than hang her still lifes in her own house.

"Just imagine," Maria said, "how valuable the walls of my home will be one day."

"This is not a joke, if you hope to be a serious painter," the men corrected, "and under the proper marital circumstance, that should be possible for you."

When a gentleman artist had completely exhausted pretending that his only concern was Maria's best future, he'd describe the wealth of his own workshop, the number of paying apprentices, the various commissions, and avid collectors who'd shown interest in recent paintings.

"I'm delighted to hear of your success," she'd say in a voice of such refined sincerity that, without question, each man left her father's house hopeful that he'd convinced Maria of his worth as a husband.

Once the door closed, before the man's boot had barely cleared the last step, any whiff of sincerity evaporated as Maria stormed through the house impersonating whichever visitor was so scarcely gone that his musk still lingered in the room. This was the moment of each afternoon I waited for.

"In our wedding bed, after you've yielded your maidenhood, I'll instruct you on how I paint the rose, Maria," she thundered, doddering about, fattened by pillows jammed under her skirt. "And do you bake, Maria? And are you economical, Maria?" She shoved a biscuit in her mouth, flinging crumbs, letting them flake down her chin and spill into her bodice. Then with great buffoonery she patted her stuffed belly, took a swig of beer, and finished her skit with a rope of belches.

"Maria!" Her father laughed despite his practical concern. As strict a man as the minister was, he was a fool for his daughter and could barely pretend to muster severity or moral indignation at Maria's impressive if immodest performance.

"Maria, you really should consider—" her father began again, but she was quick to cut him off.

"Maria," she said, mimicking the visitor's tenor as she wrapped her arms around her father. "It's a pity your father is only a minister. You have unusual talent, Maria, but not important connections."

Eventually, having regained his composure, her father kissed the top of Maria's head and instructed, "If there's a husband who advances your life, that is not wrong. A prominent name or workshop is a kind of caring. And caring for one another is what makes the greatest wealth in a marriage."

"I'll make my own wealth, Father, and happily skip the marriage," Maria said as she pulled the pillows from under her skirt.

SOME WILL CLAIM the impetuous woman I describe can't be the same Maria van Oosterwijck whose every canvas was imbued with the grace of religious commitment. As if they actually believed her still lifes were not paintings of flowers but symbols—every pink carnation a hope for resurrection, every rose a portrait of the Blessed Virgin. And surely that was Christ on each bending blade of wheat! I loved best the merchant hypocrites who commissioned her paintings, requesting sumptuous tables laden with lobsters and grapes, gleaming silver tureens, and whole sets of fine china—all that luster a celebration of their wealth. Then they required her to add a skull and an hourglass to pretend they struggled between the sin of gluttony and earthly delight. Some will claim the Maria I describe isn't the Maria of chastity and virtue they recognize, and they'll drag out the portrait of her made by her dear, droll friend Vaillant and point to the Bible in her lap. Her gray-green eyes brimmed with seemingly reverent tears. There will be mention of how, after her beloved sister died, she nobly took on the costs of her orphan nephew. *That* Maria never made a mockery of others! Or there are men and women who will, with a nod to the recklessness of their own youth, chuckle at how a well-read, earnest daughter such as Maria took to heart our age's freedoms of thought until she matured into womanly piety. Let it be said, she wasn't the first young woman who learned that keeping her gaze fixed heavenward and declaring herself resolute to God was one way to avoid life as a broodmare.

"Who really cares, Pieter," I hear Maria snap. "Let them look at my bunch of violets as proof of my chastity. Let them stomp their polished shoes till they wear holes in each sole. Just as long as they dig into their stuffed purses and hand over gold."

THEN, LIKE THAT, Maria left home for Leiden to study flower painting. For two years, she'd briefly visit home, then leave again. I did my chores waiting for the next time she'd walk through the door.

I tried to imagine her in Leiden. To imagine the city. But other than what I'd gleaned from our merchants, that the best broadcloth, wool, and serge offered in our shops came from Leiden, it might have been as far away as Aleppo. Though I knew Leiden was no great distance from where I woke each morning, at ten years old the farthest I'd traveled was from my home in Delft to Maria's home in Voorburg. And just as I'd resented Aleppo for the ink Maria cherished, I resented Leiden for her leaving us behind in Voorburg.

With her gone, whatever happened in that house was mostly nothing to remember.

Except for this: I missed being sketched.

Yes, I hadn't wanted to be her specimen of study. It had confused me to be seen. The wanting of it. And not wanting of it. But with her gone, I yearned to be drawn as I scrubbed the floor, as I pulled feathers from a duck. I longed for the discomfort, that pleasant but curious ache that flashed up my legs when I turned from the sink to find Maria watching. I felt I was less myself when she was not watching me. Without her, chores were chores. My days, simply days.

And it wasn't just me. The whole house dulled in her absence. We were like an audience waiting for the singer to sweep onto stage and, with a single note, remind us how extraordinary the human voice can be. At first hoping to replace her wit, her brother and sister wrote and performed silly plays about village life, though they soon grew bored of themselves and spent evenings recalling Maria's more clever impersonations. The minister still held forth at the table, but without Maria to lead her siblings in debate, the challenges were tepid and even the minister seemed less convinced by his own beliefs. We all waited for each letter sent home. They were read over and over until I could recite them, and soon enough I'd hear her colorful stories of Leiden quoted by neighbors and merchants in the shops.

I lined new vials of ink and pens on her desk. Each a prayer that she would return soon.

. . .

ONE DAY AT THE FAMILY MEAL, Maria, home on a visit, said, "Pieter, it's time you learned to wear a skirt. And to speak as a girl does."

Like that, with a full spoon of pea stew in my hands, the girl of me was revealed. Hadn't I known it would happen? That all that looking at me meant danger. Still, I was stunned. True, by then my chest had begun to itch, and at night in the dark, I rubbed down the puffy rise of nipples. But the cocky boy I'd become thought I'd outsmart all changes. When rubbing didn't keep me from growing, I bound my chest, winding one cotton twice tightly, followed by a second thicker bandage so my shirt buttoned flat. On humid days the stiff band across my ribs made a full breath hard to catch while I worked outside. My skin chafed. I worried that if I unbound myself at night, by morning I'd have the swollen udders of a goat. Having washed the family's clothes and cared for animals in their rut, I knew to expect my own blood. When at eleven my time came, I rinsed the darkened cloths and hid them under linens on the line to dry.

I lifted the spoon to my mouth. My face flushed hot. The sludge of peas thickened in my mouth, impossible to swallow. What would happen now? I'd be tossed from the minister's house. Without parents, there was nowhere. I had no home. How had I not prepared for this moment? If I choked right there at the table, it'd be best.

I pinched my leg. Hard. What a fool. Of course she'd seen. She'd probably always known. I wanted to stand from the table. To run to the shed. Hide behind the hutches. Bury myself under straw in the sheep pen.

Instead, I kept to the stew, forced down bite after bite. A fly landed on the tablecloth, its filmy wings shuddering. Outside a sharp call-and-response of crows. Carts passed on the road. The neighbor's mule whinnied as it did each hour. Fog pressed at the window. It seemed if I listened hard enough, I'd hear the steady threshing of fields on the edge of town. The day was unexceptional; if I was lucky, no one was paying attention.

But Maria continued, "I'll be going to Utrecht and need a maid. Pieter, you'll come with me."

A clump of stew rose back up into my mouth and I coughed. The old servant, Anke, knocked me in the side with her elbow and when I looked up, the minister, his wife, Maria's brother, her sister, and, of course, Anke, were all staring at me, their spoons held at various heights and fullness.

"Pieter?" the minister said.

I swallowed the wedge of food back down, scraped my spoon along the bottom of the bowl where the dried peas and onions stuck to the ceramic, then slid my finger along the bowl to collect the bits onto my spoon. I didn't know where I'd go or what I'd eat next; I wasn't wasting any food. I'd been an idiot to ever let myself become so comfortable as to think any day a drudge.

"Pieter?" he repeated.

"Yes, sir," I said, and felt my eyes fill. I pinched my leg again to pull down the pain. In a rush I wanted to promise that I wasn't a liar, that I was the good child who'd only done what my mother and father had asked of me. Hadn't I served well? Kept the flue clean? Shod the two horses to save the cost of a farrier? I looked at him, keeping my face composed despite the tears that had begun to fall onto the table.

"Will you go with Maria?"

"I'll need a maid," Maria burst in. "Of course, she'll come with me."

"Maria," her father scolded, "you must allow Pieter to say yes or to say no. Well, Pieter, what will you choose?"

I could hardly comprehend that I was being asked. The fly on the table, the neighbor's hawing mule, the hens with their eggs—they didn't make choices. How did one even make a choice? I felt ill-equipped. I ate as the family ate and slept on the bed I was given. I was sent to the shops with a strict list. Gathered eggs because there were eggs to be gathered.

I looked at Maria, her fingers picking at the lace on her sleeve. All those pages and pages of my hands, my face. All that looking. When had she known? From the first drawing? She pulled at a stray thread, refused to meet my eyes. It occurred to me that she was afraid of my answer. That it mattered.

In the two years she'd been in Leiden, I'd grown to hate the paltry circumference of my life. I knew every wheelbarrow and carriage that passed by the house. The paths I took each day, each dull, familiar face I nodded to made me lonely for the excitement Maria stirred. She was going away again. And she wanted me to go with her.

"Yes," I said so quietly that the minister asked me to repeat myself. "Yes, sir," I said, a touch too loud so that Anke snorted and gave me another knock in the ribs.

"Yes, what?" the minister asked, waving his spoon from side to side.

"Yes," I said. "I'll go."

Maria smiled.

"Well, that's settled," her father said, as simply as if I'd agreed to run an errand to the baker's shop. He dipped his spoon into his bowl. The others followed. Soon the table conversation turned to the week's uncommon heat. Anke brushed the fly off the table. Outside the neighbor's wife shouted, "Enough," and the gelded mule quieted. Maybe the biggest surprise of that meal was that for the others it hardly mattered. Boy or girl, a servant was a servant.

"Here's my old skirt and bodice," Maria said, pushing a bundle of folded linen into my hands after the midday meal. I'd cleaned the table and finished drying the bowls.

"What would you have me do with them?" I stood at the washbasin looking at the print of my wet fingers on the cloth. Did she want the clothes laundered or, as I had often done under Anke's strict instruction, the fabric rendered for other garments?

Maria tossed back her head, her ringlets bouncing. "Hurry and try them," she said. "Then you'll see what needs repair."

It took me some moments to realize I was meant to put on her clothes. And worse, that she meant for me to do so right there, with the kitchen curtains drawn wide and her eyes fixed on me.

"I'm to bring in the laundry before the rain," I countered, hoping to change in the shed and return to the house fully dressed.

"You'd be waiting till tomorrow." She pointed to the sun outdoors. It irked me, her making a game of this. "You understand, I can't take a boy with me when I leave for Utrecht." She took off my cap and tousled my cropped hair. Her voice softened. "Poor Pieter. Will you be now the maid? What's your given name? Ilse? Johanna?" Maria teased, "Come, Fredrika." She bobbed with mischief. "Let's make a proper girl of you."

"I'm Pieter." My voice wrinkled with embarrassment. I wouldn't say the other name. When was the last time I'd been called Gerta? Or thought myself her? From somewhere rose the last memory of my mother, her hands cupping my chin, her whisper rough against my cheek. "You'll always be my Gerta though we send you out as Pieter."

I wanted to refuse Maria. To run to the minister's study and tell him I'd misspoken at supper. I wouldn't go to Utrecht. I wanted to stay here, in his house. That I was Pieter. But had I ever said no? Was saying no anything I was allowed? Especially uttering no to Maria, when no one in the family dared refuse her.

"Gerta," I said and turned toward the rack of pans that hung from the wall. I unknotted the rope that cinched my pants. Even with my back turned, I felt her appraisal. How awkward to be rid of breeches, to step bare-assed into a linen skirt, one that had once circled Maria's waist.

"Well, Gerta, there's still more narrow to you than hip." She hiked the skirt from where it slung low, threatening to fall off. Her fingers folded and pleated, pinning tight the extra cloth. "Not to worry, Gerta, you'll fill out in good time."

Everything she said was a puzzle. Fill out? In time? And now calling me Gerta, this name I barely recognized, and how amused she sounded each time she said it.

I unknotted the tie I'd fashioned to fix the muslin cloth that wrapped my chest. With one hand I unwound the crude bind while I covered myself with the other. I snatched up the red bodice. In a scramble to get it on, I was soon stuck. My face trapped inside the boned corset. My hands thrashed above my head as I tried to wrangle the stiff fabric down. The more I thrashed, the tighter the contraption cinched around my head.

"Shall I help?" Maria laughed. Without waiting for a reply she tugged the bodice into place with two sharp yanks. "That's your first lesson that it's not all poetry and fancy embroidery, the business of being a lady." Then she pulled, snugging the ribbon lacing so tight I bit my lip to keep from yelping as the boning crushed my ribs. Looking down, what I saw was horrifying. Everything I'd worked to keep pressed flat was plumped and swollen over the fabric. When she spun me to face her, I curved my shoulders to hide the fullness. I squeezed closed my eyes. If I couldn't see, I couldn't be seen.

"Open those eyes. Soon enough you'll learn what a jiggle of flesh can get you in the world." She flicked a finger under my chin and pressed her hand against my shoulders, prodding me to stand erect. Then she fitted a bonnet cap over my coarsely mowed hair and tied a bow below my chin. "This will help till your hair grows longer," she said, standing back to regard me. "Though you're a bit bony, I can't say I'm surprised that you make a pretty girl."

Heat surged through me. I swayed and widened my stance to keep balance. Just this morning I'd been an ordinary lanky boy.

"Pieter, you can't stand that way anymore if you're to be my Gerta. You'll have to learn how to set your feet."

I shuffled from one foot to the other. How else there was to stand?

"Don't let it drop," she commanded, shoving a cream pitcher between my thighs. "Squeeze your legs, not your face." She clearly thought it all great entertainment. "Now try to walk keeping the face placid."

I took tiny steps, the pitcher clamped between my legs. When I ventured a more natural stride, it slipped, and I had to grab the pitcher before it tumbled to the floor. I tottered about the kitchen while Maria gleefully shouted, "Try to look less miserable as my maid and a bit more petite." I was miserable. If being a girl meant becoming petite, wearing heavy skirts, and falling over your own feet as you walked, I felt sorry for girls. Then I'd remember I was a girl and that it wasn't only miserable, it was impractical. I was used to the easy lope of moving through the world as a boy, scrambling to a roof in work pants, running in and out of market crowds. I loved the rough tussle with other boys in the street. So much was easier in the body of a boy.

"Have you been to Utrecht?" Before I could even shake my head, she said, "I forget you've not been anywhere." It stung to have her call it out. "You've been a good boy in this house," she continued, as if all the days I'd lived until this moment had been a child's game of pretend or a skit performed by traveling theaters when they came through the city. "You were a good boy, Pieter, but when Gerta comes to Utrecht, a whole new future will unfold for you."

And then, for the second time that day, I was offered something extraordinary. First the minister had given me the chance to choose. Now I was being told I'd have a future of my own. Call it strange, but until I stood in the kitchen in my ill-fitting new attire, I'd never imagined one. There were seasons and tasks tied to seasons. There were floods in spring and later, readying the garden for planting. When I gathered a basket brimming with cabbage, it was because the cabbage was ready to harvest. But here, for the first time, was the possibility that something altogether unknown and unimagined might happen in my own life. By choosing to accompany Maria to Utrecht, something had been set in motion. With that, I grabbed the sides of the skirt and made a shabby curtsy.

OVER THE NEXT WEEKS Maria schooled me. How to walk. How to talk. How to whiten my face with rice powder. How to stain my lips. Even the porridge spoon was to be managed in an odd new way. When eating a plate of meat, she instructed that I was to use two fingers and only lick the grease up to the two knuckles.

"But look," I said, and held out my hand, every finger sticky with fat.

"Exactly," Maria said. "You'll have to be nimbler."

As far as I could tell, becoming Gerta was all discomfort. The weighty skirts. The corset. But more severe than the pinch of the corset was the loss of the words Maria insisted must be clipped from my tongue, words forbidden in the mouth of a woman. For one who mostly kept silent, that seemed almost all my words.

"Too crude," Maria responded after my turn at the baker's counter to buy loaves of bread.

"But that's how it's done," I said.

"How Pieter did. Not how Gerta will," she scolded, impatient for me to try again.

I couldn't imagine what other way you'd ask for something as obvious as bread. I fitted the words in a different order, rummaged for a new way, but the tangle of words I unspooled made her laugh.

"First of all, not *give me*," she tutored, "but *would you kindly, sir*. Or *Sir, would it be possible to sell me two loaves?* And keep your gaze down."

What was the sense in any of that when, of course, it was possible for the baker to sell me loaves of rye? Wasn't selling loaves why the baker wore his bare feet to blistering sores kneading fresh dough every day? And why look down to regard my hands when I wanted the bread in his?

"You're the reflection of me each time you leave the house, Pieter. And Gerta's presentation must be simple and reverent."

This also made no sense. Maria was the least simple person I knew. Still, I nodded in agreement.

"Don't be fooled by what happens when I'm on this side of the doorway," she said, and with that the day's lesson was done.

I BEGAN TO WATCH more closely the stitchery of restraint when Maria left the house and how coming through the door when she tossed her hat, she shook her head with relief.

I also saw and heard the world newly. When I went to the market, the titter of laughter between maids now sounded cautious, not silly. How hadn't I noticed before that inside the shops, girls stared at their shoes and asked for but never demanded goods? I saw the blotchy red of the young maids' skin when jowly shopkeepers ogled their chests and slipped an extra frosted bun in their parcels. Their measured steps, their measured words. Maria's dulled tongue and properly clasped hands in public. I'd always admired her scorn, the jokes she played inside the family, but never realized how much effort it took to behave outside. The burden of holding herself back. I flinched at all of it.

Nevertheless, in the shed at night as the swallows swooped through, I practiced becoming Gerta. I spoke to the rabbits and pig, with modest questions. *Would you please this* and *would you please that*, while they nuzzled my hand as they always had, indifferent to my strange new mannerisms.

I soon found it wasn't so hard to manage a skirt, and Maria, pleased with my progress, sent Gerta out alone to the shops to see how she'd fare. I fared well. And while at first I'd only seen the restrictions, I began to find new pleasures, not in the bashful drop of my eyes, but in the extra bit of cheese dropped in my basket that I'd relish on the way home. Even more, as I ventured among women with a bonnet to cover my head, I liked the surprising confidences and side jokes. Under cover of gentleness, there was quick and mouthy wit. I began to crack the language of women and soon spoke with a native tongue. After all, it was my own. But for all of Maria's strict lessons, I never fully quit being Pieter, even in my corset. How could I erase all I'd known as a boy? Why would I? How much more useful to have known the world both male and female, to traverse brazenly with the rude mind of a boy or angle delicately with a girl's careful polish.

Eventually Maria said her maid, Gerta, was ready for Utrecht, though when we were alone, she continued to call me Pieter. Whatever choices I'd been offered, boy or girl was always what others insisted upon, for their own needs.

But what I did with each, that was mine to choose and shape.

AND THERE'S SOMETHING ELSE. For years, across rooms and tables, I'd watched Maria, making careful study of her moods, the casual toss of a joke when her sister was unprepared, the lilting pleasure in her voice as she read aloud, the concentrating angle of chin as she painted. I'd believed she was fully discovered, fully known to me. Yet as her maid, it became my task to dress Maria, to learn to manage the layers of her corset, underskirt, and overskirt, to lace the stomacher to her bodice stays. To say that I wasn't a nimble dresser would make my ineptitude sound endearing. It wasn't just the required precision of fitting a pearl button through the slit of a buttonhole that made me clumsy. I was shy. Shy to see her naked. Timid to touch her. All these years admiring her from across a table, and now what I put on her in the morning, in the evening I took off.

The first time I bathed her, I kneeled by the tub, a cloth ready in my hand.

"Let me enjoy the water while it's still hot," she said, splashing water on her neck and breasts.

"I'll heat more," I said, relieved to do anything other than just stare as she slipped beneath the water and popped up, her skin glistening. She pointed to the cloth. "No, stay. Scrub my back, please." She curved over herself while, with averted eyes, I lathered and rubbed down the length of her spine.

It wasn't that I'd never seen an undressed woman. No, most unfortunately, each month at Anke's bath, I'd been beckoned to scour her filthy back and neck. "Take yourself a good look, Pieter," she'd say, sitting in the tub, her long veiny breasts rolled up in her hands. "Believe me, men fall for a girl's hefty bounce and wind up with a wife whose tits sweep the floor." Then she'd release herself with a satisfied grunt and sway so that the dreadful, bumpy nipples looked that much wider and darker in the scummy water.

But washing Maria was a different sort of frightening. Her skin was so lush and firm under my hands. I tried to look away, but I didn't want to. Forgive me, all I wanted was to look. Who wouldn't? When she slipped down into the water, the length of her hair fanned out, some curls clinging like an outline, announcing how her full pale breasts fell to each side, the pink of her nipple beaded with water. I tried to be delicate as I gathered and lifted the long strands that slicked against her skin. "Oh, please." She laughed. "I won't shatter when you touch me. I like a sturdy lathering." I washed then rinsed her thick hair till each curl squeaked clean. Maria offered a limb, closing her eyes as I scrubbed each shapely leg in turn, then pumiced her feet. "That tickles," she said, wiggling and flexing as I soaped the arch of her foot. Then I soaped up the cloth again.

To help steady myself, I imagined the yard. It's crude to compare a maid's job to the care I gave our milk cow, where daily greasing with salve kept her teats from cracking. But truth all, it helped me keep calm when I ran the damp cloth up Maria's legs. Though, I admit, the following morning, sitting on the milking stool, my fingers gripping and squeezing down the softly haired teats, my thoughts drifted to the smooth skin on the inside of Maria's thigh, the dimples low on her back. Hearing again in my mind her contented low growl as jug water cascaded over her hair and down her stomach, I missed the pail, a spray of warm milk making a mess of my apron.

Slowly I began to know Maria's body. I kept neat her nails. Creamed her long fingers. Buttoned starched cuffs, my fingers tracing the marvel of blue veins on her wrist. It made me proud to be her intimate hands. To know her particularities. I learned to adjust for her gnarled, once-broken toe when helping her into a shoe. Hefted the uneven weight of her breasts as I fitted her into the stiff corset, and by evening again managed them, gently pulling a stray hair by her nipple and rubbing chickweed and lavender under the hang of her breast where she darkened from sweat. I knew to fasten a linen cloth a few days before she'd begun her monthly shed.

The yard had taught me it's more than hands that makes fine tending. More to a healthy mare than brushing her coat to a luster or picking hard mud from a shod hoof. There's also palpating and prodding a bloated belly or tending to the fester of an open sore. So, when Maria fevered, I put my nose to the skin of her neck to smell the root of her ailment. The chamber pot's rank and quality told me the shape of her health. In time I attended to Maria's every privacy.

And always, always, always, the marvel of her hair. Morning and night, dressing and undressing ended with Maria's mane of chestnut hair. I most loved evenings, when, after she'd been powdered and creamed, I unfastened the clips that held her chignon, the weight of darkness roping through my fingers. I loosened a tangle at the base of her skull, letting the long curls river down her shoulders and back. Then I took up the brush. It was bone handled, edged in rosewood, its bristles stiff. I began slowly to stimulate her scalp. Then section by section, I brushed through the locks with a rosemary oil. In the lamplight the richness of her clean hair shone, highlights of red and depths of browns. I felt her yield under the brush's steady rhythm and I loved how the constancy of my hand soothed her. Soon her chatter about whatever foolish thing a visitor had said or what was needed the next day quieted. I pressed my thumbs down her neck to release her last worries.

"That's lovely, Pieter," she said, her voice sleepy and soft. "This feels so good, doesn't it?" She touched my arm.

TWO

1661, Utrecht

"There's no one greater," Maria said. "No greater flower painter, no greater still-life painter than Jan Davidsz. de Heem." Every day that same stupid brag those first weeks we were in Utrecht. The luster of his golds. The shine on the curved barrel of a painted lute. Every day some new corner of a canvas for her to coo over, and always his name—De Heem, De Heem—incanted as if she'd been apprenticed to God himself.

I said nothing as was still my inclination. Finally, after days of Maria extolling his genius, I meekly offered, "You'll be greater."

"Pieter, don't be ridiculous." She recoiled as if I'd struck her. "Today I practically smelled the tart juice of his painted lemons. Didn't you?"

I wanted to say, "That's not juice, he's oil sloppy." I wanted to point out that any laborer who painted the front door of a house could tell you that with all the oil De Heem used, the paint would dry thin without tooth and then crackle. But I held my counsel.

In those first weeks in Utrecht, because Maria was the only woman in the workshop, I did as her father instructed and accompanied her to De Heem's studio as she settled in among the young men. Unlike the other apprentices, it was considered improper for Maria to lodge with him, so we lived in a lovely house a five-minute walk away. And what a different house it was that Maria created than the minister's home. Chairs covered in boldly patterned textiles. Emerald throws. Bright tapestry wall coverings. On tables, stairs, and room corners, she fashioned decorative tableaux—assemblages of shells, birds' nests, enameled boxes, and figurines. I shopped for exotic fruits she arranged in painted crockery. I kept the house and the ledger to tally the allowance her father provided. What pleasure I took caring for every detail without Anke's constant scold.

Those first days at the workshop, De Heem's maid, seeing an opportunity to lighten her day, set me to work in the studio. How pleased was that fat goat to doze in her yeasty kitchen while I cleaned the workshop with its rancid smells of paint-making. I was pleased to be away from her kitchen, where all I'd learn was how she expected an onion chopped. In the workshop, everything was something new to learn. I swept the floors while watching the preparation of panels and the proper way to set up and scrape a palette. I went about my every task taking study of how a studio worked.

As a maid, I suffered an assistant's occasional pinch or briny quip. If I hadn't been in skirts, I would've been fast to fists. But as Maria's maid, I kept my hands tight to the broom. Still, didn't I find ways to have fun. When one particularly pestering assistant returned to his desk, he bolted from his stool, a wayward needle having pierced his bony ass. Poor young thing! No one knew who set the needle. I let the others do the laughing and kept to the shadows, dutiful and chaste.

"Did you notice, Pieter, how De Heem encouraged me to remain close by his side all day?" Maria said as we made our way home on an evening it was raining cow tails. "It was spectacular following his every stroke to the canvas."

How could Maria have fallen into such a trance that she'd forgotten her own wary proclamations of artists eager to make a wife of a painting woman? "Don't stand too close," I wanted to scold. "He'll be quick to pluck you, not only to mix his paint but to bear a couple fat babies with his fancy strokes."

But "You'll be a better painter than him" was all I said, and jumped over a wide puddle.

"Pieter," she scolded, "what do you know?"

ONE EVENING MARIA stumbled into the house from her day at the workshop. By then, certain enough of her safety among the men in the workshop, her father had decided I would no longer accompany her, my hours better spent managing Maria's home. I went to untie the strings of her bonnet, but she pushed me away, sat down, then bounded out of the chair. She wrestled off her cap and threw it to the floor, then paced the room so distraught she couldn't pause long enough to tell me what had happened. I'd never seen her so afflicted. I worried that without my protective eye, she'd received a wayward grope or worse.

"He's threatened to toss me out." She marched about the room. "I deserve it," she moaned. "I'm useless."

The idea of Maria as useless was funny and, despite her complete dismay, I had to hold back from making a joke of that absurdity. Finally, it became clear that De Heem had called her an idiot girl when, for the third time, she'd ground red ochre too fine so, when mixed with oil, it bled and wouldn't adhere.

"'Idiot,' he said again and again and threw the paint at the wall." Maria flung her arms about to demonstrate his anger.

Her preparations! That's all it was. She could cry and fret until worn out. It would be fine. I'd take care of it for her. Even with the chores I'd been given at De Heem's workshop, there'd been ample time to watch the daily preparation of paint and see the apprentices make a poor mess of it, winding up with bladders of sorry grays and browns instead of blues and reds. Though I disliked De Heem and was loath to agree with anything he uttered, it was true that Maria had the least talent of all the apprentices for making pigment. She showed no patience for the careful grind needed to keep malachite from going gray. But why care, really? Her hours were better spent at the easel where she was in ultimate possession of patience. You just had to look at her every clean brushstroke. She was an artist, not a colorman. To me, each recipe, even the difficult ones with many stages, made obvious sense. In my days in De Heem's workshop, I'd done the watching, and now had his recipes stored and ready in my head.

"If you bring pigment home, I'll rub the paints for you," I offered when at long last, exhausted, she slumped in the chair. I readied for an arduous campaign to convince her, but it took less than a first cup of wine for her to touch my hand.

"Thank you, Pieter."

That next day, coming home, her bags were heavy with rock and plant. But her enthusiasm was back, animating every step. "I've convinced him that the problem was that I had my modesty to consider. That it wasn't proper for me to muscle the pestle in a room filled with men," she said, savoring her lie. "I said I'll bring it fresh to the studio each morning. Let me have a week, I told him. If the paint is not to your liking, I'll roll up my sleeves in the studio as the others do."

At first, she attempted to oversee my every step. Soon she quit the bossing and, along with the management of Maria's house, preparation of oil paint for De Heem's workshop became an everyday chore. It's no brag to say I was quick to it. De Heem imported many pigments I hadn't known before—Tyrian purple from the glands of a snail and red from a female bug that lives on cacti. Fancy as these new colors were, and not the least shy to trample piss-soaked woad, I tweaked De Heem's recipe and gave him a blue to rival that of any of the city's finest colormen.

But I wanted to exceed what De Heem had managed and set off to scour the shops for the purest azurite or a rare chunk of lapis, elbowing aside apprentices who clustered with purses of coins. It was fun how it unnerved them, a bonneted young woman talking crudely like a boy, and quick to thieve choice chunks of azurite from their fingers. Oh, I learned to push my breasts out a bit too for that advantage. "You're the worst of both," Maria chided, though she couldn't hide her pleasure in the quality mineral I secured and the praise she received when she brought the paint to De Heem's workshop.

Though I never liked the way Maria esteemed De Heem, I owe him for the chance to learn paint preparation. So here's forgiveness to De Heem's every indiscreet fondle, let's call them fair barter for his recipes that I honed so that when Maria was ready for her own workshop, her scarlet and yellow commanded the world's notice.

Of all the colors, I loved most the release of blue lapis. I loved the effort it took. I loved that when achieved, it was a stable hue, constant. But first of all, I loved that blue began with a great tale in a faraway mountainous land I could hardly fathom. I'd heard it described as rugged and treacherous, the mines ancient, but so remote that few had ever crossed there. I'd hold a chunk of the costly rock and try to map the journey it had already made across rough landscapes and seas and all the many hands that had held this piece of lapis lazuli before mine.

Lapis lazuli, doesn't the name alone glow brilliant? I made song of it, *lapis, lapis lazuli*, as I stood above the mortar, my whole arm, elbow, and wrist flexing the pestle in steady rhythm to pulverize the crystal fine and then finer, learning to stop breaking down the rock after its first foul release of sulfur.

"You make it sound like a magical potion," Maria said.

"Isn't it?" I said, stopping just before overgrinding, which would dull the brilliance when I worked in the binder.

Lapis, lapis lazuli, my whole body sang as I ground and milled rock, moving the particles from the granite to the alabaster mortar, melting the powder with rosins and beeswax, kneading then sifting with water until I mulled the last of the circle eights—*lapis, lapis lazuli*—I rinsed and rinsed the sediment to pull the purest, most startling blue.

"Pieter, Pieter," Maria spoke softly and lingered behind me. I leaned hard on the pestle to mull the pigment silky with poppy seed oil and a dropper of honey. "You are this painter's truest secret," she said, her whisper-like fingers at the back of my neck.

TO LOVE COLOR is to love decay. The deep black of burnt willow; the soft black of gall ink when, in spring, the wasp punctures nuts to lay her precious eggs and the oak tries to heal itself over its wounds. To love red is to love the husk of bugs. Bone of animal, bone of insect, of tree, bone of men. Dirt and soot. Blood and piss. Burnt earth. Grind, grate, pulverize, mull, the painter's palette is a ruthless art. I delighted in breaking one thing down and then, days or weeks later, my nose to a jar, breathing for the exact fetid shift.

Rot and wane. Beauty is a transformation, often a messy one at that. All the mucus, the detritus of the living. Squirt of a cuttlefish captured for sepia. The ripe purple berries macerated and festering in a shut vessel become a surprise—not purple but a soft green scumbled along a blond stalk of cattail.

"What do you think?" Maria said. She was at the table, drawing a single iris stem while I shredded leaves, stalks, and stamens of the rest of the bundle I'd brought home, tossing the purple flowers into a bowl to pulp for paint. I wasn't sure what she meant and if what pleated through my mind could be called thoughts. She asked again.

"I don't know," I said.

"I'm not asking you to know. I'm asking what you think."

I stared at the mutilated petals in the bowl. "Iris makes a good green," I said. And then, because I wasn't sure why knowing wasn't the same as thinking, I offered, "It's surprising how ground purple iris becomes bright green with a bit of alum," hoping this was what she wanted.

"There's perfect harmony between those colors," she said.

I kept my quiet. Happy I hadn't made a mistake.

"Don't you want to ask what I mean?" Maria said.

I hadn't considered asking. I didn't understand all she said about pleasing geometries, or how certain colors in relation to one another made a person feel a particular way, but I understood that without her family close, Maria required someone to converse with in her own home. I remembered at meals how easily Maria and her sister and brother had followed each other's half phrases. How, before her brother even finished telling a story, Maria knew he was shaping a lie. And when accused, he'd laugh, unapologetic. She called him Dearest Owl and her sister Mouse. They all argued without restraint. There were secrets and jokes that made them weep. They read passages aloud from books and fought over the meaning of a single word.

Without a brother or sister in Utrecht, I was to be her companion. There were nights, after brushing her hair, when she wanted me to curl close to her in her bed as her sister had, telling secrets or sharing important ideas. But what ideas did I have? What stories could I unfurl? My stories were of thieves in the market, a crate of rotting sardines, the cobbler's lazy son who patched a boot sole with a piece of moldy leather. Day by day, I tried to scrape together bits of what I'd overheard that day and at dinner polish up a story. And though I don't pretend I was ever the rival of her sister or brother for all the books they'd read or their far-flung knowledge of discoveries about the globe, Maria asked for more of my stories and, in no time was banging her fist on the dining table, shouting, "Are you saying that in front of the wife, he pinched the butter girl's bottom, Pieter?"

Happy to please her, I said, "And then one by one licked his filthy fingers," adding a lusty demonstration. The more outlandish the story, the greater her delight. I liked the way she laughed with her whole body, her feet stomping the floor.

It turns out I also had plenty of thoughts. Soon enough, I offered opinions different from hers.

I told her that the velvet face patches she claimed were all the fashion in France made her look foolish. "They're called mouches," she said, stroking a quarter moon she'd affixed to her cheek. "And worn by the finest women."

"I don't think any of the Guild men will be gluing dots on their faces," I said, and without much more resistance, she allowed me to peel the moon from her cheek.

No shortage of times she regretted the freedom of my tongue. I should amend. I spoke freely when we were alone. Outside, among others, my beliefs mirrored hers.

ONE DAY, when Maria and I were on a flat barge in the canal, she pointed to the towpath and said, "Look what happens when the two meet." I saw no one meeting on the path. Not even cows. I turned to Maria, as if by watching her I might see what it was she saw.

"No, really look." She poked the air with her finger.

"Oh." I furrowed my brow, knowing she knew I was pretending.

Finally, she relented. "Try to see what happens when the blue meets the fringe of green."

Sky and the grass? That's what she'd been staring at!

After Maria taught me to look at the seam where sky and grass stitched together, at first all I saw were swaths and edges of color. The thread of dark where a clay pitcher met the table. How a tiny distance—where an apple overlapped a pear in a bowl—could simultaneously appear vast. Or while there were some five strides between the chair and the door, why hadn't I noticed that to the eye they also touched? So many horizons, near and far, once I really began looking. There was a day Maria said, "Look," and when I said, "Oh," at light foiling in gold sheets down the face of a building, shadows purpling the edges, Maria said, "Exactly, Pieter," and a bit of distance had closed between us.

As I lit the fire in the grate, I practiced, and soon could recite some twenty shades in a flame. I wanted to describe everything to

Maria, but her enthusiasm slid easily to tedium. "Good," she said, as you'd indulge the child who's asked for the tenth time to be watched as they toss a ball in the air.

. . .

ACTUALLY, THERE'S MORE thanks owed to De Heem. It was in Utrecht preparing paint for his studio that I first learned there were days it proved wiser to take off my bonnet, don breeches and a doublet, and tuck up my blond curls to hustle for whatever rare pigment was newly off a boat. One might wonder why Maria consented, knowing I'd be arrested, mocked, and paraded through the streets if caught in men's clothes. But she hardly gave a thought to those dangers. If climbing aboard a ship, traveling impossible seas, then scaling rock faces to bring back the very best lapis had been an option, she'd have gladly sent me off to risk my life for the ultimate blue.

But I also think Maria liked how I held both within, dare I say even envied what freedom it was to move through the world as a young man, my gait open. And later, when the rustle of my skirts drew the appreciative gaze of a young man, Maria would say, "He's right to notice your glorious bounty." I can't say I know a life other than the one I've lived, but it's a wonder how much a skirt or a pair of breeches changed any given day. Inside both costumes was me. Best was learning that I was as much one as I was the other.

Some might consider me peculiar for the way I've bent my ways of being human. But I would invite even the harshest judge to spend one day drawing the anatomy of flowers. Pull apart enough of them and you learn that plants contain myriad forms. Take the spring pussy willow. Some stalks are male. Some female. And bless the willing insects that carry what's needed between them. Hazelnut and walnut house both male and female on the same tree, but the flowers claim one or the other. The hazelnut needs the orchard wind to pollinate, where the walnut in stillness shapes its own nuts. It's all varied and surprising. Not peculiar at all. Indeed, I'm as common as the lily and the rose, the sunflower and the daffodil. *A perfect flower*, the botanists call these specimens that contain both male and female. They call them *perfect, complete*. That's how I feel.

1663

AFTER TWO YEARS in the workshop of De Heem, Maria was ready for her own studio. She was determined to leave Utrecht, where she feared her own workshop would always be seen as an appendage to De Heem's, but there was the matter of the plague in Amsterdam.

Maria wasn't concerned. She wanted to leave at once. She tore up every letter her father sent pleading for her to exercise prudence and stay far from the pestilence. He begged her to remain safely in Utrecht or, better still, return home to Voorburg. Maria insisted that the news of deaths overcoming the city were an exaggeration. "People go crazy for disasters," she said. "I'd never leave my house if I listened to everyone's constant worries."

In the hopes of frightening her into restraint, her father, in florid detail, described reports of the plague's rapid progression. *This terrible illness that has overcome Amsterdam is not merely days of fever and chills*, he wrote, *nor oozing sores large as goose eggs erupting on the body. Be prepared, lovely daughter, to hack globules of blood, for your silken flesh to blacken, crackle, and tear at the lightest touch, and blood to seep from your eyes. You will pray for death long before death finally takes its claim.*

His letter made Maria laugh, and she read it aloud, mocking her father's solemn voice. She wrote back that he'd find a better audience preaching his lake of fire to his desperate parishioners than in trying to tame his daughter's spirit.

Then the minister wrote directly to me, imploring that I restrain his impetuous daughter. At first, I said nothing, knowing any attempt at containment would only flame Maria's will. Then, I told her I was happy to risk my own health following her to Amsterdam, though I wondered who'd be there to patronize her new workshop when all the finest homes had been shuttered, the wealthy having run off to the countryside. If she wanted to sell paintings cheaply to brighten the final days of the city's infected poor, I'd gladly help. But as for finding worthwhile pigment, there'd be scant choice with the ports closed. Talk of financial constraint curbed Maria's enthusiasm; nevertheless, keeping her from moving was a constant battle.

I didn't wish it upon Utrecht, but just when Maria declared the plague was a thing of the past, despite no reports verifying the claim, and insisted I start packing for Amsterdam, there was an outbreak of plague by the North and South Gates. It seemed obvious that this should quiet her, but Maria's first reaction was to urge me to pack faster. "If it's come here then we might as well go. Anyway, it only afflicts the poor. We'll be fine." she said. Cold as she sounded, she was mostly right. The wretched, cramped conditions fueled contamination in those neighborhoods. But the people of Utrecht, remembering other plague years where infection had spread beyond the poor to kill half the town, quickly imposed strict ordinances and quarantines. There were sanctions on imported straw and meat, hemp and flax, even cucumbers from local villages. Suddenly, it wasn't easy to find the brown sugar Maria loved to sprinkle on fruit.

"If this scarcity annoys you, imagine Amsterdam," I said. I didn't bother with descriptions of plague houses, boils, bleeding eyes, or the steady clang of bells marking each death, but instead of Amsterdam bakeshops without a speck of flour. When we got there she'd better be ready to forgo the quince jam from Constantinople she loved to slather on biscuits each afternoon. And forget her Chinese face creams.

"Enough, enough!" she cried out when I invoked daily life without imported grapefruit and pomegranate.

To its credit, Utrecht managed to squelch the early strain of illness, and the death bells ceased. For two more years, Maria stayed on with De Heem as the plague continued to ravage Amsterdam. He was more than glad to keep her, and it was there, through his introductions, that she made her first sales of paintings signed *Van Oosterwijck*. I was now shy of eighteen, no longer the slim-hipped freshly emerged girl who'd arrived in the city. For all my caution, I was also eager to get to Amsterdam and on to my next future. But I used this time to further refine my knowledge of paint preparation and heighten my attentions as Maria's maid. Now fuller chested and bottomed, I sewed dresses more refined than other maids and learned to comport myself in the manner I thought fitting for the servant of a famous woman painter. Maria gave me books to read, and as I read aloud to her, she polished the ways I shaped my words.

At last we learned river and canal travel had fully resumed. That bunches of straw marked no more Amsterdam doorways. That their dead had been shoveled under. Yes, more than a tenth of Amsterdam had died, but what mattered to Maria was that the wealthy had returned, the ports were full and merchants hopeful.

"Now Pieter, *this* is the right moment," she said as if she'd always erred on the side of caution. "After all those boring days watching birds and harvesting mushrooms in the countryside, the good people of Amsterdam will return to their city hungry for delicacies, great gatherings, and art. And the workshop of Maria van Oosterwijck will be fresh and exciting."

It was then we quit Utrecht to make a life in Amsterdam.

THREE

1665, Amsterdam

THE AMSTERDAM HOME WAS PAID for by the sales of Maria's paintings. She'd begun selling that prosperously in Utrecht. However, it was the slant of Maria's father's hand on the lease, thanks to a city law requiring a man's signature. Oh, it made Maria furious. And nasty. For weeks no matter which way I set a room—the pink silk chair angled by the window, an Italian glass lantern displayed on the polished walnut desk—she insisted it was a hideous arrangement. I moved all the furniture again. Now the pink chair in conversation with the purple settee. But the next placement, she raged, was even worse. "Pieter, this house is shit," she said as if I'd forced her to spend her money on it.

I propped a carmine pillow first on the silk chair, then on the carved wood one. Maria clicked her tongue with disgust. I wanted to shake her, bristle her out of her foul, sullen weather. "Are you still a painter?" I asked as Maria grabbed the red pillow by a gold tassel and paced the room, trying it first on the settee, then on a third chair, before shoving it onto a corner bench.

"Oh, forgive me, I've clearly stumbled into the wrong painter's home," I continued. "It seems you're simply an industrious wife making a comfortable home for your artist husband. The painter I work for, however, has important work to complete. I'm going out to find her Spanish yellow." And with that I walked over to the bench and threw the pillow to the floor, where it landed with a thud.

She whipped around as if yanked by rough hands. "You don't know how to pick. I'll have to go with you."

"Well, be quick about it," I said, stomping up the stairs to my room. "Picked-over ochre won't make you happy."

My room. In our fine canal house. Perhaps it's wildly presumptuous—a shabby footnote like myself—to determine what was important in Maria's life. Or worse, to call the house *ours*.

"Pieter," Maria shouted from the bottom of the stairs. "Aren't you ready?"

I pushed aside the curtains to look down on the street where a girl hurried, two full baskets weighted in her hands. She veered among the horses and pigs, the men and women hauling sacks and pushing carts. I imagined the scolding she feared if her baskets spilled, fruit toppling into the fetid canal. I wanted this hurried girl to look up and, for a brief moment, smart with envy to see a young woman in a room with lilac silk curtains. I was a woman who no longer slept among the animals or on a bed in the kitchen. Now I went to a room with washed white walls and tall windows. Now I slept in a bed with finely pressed linens. I had my own desk and upholstered chair. In the cabinet where I grabbed my cloak hung my very own three dresses and two petticoats. I touched the lace set on the cuffs of the dress I wore when I accompanied Maria on her visits. In a drawer below, even my neatly folded men's clothes were made of fine fabric.

"For Christ, Pieter, do I need to light a fire under your petticoat?" Maria shouted. "I'll set your ass aflame if all the best yellow's gone to Willem van Aelst."

I smoothed my hands down the brushed wool of my cloak. "Coming," I said, and descended slowly, ladylike, my well-creamed hands sliding along the oiled banister.

ARM IN ARM, those first months, we walked the fine canal ring of the city where wealthy men and women took their daily strolls. Maria hugged close, shivering at the possibility that anyone might approach for an introduction. If among those who are considered shy there are both the perpetually retiring and the initially restrained, Maria belonged to the latter category. Easy-tongued with friends, spinning conversation like a glass smith blows and stretches a vase, she was initially choked in the presence of strangers, as if overtaken with illness, her throat dried, her skin itched and blotched rosy.

It didn't matter that she was beautiful, her face elegantly balanced between finely boned and plump. Or that her reputation as an artist of talent and interest had been quickly recognized. It didn't matter that after the initial bashfulness, she became her boisterous, opinionated self. All certainty, opinion, spark, distinction, intelligence, daring, and wit thinned in a crowd of unknown faces. I reminded her that in Utrecht, she'd suffered the same reserve and within weeks was pestered by social promises and the unwanted confidences of her many new friends. "That was different," she responded with certainty.

As each stranger passed, she clung tighter to me. "Say anything," she begged, her head tilted toward me in an approximation of intimate conversation. As it turned out, I'd a talent for wicked nicknames, which I spun to make her laugh and look engaged as we walked the canals. Because she found it unbearable to raise her eyes to acknowledge passing couples, I was tasked with murmuring, "Good afternoon," nodding effusively to the well-clad merchants and wives who wished me a good day as if I belonged strolling in their midst.

"Good afternoon," I said over and over. Then, to relax Maria, I held her hands in mine and in a firm voice instructed, "Stopper your nose. Dreadful Madam Sausage's silk skirts are leaking farts from eating so much cabbage." Maria's laugh rang out and, forgetting her fear, she lifted her head to catch sight of which lady I'd dubbed Madam Sausage. "On behalf of the great still-life artist Maria van Oosterwijck, a good afternoon to all," I called out as we crossed a bridge, my voice bouncing off the bricks and water. Her need made me feel ridiculously bold.

She pinched my waist. "Pieter! You've gone crazy."

"Would you rather I stay home, and you take your walk alone?" I teased, beginning to disentangle from her grasp.

"Don't leave me." She tugged me back in place—as if I'd ever consider leaving her!—and we continued on our route, me conjuring ever more outrageous names to delight her.

Those days on the Herengracht, I hoped some thought me her adoring younger sister.

OF COURSE, too soon too many invitations arrived.

"A husband who proves capable of babble with the dull souls I was forced to suffer tonight is the only recommendation for marriage," she announced upon returning from her first salon. "I might seriously consider putting up with the rest of marriage for that relief alone."

But just as I'd promised, soon all shyness shook from her. Then came the requests for dinners and concerts and no end of those who wished to claim her time. What distraction! It unsettled a day's focus—all that fuss deciding between a buckled or laced shoe for a concert.

How much better spent were long days in the workshop, Maria with a scarlet smock buttoned over her work dress. Did she ever look more striking than when she was so entirely absorbed? Brow wrinkled, her full mouth puckered into a bow while her brush stippled the fuzzy lamb leaf curled over itself or the stem's prickled surface. Her mahogany curls massed in a twist, and, because she always needed three paintbrushes at her ready, two brushes poked out of her hair as she worked. She muttered instructions to herself, creating a rhythm between her voice and her brushstrokes. Perched on her painting stool, she looked like a dancer, dipping right and left as she exchanged the brush in her hand for one nestled in her hair. I went about my chores, careful not to disrupt that brilliant concentration, determined to give her quiet where the outside world did not exist. If it so happened that an unworthy invitation or three were accidentally tossed in the kitchen fire, just blame it on a certain maid's lack of tidiness.

ONE MORNING in the first months in this new city, I found myself lost in a maze of crowded streets, desperate for pliers or a tincture to relieve a tooth pain I'd nursed for days. I'd hoped to find a specific apothecary when, careening around an angled corner, another shop materialized. Looking through the window at shelves of strictly organized jars of herb, fungi, and uncloudy extract, I could see this shop was of an altogether different quality than the usual druggist's with its watered-down tonics. Then I noticed the two walls stacked floor to ceiling with pigment and stone, the range and quality notable even through the window. I hurried inside, my aching mouth forgotten.

You'd think that in a city with shelves stocked with everything you had never known you needed, and more arriving each day from afar, finding excellent pigment would be simple. However, it was only simple if you were simple to please. An abundance of colormen hawked rainbows of bladders, but when the color squeezed out, it ran chalky and cheap. Most apothecaries weren't better, despite signs that boasted the best pigment from all directions on the seas. With a glance I could see who cut with extra clay—and more than once I rubbed a bit of pigment between two fingers and felt the poor, uneven grain.

I lingered at the back of the store. The proprietor, a tall lanky man with a long face made of a hatch of angles and a tangle of dark hair that threatened to cover his eyes, managed customer after customer. He vaulted up and down ladders, pulling out drawers, all his limbs in motion as he recited what he believed was needed and how it should be administered. I was glad for the lengthy line of shoppers allowing me time to consider his manner and, more importantly, the quality of his products. I was impressed on both accounts. With one patron he was garrulous. With the next, quiet and exact. When an elderly gentleman hobbled forward barking an order, the shopkeeper responded gruffly but brought the tied package around the counter to confer privately with the man, their foreheads practically touching as the gentleman wept.

"You won't need that," he remarked to a woman after she'd rattled off a lengthy list. "This salve I make will do better work than all you've asked for." When the woman argued, he was terse but polite, explaining what was unnecessary on her list. "If you insist," he said, his bushy eyebrows aslant, after she demanded he fulfill every last item, "I'll happily take three times your money for three times less the worth." Had I ever heard a shopkeeper say, "You won't need that"? More often a fretful mother was convinced to purchase ten tinctures to solve a simple rash on a baby's bum.

When it was my turn, I stepped up, ready to make inquiries. Before I had a chance to ask for orpiment or from where his reds hailed, the proprietor leaned forward over the high counter, his elbows jutting out so that he framed a triangle. "I see already you won't be easy to please. But how can I try?" he said.

"Would you rather I take my business elsewhere?"

"No, no." His face broke open with amusement. "But I see you have impeccable standards. Not only one who wants the very best but one who's able to discern it's rare."

It was disconcerting to be so carefully noticed, and though it was a compliment, I found I wanted him to be unable to fulfill my order to prove I was not the difficulty so much as the quality of his goods. Yet, the goods were superior. When I asked to see orpiment, with a cheery grin he also brought down Indian yellow, offering it might be more to my satisfaction. The gum sticks of gamboge were the best I'd seen in any shop. "Interesting question," he said appraisingly when I asked if his malachite was Arabian or Russian, then he pulled out a drawer of both and provided an African malachite for additional scrutiny. There was a bright whistle to him as he weighed and pouched, pleased to have exactly what I needed.

"Luyc," he said with a slight nod, his mop of hair flopping forward, then back. "That's the shop's name and mine. I see you're a painter. What's your name, if I might ask?"

"Gerta." I forced myself to meet his stare. And then with a measure of defiance said, "Gerta Pieters. I prepare paint for the workshop of the painter Maria van Oosterwijck."

"Gerta, Gerta," Luyc trilled my name. "The Van Oosterwijck workshop is clearly lucky to have you. Though you hardly need me to confirm what you already know. No shortage of fools squint at a cake of indigo, praise it as lapis, and believe themselves discerning."

I fidgeted while he bundled all the vials and pouches into a large parcel. It wasn't that I was a stranger to the flatteries and flirtations of shopkeepers, or to what a flatter and flirt back might yield. What unsettled me was that he wasn't flirting. His words were in earnest.

"I hope I'll see you back, Gerta, after you've judged my pigment's worth," he said.

"I see the worth already." It was not my usual way, to offer praise that a shopkeeper might use against me on my next visit. But his straightforwardness had proved disarming.

As I turned to hurry out, Luyc reached out and stopped me with his hand. "You'll find a small parcel with a paste of ginger root, peppermint, Spilanthes, and thyme for that pesky tooth I saw you nursing when you came in. Pack it thickly, Gerta, then tomorrow rinse with the garlic chamomile wash I've also sent with you. Two days of paste and rinse, and that tooth won't be lost."

EACH COLOR, each preparation of paint, has its quirks and difficulties, its mysteries and inconsistencies. I was often made less crazy by fumes of mercury than managing the instability of certain paints.

"Well, that's most people," Maria said as we worked in the studio.

"Speak for yourself," I teased.

When had this happened? That I teased Maria? More than teased; indeed, we'd developed our own playful language. Color had become our secret code. We called one painter Orpiment for his toxic tongue. Another Sap Green for his fickle, inconstant nature. We called Willem van Aelst Willem Lead White for the wide flakes of dandruff that speckled his jacket. Not to mention that the man reeked of the vinegar and shit necessary to the stack process for that shade.

I wish I could avoid all mention of Willem, but I suppose it's better to get something said of the well-considered flower painter, since others are quick to rumor and spread their oily lies about Maria and Willem. He might have been highly regarded as a painter, but I had no regard for his character. A drunk. A lech. Unfortunately, others excused his behavior. He sold well and made it his business to boast about it to Maria every chance he got.

When Maria took the house in Amsterdam, she'd briefly apprenticed in his studio and for years she held a student's awe for Willem, crediting him with her composition and glaze technique. I wanted to believe her fawning was simply expedient, that aligning herself with Willem van Aelst was a means to establish her presence in the city. But Maria choosing a house so close to his that, through a shared courtyard, they saw into one another's workshops was a foolishness I couldn't stomach. Though stomach it I did. As if I had a choice! While Maria claimed to want to know all my thoughts, I knew better. She wanted companionship, that much was true—meals where we lingered at the table, arguing with lively opinion, so that you might have mistaken us then as two friends eating supper. But it wasn't that simple. When it came to Van Aelst, she believed him essential to her career, and I treaded lightly. That was, until the idiocy of his marriage proposal.

Repulsive as it is for me to say, Willem van Aelst, fat, sheeted in dandruff, barely able to hold a brush with his boozy shakes, made Maria a marital offer. The sheer nerve of that disgusting offer. Oh, how he still riles me! Balls be all, now I'm in a snit. Let me take a breath. And, though I'd rather never to speak of his bulbous face, let me get this nasty moment over with.

"Surprise, surprise, another morning and Lead White's still sleeping," Maria said as she slashed her brush against the window, leaving another white mark. Her studio window was already cloudy with them.

"Too bad," I said, "I bet you were dreaming again of his foul breath on your tit."

"No, I dreamed I offered you to him." She hoisted the back of my skirts. "He said he'd happily take a girl who knew her way around animals."

I swatted her off. "You want me to make a fright of this paint?"

"Make a mess and I'll send you back to nowhere." This was Maria's favorite threat.

"Before I go, I'll tell Willem Lead White that you dream to be his faithful wife, mixing his paints by day and every night playing with his flop of a prick. Or better yet, I'll leave a sack of pickled snakes at his door to make clear what you think of his proposal."

"That won't do," she said. "I need Willem more than he needs me." I turned away, sickened.

Though it turned out, instead of snakes at his front door, Maria had a cleverer plan, one that was elegant and assured. She would announce to Willem that if they were to be wed, she needed proof of a pious husband who woke early and put in a full, honest day's work.

"Let's simply wave to each other early each morning for one year," she proposed, her hands clasped theatrically. "Each day that you don't wave back before noon, I'll make a mark on the window." She acted if she expected the very best of her Willem. As though their shared future was all she longed for. She made her challenge sound as if lifted from a fairy tale, though it was more a drunkard's bet since Willem's boozing was legendary.

Hungover or stupid with romantic idiocy, Willem said, "Excellent, my darling, I'll have a year to dream of you as my wife." Who knows if his soggy mind dreamed at all, but he never woke before noon. And every day Maria had the pleasure of another white slash of paint on the glass.

"Don't send me back before I can happily wash this window clean when the year's up," I said.

"Not to worry," she said, turning back to her canvas. "Before I send you back to nowhere, you'll be rump up while snubbed Willem enjoys my promised pity fuck."

When could Maria ever resist having the last word on the matter?

ONE AFTERNOON while I sat at the table shelling peas, she asked, "Will you sit for me?"

It was the oddest question. Wasn't she across the table drawing me? When had she ever asked my permission? Just as Maria had drawn me when I was a boy working in her father's home, now she filled sketchbooks with me polishing the floor, my skirt bunched and knotted to keep it dry. I lifted the bowl of peas to show that there was ample left.

"No, when you're done, Pieter."

"And when am I ever done?" I countered. There were meals and washing and the day's paint to prepare. Holding a pose meant the kilter of work would be off. Something left undone. I hurried to finish the peas.

"I want to draw as they do with the model. Can we do that, Pieter?" Her voice was tentative. "I'm always excluded."

I understood then that she did not want to draw me about my chores, but to make a study of my naked shape. The old feeling of shame flushed through me though it had been many years since that hidden girl had been revealed in Maria's father's kitchen. I wished I could say I was bolder. That I said, *Draw me however you need*. But I didn't feel bold. Even standing fully dressed, I felt too naked. I tried to reason with myself. There was scant privacy in the house, barely a scarf of modesty to wrap up oneself in. I wasn't at all unaccustomed to being seen in my ablutions and toilette. Hadn't we on many bitter nights, like any lady and her maid, curled close in a single bed to keep warm?

"I don't want to," I said, and turned back to the bowl of peas.

"Please? I'll help." She reached into the bowl and began shelling. We worked in silence until we'd finished the lot of them, then she continued, "It would be a kindness. I can't go anywhere else for this."

I realized she wouldn't push any further. That if I stood and went on to the next chore, she'd not ask again. That it had taken everything she had to ask as she did. It made me feel powerful and as if I might cry. No matter what she did in the world, no matter the respect our studio was beginning to accrue, she'd never be allowed to join them when the men drew the model. Eventually I stood from the table and fumbled thick-thumbed at my garments.

Maria stepped behind me and untied my apron. "Let me help, Pieter." Turning me to face her, button by button, she unfastened my blouse. "Isn't it odd?" Her breath tickled across my face. "You've clothed and unclothed me for years, and, for the first time,

I'm the one undressing you." She slid the blouse from my shoulders and unfastened my corset. She reached behind and untied the waist of my skirts, letting them rustle to the ground. The air, sudden against my skin. My skin, a sudden vast expanse. And her so close. "You're lovely, Pieter," she said. There was such tenderness in her appraisal that I wanted to push her hands from me. This was entirely new. Terrifying and stirring. To be called lovely by Maria.

She took my hand, guiding me across the room. Then she positioned me, my one hand resting on the chair's back, the other fitted at my hip. Taking a few steps back, she regarded me. Then she was again beside me, covering my hand with hers. "Like this," she said, sliding our hands across my bare waist. "Yes, that's it."

A flitter low in my stomach. My own skin felt foreign. *I am in the kitchen. I am in the kitchen*, I repeated to myself, as if posing naked in the kitchen was as common as shelling peas.

It was a relief when Maria took a seat. I expected her to begin drawing, but she continued to stare.

"Am I doing something wrong?" I felt unsteady on my legs. A chatter in my body that I couldn't understand any better than the far-flung tongues of men off ships in the port.

"No," Maria said finally, "I'm taking you in, Pieter. You're perfect." Soon she was alternating her gaze between the sketchbook and me while I stared straight ahead at the cupboard, which looked in need of a good straightening. What I would have given to wash and restack bowls rather than stand in the middle of the kitchen with a damp breeze tickling my ass. I didn't need another reason to curse the Guild for prohibiting Maria's membership, but there were plenty curses that coursed through me that morning. The more she looked back and forth from me to the drawing, the more I felt both invisible and entirely too visible. *Just pretend you're a bowl of fruit*, I said to myself to quiet the gooseflesh that pimpled my skin. There was no quieting any of me. Neither the rush of mind nor heart.

"Turn a little," she said. "From the waist, twist. Yes, like that."

She spoke to herself as she sketched. Stopped. Nodded. "More length," she corrected. Then, "Check that proportion."

"Who knew you were so long-waisted, Pieter?" she said absently to me.

I was long-waisted? Suddenly I was desperate to see myself. Needed to see how it was that I looked. I knew my own unclothed body as I washed or dressed. But to see the whole of me. I never had.

"I want to look," I said after I'd held another pose.

"Of course," she said. "Come look at your handsome loveliness."

Then there was the business of crossing the room. Walking even that small distance with her watching seemed impossible. I grabbed my apron from the chair, bunching it against my frame. Then hurried behind her. It seems funny that having been sketched for years, looking at myself then should have felt so odd. Yet it was. Disorienting to see on paper what I'd never seen and couldn't see on my own. How in a drawing of me turned to one side, I could see a side view of the way my breast scooped upward as it connected with the hollow of my underarm. I saw the roundness of my calves and the sturdy thick ankles so unlike Maria's fine bones. I'd never wondered about my back. Now here it was—a stitchery of taut muscles, winged blades, and two lines tapering to a waist before the muscular swell of buttocks.

"This is me?" Even as I asked the question, I saw the familiar square jaw and broad nose that Maria had sketched so many times.

"Yes." Her tone was amused. "Do you approve, Pieter?" When I didn't answer, she asked it again. Then seemingly done with waiting, said, "No bother. You'll learn your own loveliness."

I certainly had never thought myself lovely or even handsome. And I never came to think I was, though soon enough being drawn without a thread of clothing on but for red wool stockings tied above the knee or a feathered hat on my head became as commonplace as being sketched hanging bedclothes on the line.

FOUR

They were calling it the year of lost boats. Boats were sunk or pirated near weekly, though sometimes it seemed they purposely delayed arrival to drive up a price. For months there'd been a shortage of red. Or rather, of good red. Even Luyc's shop, where I'd secured fine cochineal before, could offer nothing but Indian Lake or Persian Kermes. I'd scoured every shop and stall in the city. I'd found cinnabar, rose madder, brazilwood, and pounds of ochre, but those reds mixed muddy or blackened. Shopkeepers offered shards of dragon's blood, spinning tales of elephants toppling dragons. But what I coveted for the studio was the Spanish bug: dried cochineal from South America, which made the purest crimson. Now, after weeks of prowling the docks, hanging around for any mumblings about ships carrying color, the sight of Emerald Boots in his finery camped before a fire let me know that perhaps the boat I needed was coming this night.

"What's coming in?" I asked, moving close to the small fire where he sat, his tall green boots gleaming in the light of the flames. I was no stranger to the port. The harbor at night bustled loud as day, with the sounds of boats unloading at all hours and rowdy sailors, who after they finished hauling never circled far for mischief and pleasure. It was best to keep my business efficient, never lingering, knowing that trouble might flare. But these last weeks, I'd been at the docks more freezing nights than I preferred, waiting for a shipment of bugs to arrive. I squatted by the man's fire. From my pants I pulled a silver flask.

"Share your heat if you're taking mine," he said, muscling it out of my hands. I did a quick check of his face for sores or plague, though his features were shadowed under a mink hat with ostrich plumes, but his lips were already wrapped sloppily around the flask. Drink dribbled down his chin into the folds of his neck. He started to hand it back, then thought the better and took another swig, longer this time.

Over the flame I watched his face. My choice of warming at Emerald Boots's fire hadn't been random. This man, with his plumed hat and green boots, was neither an idle boatman nor a Portuguese Jew waiting for small quantities of merchandise. No, I'd gone to the dye works some months back in my search for the ingredients to make red and, seeing him in charge, let him flirt and hope to handle the sweet maid, Gerta, in exchange for a hefty pouch of bugs.

I wiped the flask's lip against the wool of my pants then took my swallow. From my bag I brought out a few pieces of wood to throw on his fire. A friendly gesture, one that let him know my flask would be staying close. It was stinging cold, a night that promised to be longer than all the hours a night could hold.

"What do you hear of what's coming into port?"

"What do you need to hear, boy?" he asked.

"I want the Spanish ship."

"What do I know?" he slurred. "What do I know of ships? What do I know and why do you care?"

"You're not out here risking a frozen ball sack all for a free drink," I said, holding my flask aloft. "There's someone I know quite interested in Spanish bugs."

The slight cock of his head told me that soon enough I'd have an answer. "Bugs?" he said. "Not enough filth and disease in this rich city, someone needs bugs imported from Spain?" He reached out his arm. His many rings glinted in the firelight. I handed over the drink and let him take his good time. I had all night, and plenty of wood and drink in my bag.

"Someone I know will pay well for a crate of red." I pushed another log on the fire.

"Red? I thought it was bugs you were after," he said.

I smiled at his game, but truth be all, I was growing impatient with his feigned ignorance. And cold. I considered that perhaps I'd judged wrong, and it might have been swifter if I'd shown up at his fire with tits hoisted and my bottom loose in my skirts.

I poked at embers. "Red bugs," I said, and named a price. A fine price. Nothing he'd ignore.

He shifted on the stool, working calculations. Easy enough for him to lose a crate. It wasn't news that crates often disappeared, or were snatched and emptied practically midair, traders grabbing goods and flinging money at the sailors disembarking so that nothing was left but splintered wood by the time they reached shore.

The numbers between us went as expected; each of us daring the other to walk away. Generous silences. And generous sharing of drink. Finally, as dawn came and we watched as the great crossed branches of the Spanish flag entered the port, we arrived at the price I'd offered when the moon was still high.

"Those damn boatmen," I joked, "tell me one you can trust." I handed him a third flask to finish and a roll of money.

"Damn thieving boatmen, indeed. Can't ever trust them not to lose a crate of bugs," he said with a last guzzle, then pocketed my flask.

FIVE

THE STILL LIFE IS METICULOUS WORK. Finishing a single painting might easily take a year or two. Six months if you have a fast, sure hand, a composition that isn't too fussy, and a few good apprentices. The other Amsterdam workshops were crowded with boys whose parents paid healthy money for their sons to study under Guild masters. There they learned to grind paint, prepare boards, and study the still life. Those who rose to assistant underpainted and worked backgrounds. The best assistants painted the lesser parts of a canvas until the day when hopefully, with enough talent, they produced their own canvas worthy of invitation to the Guild. What family would toss off their coin and send a son to study under a woman excluded from its membership?

Was it any mystery then that production was higher in other workshops in the city? That I cared for the finest still-life and flower painter in Amsterdam, I had no doubt, and I knew I contributed the best pigment for her work. But without apprentices to assume the basic studio work, she'd produce too few paintings and would never achieve the acclaim and financial reward she deserved. More was required of me.

UPSTAIRS AT MY DESK, after Maria had gone to sleep, I began. I thought it would be easy. After all the years at Maria's side watching her create volume with the direction of brushstrokes and use veils of dark glaze layered over lighter paint to lend texture and substance, I'd believed I would be better than a beginner. But I wasn't. Struggling to even hold a piece of charcoal at the correct angle, I made a mess of every attempt at a flower, the petals fanned like a child's crude doodle. I scrawled, erased, and shredded paper each night. Every morning I twisted the failed drawings and used them to kindle the kitchen fire. After weeks of humbling effort, I remembered how often Maria looked at a finished canvas, declaring, "It all begins with the line." So, I started again. The broken line. The enclosed line. Page after page, I practiced. And after many nights, when the lines became increasingly straight and certain, I graduated to basic shapes. Cup, cylinder, cone, triangle.

Then, on to the tulip, that simplest of flowers. Funny to call it simple when collectors went into debt for a single stem. Still, the tulip's gift to an artist is its straightforward shape. That basic cup, elongated. And from that oval, a shaping of three petals and three sepals. In time I mastered the snowdrop. Then the rose. Then grapes mounded on a vine. Then columbine. Madonna lily. Sunflower. Every night hoping it was enough, I saw it still was not. There was more. Insects. Goblets. Vases. Napkins. I studied flowers in the manner she studied their anatomy at the Hortus Medicus. And then more practice to create volume, to accomplish tonal range from highlight to darkest shadow. Then cross-hatching. Then blending, smudging with bits of coarse paper and dust.

Then I set about learning to paint in the same methodical way I'd taught myself to sketch. I practiced readying a canvas or oak panel with layers—glue ground mixed with ochre applied to the panel then pumiced smooth, followed by a primer of ochre and iron white. When it came to painting, I knew to follow fat over lean, so that each layer was more flexible and slower to dry than the one before. I learned drybrush, wet on wet, and glazing. I painted pale cabbages, mixing red lake with white. Before tackling shading and depth in a bunch of grapes, I painted single grapes—scumbling a base of blue, then layering white and then yellow so that each grape glistened juicy with reflected light. I kept my strokes short. And kept the brush's tip fine. Always, I worked to school my hand close to Maria's, to hold a brush exactly as she held a brush.

But something more happened. Just as I'd been reshaped by daily life as a boy and then as a woman, I was changing again. Every night, I entered the mind of art. And when I looked up from the desk to find the streetlamps extinguished and the first gray smear of dawn, I rose and went about the housework. But my every task was altered. Now I noticed light as it sliced across the coverlet, where it fell on a wet tin pot. On the way to the shops, stopping to watch a boy piss in the canal while his other hand grabbed tight to his mother's skirt, my finger traced the taut bow of his body's curve against my apron. At the fish market, while I admired the high lacquer of silver herring piled on ice, the monger rapped my hand twice, reminding me to order. Painting had queered me. It had rearranged my place in the world. Less in how the world saw me than in how I observed its infinite possible compositions.

How strange I'd become, stalling at the market to admire the blunt shapes of a goat carcass hanging from hooks, the glistening meat and ribs. Or so distracted by the shades of the neighbor girl's ivory skin and the starched white of her collar, I hardly heard her frisky gossip. I tell you, pigment and painting transformed me more than a skirt or pants. As I stared at the rich purple of a split-open cherry, the girl in line behind me pinched me and scolded, "Who are you dreaming of? You're like a bee drunk and lazy with love."

"You couldn't imagine" was my cheeky retort.

Hardly lazy, I was more alive. Alive with the wonderful secret I carried. That I was someone different than anyone imagined.

I LISTENED FOR HER SHOES, thick on the workshop stairs, and, as always, she jumped the last two, eager to start. I waited. Then heard the troubled intake of her swallow. Her feet scraping in place. How I longed to spin around and see her progression from horror to curiosity as I raised a brush to her newest canvas, a floral arrangement she'd begun the day before, transferring the flowers and grasses from sketches made months earlier at the gardens. But not a sound from Maria, just the rasp of her shoes.

With a confident hand, I continued underpainting, using lead white with linseed oil. I'd added a gobbet of raw umber, something she never did. I stepped back. Regarded the canvas. Dipping my brush directly into the umber thinned with a little oil, I drew a large triangle on the canvas.

Behind me, she gasped. "Pieter..."

I'll say this more directly. With that triangle, I'd indicated an imbalance in *her* composition. I'd corrected Maria's painting.

It was bold. Not anything I'd planned. Maria often made early corrections, an opportunity to intervene before problems of composition had compromised a painting.

Her boots roughed against the wood, each scuff deliberate and percussive. I had not anticipated how excruciating it would be, listening to her progression as she made her way across the studio.

Then she was beside me. Resisting so much as a glance to gauge her reaction, I continued amending the composition.

"When you're done," she said, her voice straining to sound as if nothing unusual was occurring, "please prepare Venetian red for my second canvas while I tend to a few more changes on this one." She slipped the brush from my fingers, then continued the work on the composition. Her reaction was as I'd hoped. Pragmatic. She needed an apprentice. And she knew it. If she was annoyed by anything that morning, it was only that she hadn't realized before me that I'd become her apprentice. Though, of course, eventually that's what she told the others. That she'd taught her maid. That she'd done what no one else had done before and turned a servant girl into a painter.

THOUGH FOR A GOOD LONG WHILE, she didn't speak of it to anyone—it was her secret. Our secret. And I would've chosen to remain a secret. My learning to paint was meant only to enhance her reputation. It was never meant to be a gimmick to dazzle the men who came to her parties. But later, when it dazzled them— Dirk Schelte, Willem van Aelst, Constantijn Huygens, Wallerant Vaillant, and all the others—Maria ensured I was simply a reflection of her own light. How did Huygens later say it in his poem of tribute to her? That I was the moon to her sun?

By the time they knew I was her apprentice, Maria's fame had surpassed many of the Guild's men. Cosimo de Medici had already bought the first of the paintings he'd purchase from her. Many others too. Yet, absurdly, it was teaching me that pressed upon the limits of their imagination. Every day traders brought back fantastic oddities from the farthest places imaginable. It was no longer remarkable to see a rhinoceros or an armadillo led along a canal.

But to watch me paint a withering peony with a skill that rivaled any man's brush stretched their minds in ways they could barely grasp. It still galls me. Not even so much that I became the sideshow curiosity, but that in all the years it never occurred to anyone that I might have taught myself.

ONCE MY APPRENTICESHIP BEGAN, it seemed impossible that it had ever been any other way. I still opened the workshop early to prepare Maria's paint, but having learned to paint and manage paint's viscosity, I tweaked every recipe. After her initial drawing and composition, it became my duty to underpaint. Soon she asked me to scumble green before applying a black background. Other still-life painters make this a single step, but Maria preferred separating underpainting from dead-coloring. It gave her more opportunities to add to her original vision, kept her possibilities fluid. Soon she was asking me to lay in the flower shapes with simple masses of pink, yellow, or red for additional depth.

If I sound a braggart when I say that once I started to help with the early parts of the canvas, Maria's work rose to a new level, so be it. It was what I'd anticipated, a simple calculation. My undertaking the rough work meant all her concentration was applied to her exceptional brushwork. Production increased. And sales. Greater attention and more commissions. There were comments that her painting was achieving greater luminosity and dimensionality, and it was true. Maria knew it. We both knew it. Nothing needed to be said.

"**KEEP GOING, PIETER**," Maria said, her tone offhand, as if it was nothing unusual that now I was being told to paint the actual flowers in the still life. Only a few apprentices, the very best apprentices, were allowed fine brushwork. Most were relegated to painting backgrounds or the dark clothes of a portrait's subject. But my Maria—clever and preemptive—made sure she gave the order before I took it upon myself this time. I didn't ask how she knew that late each evening with what paint was left on her palette, I continued my training. I didn't show surprise or wait for further instruction. I didn't select a lesser flower tucked in the background. Instead, lifting her finest brush, I began to paint the signature sunflower that crowned her composition.

THESE ARE THE DAYS I love most to remember. Hours we painted in silence, though just as often, one of us would spin out a joke that pitched us into raucous barks. Two women alone in the studio, we farted and cursed. Though we'd lived far from the house of her father for seven years, though I'd prepared her paint since Utrecht, being her full assistant and painting beside her brought us a new closeness. It challenges me to fully describe the rhythm of this life together. Or what exactly I became in that house. Her maid, yes. Her assistant, yes. But I was also her daily companion, the person she called for when troubled by a dream. I knew when to be which and what was expected of each task. That sounds more difficult than it was. The romp and ease I'd had with childhood boys, I now had with her. One steamy day, Maria declared us tropical pirates. "Tops off," she decreed. We hung sheets over the windows and, wearing only underskirts, worked bare-chested long into the evening. When I had to leave the studio, I hurried out to the markets, eager to return and entertain her with outlandish scandals from the poultry and butter shops. She brought home the dinner arguments of philosophers and poets.

For our midday meals, more often than not, I carried bowls of soup down to the workshop for us. After, I would pull out an inlaid wooden box, pop the latch, and with a flourish brandish two bone pipes. I'd fill each with tamped tobacco, slip a stem between my lips, strike a match, and light hers first.

"Soon all of Europe will praise Maria," I'd shout through a billow of smoke.

"Mere praise?" she'd say, her pipe fitted at the side of her mouth. "I want their money, too."

"Oh, plenty of money. Commissions from every palace," I'd promise. If she had to suffer the boastings of a Guild she couldn't join, then, puffing my pipe, I vowed to create for her a much bigger world.

"I'VE DECIDED YOU'RE A MASTER BAKER. A French baker," I said at the close of a long day in the workshop.

"Really? I'd been suffering under the belief I was a formidable Dutch painter."

"All week I've been trying to understand how your sheer glaze layers, one after another, create the density of the sunflower. Now I understand. You're like a baker in Paris composing the mille-feuille—a thousand semitransparent layers building a thick pastry of delight."

Maria clapped her hands. Then took a deep bow. "Merci! Merci! A baker, c'est moi. One hundred points for you, Pieter."

This was one of our games, devising professions and nicknames for each other. Points awarded for originality and aptness. After she rejected a verdigris not once but three times, saying it was too pale, too thin, and then too dark, I named her Mule Driver.

Hummingbird when she kept changing the composition, shifting flowers on a panel. But for that evening she was happily Madame Boulangère, sprinkling conversation with what she called bons mots.

The next morning as I laced her corset, she said, "I've decided you're the butterfly."

"No talking," I reminded. Too much air in and out of her lungs kept me from adequately tightening the straps.

"*Pieter's the butterfly*, I thought when I woke this morning, and right away awarded myself eight hundred points."

"You can't give your own points!" I pulled the laces so hard that she squealed.

"It's so brilliant, I'm surprised it's just occurred to me. Your metamorphosis. Boy to girl. Servant to painter. And now as you paint canvas to canvas, seeding my work like pollen."

By the end of that day, she'd added a monarch to the painting on the easel. "There you are, Butterfly. No one but us will know it is you." And promptly she awarded herself another eight hundred points.

"Slower," Maria said. "You aren't mopping kitchen tiles." I threw my paint rag at her, and in a flash, she'd snatched it and flung it back. "You want to be done. That's not how glaze works."

"I know," I whined like an ill-tempered child. Since the day I'd named her the baker, I'd come to recognize that my own glazing skills were insufficient and had asked for lessons. Though I knew she delighted in instructing, I hated being slow to learn to finesse a technique.

"I know you know," she mocked. "But have you the requisite restraint, Pieter?"

"How can you be such a master when you're the most impatient person in the world?" I hunched over the glass, mixing droplets of flax oil into the crimson.

"Despite common belief, impatience and patience are both virtues. And both vices. One needs to be discerning, which is more bother than most people will manage. But today, we're considering something simpler yet ultimately subtler. Letting the opaque ochre fully dry before layering crimson glazes. It involves courage, Pieter. Having the courage to wait before rushing forward with the next transparency. One tires and wants to be done. Even at the risk of the surface cracking or muddying. So my courage here is more powerful than my impatience."

My troubles with layering gave Maria the occasion to expound in what was perhaps her favorite of all the games, in which she'd bend whatever word I offered—transparency, opacity, texture, form—into a discourse on a philosophy of living. There was nothing about life that she couldn't speak to through the lens of art. Consistency. Courage. Permanence. Art was, she maintained, the supreme measure, the truest lens of morality. She held forth passionately. More than one bone pipe she smashed at the apex of a diatribe. It wasn't lost on me that however skeptical she was of religion, she was a minister's daughter.

ONCE A MONTH, all the men descended on us for a grand dinner. Maria honed the guest list for each gathering, inviting a mix of the city's philosophers, dealers, scientists, poets, merchants, collectors, regents, and painters, always including whatever foreign dignitaries and other esteemed men were visiting Amsterdam. The wives, as afterthought, of course were invited. Without a place in the Guild or a painter for a husband, Maria argued these dinners were necessary.

She took these nights of food and conversation so seriously that for me it meant days of preparation away from the workshop.

For a week before I'd scour the markets, searching for whatever new delicacy had arrived from who-knew-where that Maria needed to complete her table. Every platter was to be presented like a painter's vanitas—abundantly heaped with lobster, oysters, rice perfumed with slivered ginger, mango, another platter of the ripest fruits and cheeses. There were forget-me-nots served with softened butter. Bream stuffed with grapes and anchovy. When I wasn't in the markets, I garlanded the rooms with braids of fresh flowers. Silk ribbons threaded with tiny bells hung from rafters. The rooms gleamed, each silver goblet and pitcher polished. Every spoon's reflection considered.

Then the philosophers, dealers, scientists, poets, merchants, collectors, regents, and painters arrived. It quickly became one of the city's most desirable invites, particularly when Maria's esteemed friend, Constantijn Huygens, was in town. Huygens had taken an interest in Maria since she was a young girl when he'd built his grand home, Hofwijck, in Voorburg, claiming he needed relief from what he called the terrible demands of the vast world. These terrible demands, as far as I could tell, were the stuff of dining with kings, serving as knighted secretary to the Prince of Orange, and corresponding with the most prestigious men and women of Europe. Artist, translator, musician, statesman, Huygens's splendid name was trumpeted by all. Whom hadn't he befriended? Which painter's career, not to mention pocket, hadn't been shaped by Constantijn Huygens?

On the nights we entertained, I stood, crisped and tidied in uniform, serving seconds and pouring drink and more drink. Amid their talk, hands wandered, patted, grabbed. I sashayed and bent away but was ordered by Maria never to give a single one of them a well-deserved punch or unkind word. They postured and preened until, glutted, they wobbled and belched from our home.

Let me now say clearly, I detested these men. Even a gentleman as kindly mannered as Huygens. They were an intrusion, a distraction. While they shoved their mouths full of pies layered with heron, swan, and pigeon, they blathered on, heralding their importance. Always their importance! Their important ideas! Their important careers! Oh, how I would have liked to give them each a lace fan to circulate the foul winds from all that gassy pretense.

Even more, I detested the way Maria fashioned herself for them. I don't just mean the outlay of her most sumptuous satins or the powdering and curling of her hair. It was the way she made herself slightly less acute, less brazen, less intensely herself. Her unruly laughter trimmed to a sparrow's pert trill.

"It's what they need a woman like me to be," she'd say the next morning in the studio. I angled my shoulder away, focused on work. "And Pieter, I need them." She stood so close our arms touched. I stepped away.

I couldn't argue, still I detested that she needed them and the way the dealers sold her as a novelty. *A woman painter, my God! And she paints as if angels sit on each of her delicate fingers. So pretty, yet unmarried. Such a mystery!* The poets couldn't resist calling her a virgin in every one of their idiotic poems.

It seemed impossible for them to imagine a passionate and formidable woman, unmarried, and not in need of a man. It hadn't mattered that Willem was a scaly, poxy, nasty balls of a drunk; it surprised many that Maria turned him down. The only explanation anyone could muster for her refusal was pure devotion. The devout virgin painter. That daft story chased her for years. Please! And the important men who visited—Dirk Schelte, Wallerant Vaillant, Constantijn Huygens, and plenty of others who knew better, who, in private, well enjoyed her bawdy lip—still found it convenient to speak (*wink, wink*) of her purity as truth. I detested those men for upholding an ideal of the religious Maria, while some clearly reveled in private dreams of owning her. How they recognized her originality even as they desired to make her less than herself.

Most of all I hated how those insufferable gatherings took her away from the studio. I turned my silence against her. "Pieter," she said, "don't be such a bully." She wedged herself in front of the easel where I glazed the petals of a delphinium. "Pieter, what would you have me do?" She wrestled from me a brush loaded with ultramarine. In two swift flourishes she'd lined a mustache above her lips. "Of course, I'm the equal of any of them. But these evenings matter. Already I've been invited to the home of Jan Six. You'll come with me. You'll see his collection."

I grabbed back my brush. Even knowing that the invitation would lead to a commission, I wouldn't soften to her that easily.

"Please," she said. "I order you to stop being angry so we can finally talk about Willem hauling himself up on the table and oinking like a pig."

There it was: that divine rude mouth ordering me around. Of course, I buckled. I loved her insistence. "I barely restrained from shoving a fat apple in his mouth," I said.

She pretended to twirl her painted blue mustache with her long pretty finger. "An apple in his mouth," she sang, "and a lobster claw up his ass!"

SIX

Because he will have consequence, I must speak now of the nephew, Jacobus. Though this far I've tried to keep him absent from this story.

Yes, yes, I know, the poor child, his adoring mother lost to fevers. But which of us has not lost someone to fever? No one cried for the child I was. Mother gone, father gone, and no wealthy aunt in Amsterdam. There were the early months, after the death of Maria's sister, when the boy was placed in one of the crowded orphanages. Then, for a bit it seemed he might be sent off, as many orphans are, posted as a shipboy for the East India Company. Call me harsh, but there are worse fates for a child, and I reassured Maria her nephew would receive a worldly education, learn a trade, and, with time and age, possibly rise the ranks to boatswain or quartermaster. Many a farm boy, I said, trying to make it sound romantic, dreams of his chance to go beyond the flat lands on a voyage east.

"Only to die at sea with putrid, scurvy-blackened gums," Maria countered, having received persuasive counsel that it would not look decent for a wealthy artist aunt to abandon the boy. Weren't those who advised her quick to count her money! I suggested that a larger home on a better street would be a more impressive display of Maria's wealth than the burden of a phlegmy child. But they regaled her with stories of the life aboard—bowls of porridge and rancid butter, rats, disease—and she was told dangers on land were no less extreme, impressed into years of service by Soul Sellers who'd fleece a boy a third of his pay and burden him with debt before he'd even thrown his horse blanket onto a ship's hammock. So Maria stepped in and took on the boy's management, paying for his necessities and schooling. And as patrons extolled her virtue as sister and aunt, she began trumpeting that the boy was certainly her greatest joy, announcing that, in the memory of her dear lost sister, she'd devoted herself to ensuring the rest of his life be filled with better fortune.

Of course, it won't surprise you that regardless of her purported devotion, the daily charge of the child was left to me. From the start I had no fondness for him. He was always mewling about, behaving as if he were entitled to a golden throne of misery, as if a mother's death weren't the common lot of many children. He lived at school, so at least he was mostly out of my way. Still, there were holidays. Too many. And with each holiday, he returned a little taller and a lot hungrier. It all meant more chores for me.

He was a child resistant to manners, and my slightest nudge or slap about the ears was treated as if he were a lamb and I the cruel shepherdess. Whatever manners his own good mother, rest the soul, had managed to teach him, or that I tried to enforce, Maria's spoiling corrupted, and the child became increasingly petulant, ungrateful, and needy. Soon, Jacobus learned that when he cried, Maria came running, quick to prove herself the doting aunt. She'd clasp him to her bosom and say, "Hush, darling," while stroking his fat cheeks. He'd cling to her while accusing me of unkindness, and she'd scold me that I must only remember my own lowly childhood to want to better his.

Maybe I should've been proud of her care for the orphan. And, yes, perhaps I might've been a better help. I might've made his parenting seem like something we both wanted, even privately joke how we'd taken on this orphan, like a parrot, as the lucky mascot of the workshop. Instead, my mind reeled nastily, needling at her every show of maternal devotion. Distractions, wasn't that what she'd always called small children? Wasn't it proof that when the boy was underfoot, she hardly spent a full day in the workshop before heading out to show him off like a little pet and to find ever more amusements for him? On Sundays the two of them would venture to church, Maria parading the nephew in fine clothes. Other days off they went to the Hortus Medicus, hand in hand, the lunch of fresh herring, cherries, and lemon buns I'd prepared recklessly swinging in a basket from Jacobus's free hand. I won't deny it hurt to have her leave the house without so much as a goodbye.

I'd set hard to my duties, but in truth mostly I fussed about, waiting for them to return, tormented, imagining all the time she wasted on him. What I clipped to the laundry line were not the sleeves of her damp blouse or his trousers, but a vision of the two of them cavorting in the medical school gardens where Maria and I had spent many a quiet afternoon. I ached imagining them there. And worse, she'd arrive home from our gardens with her sketchbook filled not with studies of flowers but drawings of Jacobus jumping and running, just as she'd once drawn me as a child. I've little right to call the Hortus Medicus *our* gardens, but which of us controls well the possessiveness that broils through the mind when affection is turned from us and shined on another?

Horrible to confess that I was jealous of a child. An orphan at that. Worse still to admit I saw him as my enemy and looked for small ways he might be vanquished. It was my charge to play with Jacobus, and I'd wrap a cloth tightly about his eyes and watch him bang into sharp corners or fall into the pig trough while I hid, calling his name. When he cried to Maria that I was unfair at games, I sent him out with a pocketknife to play mumblety-peg with the rough neighbor boys. I knew that Jacobus would soon become a toy for these older boys, that they'd tie him up and light a fire by his feet or dare him to do increasingly dangerous stunts like stilt-walking the narrow stone walls on a canal bridge. When he arrived home wet and bloody, I cleaned him up, ministering to his wounds with theatrical care, though I was certain to choose a healing ointment that had its own sting. And when he flung about the rude words he'd picked up from older children, I showed deep moral concern by washing his mouth out with dishwater.

I'd count the days until I packed him for school again. Then, with genuine care, I'd fold his stockings and vests. For that last week I gladly prepared all his favorite meals. Maria would perform her requisite crying over how she'd miss Jacobus, but I knew she was delighted that soon she'd be back to life without constant distraction. She'd done her duty. Once he was gone, I gladly suffered the occasional letter he wrote to Maria because our home was again as it was meant to be, ours. Maria's and mine.

SEVEN

1668

After seeing Maria up the staircase of the formidable home of Jan Six, I entered through the servant's entrance.

"A fancy one, this one thinks she is," a maid snickered as I hung my cloak on a hook. I was used to servant's snorts and sidelong glances. Far less than envy of my good silk dress and fur-lined cloak has smeared cruel a servant's heart. No warm cup of drink was offered. I didn't care a toss. I wasn't intending to settle in the kitchen to make pleasantries. It would only make their tongues lash faster when they learned I was meant to find my way upstairs to accompany Maria on her visit.

Once upstairs I was in awe. I'd accompanied Maria to many of the best homes in Amsterdam, but this was different. The painted walls, the array of marbles—pink, green, and a remarkable white one cut with veins of blue. The front hall was a floor-to-ceiling gallery; the sheer quantity of art was overwhelming. And in the center of all was Jan Six, who received Maria as if he were the one impressed that she'd bothered to take the time to visit his home.

"It's a great honor," he said. "I hope you'll find it an afternoon well spent." Then he commenced to talk Maria through his collection, painting by painting. He was unlike other collectors I'd encountered while at Maria's side. His bearing was commanding, but he led with curiosity, not the arrogance of acquisition. Each work of art seemed entirely personal to him, many connected to ideas of science, philosophy. He stopped in front of a small landscape to tell Maria about a dream he had for weeks after he'd hung the painting. "Soon after that, I began to write a new play. This painting was the gate. Though I can't say exactly how," he said.

Maria took her time before the landscape, though it was obvious to me she didn't think it worth much consideration. "Maybe you were simply ready to write it," she said, pivoting to regard three small etchings.

"No mirror of nature, this one," Maria pronounced, her voice ribboned with disgust. "Well," she said, facing another, "so much for that shabby hand."

Jan Six laughed at how quick Maria was to point out where neat brushstrokes faltered. He seemed charmed by her disdain, her daring to judge his taste and the worth of the collection. And I walked behind her, pausing when she paused. Quickening past paintings when she barely bothered a glance. Though at each I wanted to linger.

"Come," Jan Six said, leading her toward another room. "There's plenty more for you to admire or trounce. Most of all, Maria, I'll want to know what you think of my portrait."

Everyone in Amsterdam knew of the portrait. Rembrandt had painted it long before Maria and I moved to the city. We also knew it wasn't the first, that Rembrandt was known to have repeatedly sketched Jan Six with the same ease with which he drew washerwomen and drunks in the streets. It was the envy of other artists that the two men were close friends, that Six spent afternoons in the studio, reading from his play while Rembrandt etched him or made illustrations to accompany it. It was also known that Jan Six generously loaned him money, saving him more than once from bankruptcy.

I followed them into a large room. There, alone on one wall, was the portrait. Jan Six watched Maria as she moved very close, her face almost touching the canvas, then she stepped back, then even farther back to the far wall. She repeated this back and forth. Small sounds tsked through her pressed lips. Jan Six watched as she bent close to examine sections of paint. Finally she said, "Is it really a surprise to anyone that the man's broke and can't get a worthwhile commission?"

"Gerta," Jan Six called without looking back. "If Maria won't say anything substantial or even pleasant, at least you might. How do I look in the painting?"

I knew a quiet "Lovely, sir" was the correct answer, given my position. But I couldn't speak. I was still fixed in the entry door, as if stopped by a wall of wind, overtaken by what I was seeing. It was unlike any painting I'd ever seen. Everything I'd learned in Maria's studio was committed to erasing the very fact of paint. This portrait of Jan Six erased nothing. Here, the brushstrokes heralded paint. Here, in passages, the work nearly appeared sloppy, but also perfect and exact. Grand and intimate. All at once.

Despite the finery of the cloth and pearls, this was not the conventional boast of the wealthy. Here was a man, the painting declared, with no need to brag. Not about pearls or the finely starched wings of his collar. Here was a man, the painting declared, who stood in light, his head cocked in inquiry, in open thought. A vivid, worldly man. How had Rembrandt so completely captured the essence and substance of this man who stood here in the room with me?

I stared at the painted left hand of Jan Six. Felt the texture of his skin, the release and the tension after the glove had been pulled off. While the right hand, which clasped the gloves, was carefully wrought, the veins and intricate workings of the hand distinct, the left hand was worked wet on wet so that it appeared raw and unfinished. The contrast between the two was uncanny. I couldn't say any of this. And, if I opened my mouth, I couldn't trust myself not to.

"Gerta, nothing?" He'd taken Maria's arm. "Your maid's too timid to say I'm not as handsome in the painting as she finds me in my home." His painted face was, in fact, not very flattering. Bloated and pocked, every flaw exaggerated, yet his gaze was thoughtful. Compelling.

"Well, sir," I started, though I can't say how I found my voice. Maybe Jan Six, the man with the open, curious face that had been so spectacularly captured in the painting, would not be affronted if a maid spoke truthfully about what she saw. "I've never seen a painting like this before," I offered as a neutral first test. Not dishonest, but an invitation for him to ask a next question.

Jan Six laughed. "I bet you haven't." He never turned to look at me.

"You know I'm originally from the Delft area," Maria said, leaning into Jan Six, steering him through the open double doors of the next room. "The merchant Van Uchelen has a fine painting by one of our Delft painters, Vermeer. I wonder, do you have one? I prefer that refined palette and hand to this aggressive hand, that's clearly more eager to get it done fast than to get it right."

"I took you to be less of a conservative, Maria." Jan Six's tone was playful.

When they were well into the next room, their muffled, teasing voices having transitioned to suitable pleasantries, I allowed myself to draw close to the portrait of Jan Six. God help me, I couldn't stop what I did next. I put my hands to the painting, running my fingers along the scarlet cloak that hung from his shoulder, following the simple dabs and traces of color, the shadows, the closures—rough, confident, perfect. I mimicked the gestures of Rembrandt's hand, how it had arced, a flicker of dry brush on the sleeve, a daub of white where the light edged the cloth. If I had any doubt this was choice not skill, I needed only to regard the precisely painted white collar framing the face of Jan Six. It was perfect.

"We lost you, Gerta."

I spun around to see Jan Six was leaning against a wall, his head angled exactly as in the painting. How long had he been watching? Had he seen my hands trace the ropey veins on his ungloved hand? Had he seen my fingers pop down the front of the white shirt, making a bob at each thick closed button and a fast smudge on the open ones?

"I've never seen a painting like this before," I said, deciding it was best to just repeat myself.

"Well, I suppose I can be grateful that at least the maid likes it better than her mistress," he said. "Come along. Maria only seems interested in where I intend to hang the painting of hers that I've commissioned."

RESTORATION DAYS. That's what Maria called it when we took a ferry to the countryside, arranging for the boatman to collect us before nightfall. She promised we'd go once a month, but more often demands fastened us to the workshop. Still surely there were many months when we went off to gather specimens and hunt for mushrooms, though I fear I've blended them into this one particular perfect spring day. The air grassy and cool. The deep blue sky speckled with lambswool clouds. Maria, whom I'd dragged from the studio, had turned exuberant, practically riotous, as soon as we were on the boat, rousing the boatman with his bashful stutter into practicing tongue twisters. I'd packed us lunch, a blanket, a book of poetry by the toast of Amsterdam, Cornelia van der Veer, and a wet cloth to keep moist any irises and lilies we picked. Also, watercolors and two small panels to tempt Maria to paint.

"I'm restoring today, not painting. Anyway, I hate nature," she said. It was one of her favorite outrageous claims. That she detested the mess of nature. That it was always preferable to paint the lily or wild rose in the studio. The freedom to create a bouquet of flowers that bloomed in different months was her first justification. The second was that an arrangement and vase implied a human presence even if not visible in the painting. To her, that particular human, who didn't appear on the canvas, was her true subject. The out-of-doors was for bringing indoors what needed to be trimmed and properly sized for people's appreciation.

"To paint this would be a bore," she said, her arms opening in a grand gesture to our surroundings. "Is there anything more limited? Grass, more grass, and a few bearded irises on the bank?"

"You're making a ridiculous argument," I said. "Look at the field. The wind blowing through it like a horse's mane."

"I look and see monotony. Pretty. But dull. That's why it restores me. Show me something different." She placed the canvas in my lap.

I dropped it on the cloth. "What if someone sees me?"

"It's us and a couple of cows. Anyway, no one knows us. We're just two women out for a spring picnic."

She took out the book, lay back on the blanket, and read aloud one of the friendship poems Van der Veer had written to the poet Katerina Lescailje. I held the panel in my lap, uncertain what to do. I'd never worked a canvas without her composition. Every brushstroke I made was in imitation of hers. That was my task, and I was proud to have developed my hand to mirror hers. Now, out in the open, she asked me to paint what I saw. Did I even know how to see on my own? Why had I said any foolishness about wind? How could I paint a force visible only by the way it bends grass and shakes through leaves?

"We should get the flowers back to the studio before they wilt," I said.

"What's the rush? I'm barely restored. And the ferry's not coming for hours. That is, if I haven't scared him off entirely." Maria rolled over onto her stomach. "Plus, I have to get through this interminable poem. Pretend I'm not here and show me."

I made myself ignore her and look again at the field. And the more I looked and felt and listened, I forgot to feel worried. Soon the spring breeze against my cheek, its whistle through grass, began to move my hand. And without thinking *How will I possibly compose this vastness*, I worked in washes of color, not trying to keep edges defined, barely rinsing the brush or blotting excess water, and soon, there on the canvas, was the throw of wind across the field, the rising trill of spring peepers and the muddy marsh tang of the canal. I painted a lone tree leaning at the rise of the hill. Then the great press of the opaline sky, a wedge of storm collecting to the west.

I pretended I didn't notice Maria looking up from her book to watch me.

"She's witty," Maria said at one point, breaking from the long poem, "but definitely more in love with her own wit than her friendship." Once she paused, and instead of another wry comment about the poem, said, "That's exactly what it is. A vision I don't have. Utterly your own."

What a thing to hear. That what I'd painted was mine. Only mine. At her encouragement, I painted the second panel as well.

"You make me want to go to that place," she said when I'd finished. She held the painting in her hands and looking between the canvas and the field said, "I swear, Pieter, it's more interesting to me than where we are. One day the world will know your name." And then, as if the perfect day had not already surprised me sufficiently, Maria threw her arms around me and said, "One day I'll compose truer praise of our friendship than these clunky rhymes about her supposed beloved."

IN LATE SUMMER in the streets of Amsterdam, people lingered on corners as if storing a harvest of dry August light. But I didn't. My boots clipped against the stones. In the months since I'd been at Jan Six's, the portrait and its painter were almost all I could think of. That I lived in the same city as the Master—which is how I thought of Rembrandt—astonished me. Just to think that he was moving paint an easy morning's walk from our house made me breathless. I looked for him in the streets, his hat and cape. In the market, I struck up conversations with his old assistants, who cringed when admitting to having once worked with him. I pushed them to reveal the proportion of smalt and earth red in his shadow blacks. And was it true that he insisted on only using burnt porcine bones for bone black? "Who cares? He's forgotten now," one old student tossed off, though when pressed, he reluctantly conceded that no painter in Europe matched Rembrandt's range, his curiosity, or sheer skill. At Maria's dinners I'd heard the gossip of his miserable state of affairs. They delighted that he was no longer living in a fine house where students doubled up at desks, some working out of cupboards, all paying exorbitant sums to assist him. And they joked that when the debt collectors were done with him, he'd end up in the same filthy streets where he'd squatted to draw a woman washing socks. To them, even the griefs he'd suffered were proof of his worthlessness and vice.

I made it clear to Maria that I didn't care if she and all the city barely considered his art worth consideration. Or that in his penury, what remained was mostly rumors of extravagant debt and loss. Maria wasn't eager to hear of my infatuation with his draftsmanship or that I thought of him as the Master, but I kept true to what I'd seen looking at the portrait of Jan Six. Though maybe I also enjoyed the stripe of jealousy in her voice. For all my boldness, I wasn't so foolish that I'd said where I was going that morning. She thought I was out scouring the shops for melons. We'd heard of a new import, flesh the color of a peony and sweeter than spooning sugar.

I rushed down the street—Pietered up, as I'd come to think of it, in man's breeches, vest, fitted waistcoat, cap, and a scarf loosely knotted at my throat—until I arrived at the small house. The narrow door was nicked and poorly painted.

"Well?" a woman gruffed, answering the door after I'd knocked and knocked. "Well," she repeated, waving a kitchen knife accusatorily.

"I have something for him," I said, intruding my boot over the threshold.

I had only the flimsiest of plans. To get inside. To stand near him. To bring him my few gifts. To watch the great painter whose painting I'd put my hands to and felt the raised strokes that carved space and light.

"Give it here." She kicked my foot back. Her empty hand jutted at me.

"I was told by Jan Six that I must deliver my parcel only to him. Not even to the hands of his assistants." I stood tall, impressed by my lie.

"Oh, right, assistants." She laughed bitterly. "His many, many assistants."

Just then a girl called from another room and the woman, flustered by annoyance in all directions, motioned me with the knife. "Jan Six sent you? Be quick then." She pushed me inside and pointed to a crooked staircase.

"Here I come," she called, and bustled through the hallway, her wide hips practically touching both walls.

Now that I was inside the house, I needed to catch up with myself. Soon I'd be in the Master's room. I climbed the stairs slowly. Each footfall echoed up the rickety staircase. Stopping near the top, I felt the emptiness of the room just before me. He was alone. I was certain of this. A thick, phlegmy cough. Then hawking. A boot clomped against floorboards as if to force the expulsions. How could I enter that room? I'd heard the terrible stories about him. Cruel, furious, quick to deliver a tongue-whipping or worse. The more intense his public disfavor, the more unrepentant he'd become, sometimes feigning deafness, even to the last few patrons he desperately needed. How would he react to my unannounced visit?

I sat on the landing just outside the door. Amber light slashed across the floorboards and my pants. The mustache tickled my lip. Why had I even come? I'd wanted to present the Great Master with a bladder of fine Spanish red and a bottle of walnut ink, tied, as I always did for Maria, with a strand of fresh thyme. Now that seemed too paltry. A measly bottle of ink. Paint stolen from Maria's studio. Why risk it? I could leave, avoid the lies concerning the missing paint. Then, an eruption. A fat breath-halting snort. Another and another till the snoring softened, steadied. Before I could ask myself another question, I ducked inside his studio.

He sat on a squat stool in the middle of the room, neck knocked forward, back slumped, his arms resting heavy on his knees. He snorted and slept. Above him, on the easel, was his face. It loomed out of the grit and muddy tones, staring at me from across the room.

In fact, his face was everywhere. On easels and hung on the bare walls were other self-portraits. Each painting looked to have been completed in a single sitting, layers applied before the last had dried. As if he were in a great rush to paint his face before he expired. The whole room sang with the aged, spoiled face of Rembrandt. Over and over, the ruined perfection. The room was damp, barely heated, and sooty light filtered through the window, but I was filled with awe. My blood trembled. Maria's father, the minister, might have called the sensation that filled my body a holy wonder. But that's not right either. All these years later, and I still can't find the words.

The floor groaned as I stepped toward him. He honked a great sneeze and startled upright. I froze until his body eased and he sagged again, relaxing into his wheezy sleep. I edged closer until I stood directly behind him. So near I might have lifted a wispy curl of his thin hair around my finger or straightened the dirty cap on his head.

Up on the easel—pitted skin, slack jowls, spidery veins—the sweating pocked face of an old broken man. His portrait of Jan Six was no preparation for this painting, nor for any of the self-portraits in the room. In each, a sorrowful man kept final watch over his living counterpart, who drooled and snored on his painter's stool. If there was a shred of nobility in the scene, it was the nobility of honest self-appraisal. With each stroke and jab with the brush, with the thick impasto of mottled skin, he'd abandoned every available artifice, declared: No time left for refinement! Here was paint intimate, rough, and monumental. Out of nothing, he conjured everything. With a restrained palette of black, brown, and a bit of ochre at the cuff of his sleeve, he'd claimed his poverty, the wreckage of a life without apology.

I was no stranger to transience. In every still life, I painted dead flies and withered petals. But I took pride in rendering with ultimate delicacy what endured and what was fading. The refinement of diminishment, that was my goal, to make the dying as beautiful as what remained. No, to make a cleaner, more perfect world than our actual one. Now he challenged everything I'd understood about the purpose of art. His paint willfully fatty. His brushstrokes like scars. He refused to tidy the calamity of living. His refusal, a declaration of survival.

"Come on, he's finished. He's nothing." I imagined Maria's goad. "Look again at this ugly painting, will you, Gerta? I get more for a vase of flowers then he'd get painting the entire Bible. Choose your master." I could hear her laughing.

I reached into my sack and brought forth the bottle of ink and the bladder of paint. I crouched and put the ink by his feet. There was no red on his palette. Could he no longer afford it? On the palette I squirted a hefty mound of the rich red so that he'd see it when he woke.

A residue of paint was gobbed on my finger and, before I understood what I was doing, my finger pushed the crimson paint across the ochre cuff of the sleeve. I pressed two fingers into the paint and swept more and then more red along the cuff. Then, ever so lightly, I smudged my finger along the *tsk* of his bottom lip. I imagined that he'd wake and, without even questioning the sudden appearance of red on his canvas, the hefty mound of expensive Spanish red on the palette, or the remaining bladder by his foot, his brush would do what was needed. As if his very need of red had conjured it. Then, with the very best red to be found in the city, he'd feather red veins and rouge the chafed skin and elegantly frame his hands in red cuffs.

I unspooled the metal coil from a paintbrush to mend the bristles. The hairs clumped, frayed, worn beyond repair. Every brush needed such attention. The fine hairs looked like dandelion gone to seed. The palettes needed scraping. The whole studio was in disrepair. I should stay. Serve him. Keep a small bed in the corner of the studio. "Choose your master," I imagined Maria saying again.

"Yes, you certainly do love your silk and fine cream," Maria liked to say. It was true. I was a child from the pig shed who now slept on a high bed dressed in linens and silk. But it wasn't only that I'd grown used to the comforts of a closet of crimped petticoats with bows of imported lace. It was much more. She'd shaped the way my eyes saw the world and led me to the words I had to describe it. She'd encouraged me to have my own words and vision. She'd called me her true friend.

Rembrandt grunted, wrestled his ungainly body upward. I rewound the coil, dipped the damaged brush into the red paint, and leaned it against the bladder. Then, before his eyes could blink open, I bolted, tripping down the unlit narrow stairs.

EIGHT

1670

"A MARVEL, MARIA." Constantijn Huygens's forefinger traced close to the still life, mapping the movement between two flowers, pausing to pet the air where a tulip petal had begun unhinging from its stem and rested against a broad leaf like a face against a steady arm. "You're doing something very new, Maria. You've reached a new level."

Maria fiddled with her lace cuffs. Her shoes, clicking on the floor like a fan dancer, tapping this way and that, barely able to contain her pleasure at Huygens's admiration. On his word, painters' work had been well-placed and sold. He'd already made two notable sales of Maria's work, most recently to Cosimo de Medici.

It was fall, the studio windows and door open on the unexpectedly warm day. Soft afternoon light filtered through the room. I lingered just outside the garden door with a tray of cups and plates gathered from the picnic they'd enjoyed at the outdoor table.

"You feel the exact slight pressure of the petal as it weights the frond," he exclaimed, as if this were his revelation and not Maria's observation impeccably executed. "Goodness." Huygens bent closer and closer to the painting as if attempting to inhale the flowers' fragrance. She painted with a fierce—that was the word he used—a fierce realism that brought the viewer to his knees. "This is really something."

Maria stood at his side. Such praise, delivered by one unequivocally confident of his opinion, was everything to her. She trembled, overwhelmed by his approval. Of course she did—he'd been a looming presence in her life ever since she'd been a girl in Voorburg. And now he was her most connected enthusiast.

"Such roses!" he trilled. Compared to their vividness, he claimed everyone else's were paltry blossoms. "And that butterfly! Oh, I know who absolutely needs this in his collection." All the right names were said. Names Maria longed to hear. A painting for the Emperor Leopold. An Italian count. And wait till Cosimo stands before this painting; he'll need this one, too.

I listened with delight to Huygens's celebration of the work. Wasn't this exactly what I'd foreseen? That my help in the workshop would allow Maria to concentrate her attentions and refine her style? The Emperor. Medici. Wasn't this all I'd wanted? For her. For our workshop.

"Maria, I have no reason really to be so proud. But, darling, I am beyond proud. My whole body sings with pride." Huygens's hand grasped hers then quickly circled her waist. He tugged her tight to his side.

"Oh, I beg you take full credit." She actually cooed. She was impressive, very skilled at the rhythm of the flirt—at once poking fun at his claim and honoring his importance in her life.

"I'll have no problem at all placing these paintings." Constantijn walked between them, all the while keeping Maria clipped to him like a shiny new brooch. "And I'll be placing you very well."

I returned to the outdoor table to gather their soiled napkins and continued listening in. Maria kept up the banter. She was nothing less than I expected. Smart and funny, goading him to catch fat sums for each. Then there was quiet. An odd quiet. I edged closer to the door, worried that he had pulled too close to her and I might need to make a timely entrance.

Instead, Constantijn stood alone in the far corner in front of a small painting. "When did you do this?" he asked, leaning closer.

Maria walked briskly back to her worktable. She busied herself scraping dried paint from her palette, working a knife blade into a scab of green.

He remained fixed before the painting. His fingers doing that strange fluttering he did when concentrating, all ten fingers whisking in the air as if playing arpeggios on an invisible instrument.

"When did you paint this?" he asked again.

"I didn't." Her voice sounded strangled as if she'd been snuck up on. Red spread up her neck.

"Well, tell, tell, tell," he chirped. "Where did you buy it?" He leaned so close his lips practically kissed the panel. "It's superb. Quite particular."

"I didn't buy it." Maria's voice thinned like she couldn't quite find her breath. "It's . . ." I waited for her to reverse and claim it.

"Well, you must tell me."

"It's Gerta's." My name caught in her throat, a surprise confession.

"Gerta?" His fingers fluttered in the air over a curling tendril on the canvas. "Gerta who?"

"My maid, Gerta," Maria said. "I've been teaching her."

He laughed, a beefy low-in-the-throat laugh. "Stop this. Stop playing. Who is it? I could tell the style and subject weren't yours."

"Gerta, come in," Maria said. She sounded small and stiff, and I understood that what she really meant was *Gerta, I've made a terrible mistake. I'm a trapped fox. You must free me.* So I turned back into the courtyard to gather the cloth from the table. "Gerta," her voice spiked.

I stepped through the doorway. My whole body burned as if I'd rolled in nettles. As soon as she'd spoken my name, I'd understood that our secret, our private life together in the studio could be lost. She understood too. Our world was changing. Had already changed. Right there, through the open windows and door, I'd heard him say *Superb*. And she'd heard it too. I trembled just as Maria had trembled when he'd spoken of her work. Her face was racked with pain. His filled with wonder and curiosity. At that threshold, I felt pulled in both directions. I stood, trying to balance the tray of dirty dishes in my hands.

"Gerta," Maria snapped as Constantijn continued to refuse to believe that the small painted panel could be mine. "Put down the tray. Do a quick study of the dishes and napkins."

Not *Please, Gerta*.

Not *Please come in and put this pawsy fucker in his place, make him dribble wee in his pants*.

It was *Gerta, do*.

I sat at the small table and opened the box of watercolor cakes, choosing a wide, flat brush and a fine one. I heard Maria walk across the studio to take Constantijn by the hand and position him behind my wood chair. I didn't look up.

"You've seen my maid before," Maria said, as if I were not in the room. "A surprisingly capable learner, the girl. First, I taught her to prepare my paints. Next the stretching and preparation of canvas. And then—though like you, I hardly imagined it could be done—I began to teach her to draw."

I longed to show him how deftly I could wield a paintbrush and in a few quick strokes sketch the jumble of stacked cups and plates, the spiral rind of an orange, a crust of bread and the cutlery peeking out from the folds of tossed napkins. I longed to swiftly create dimensionality, the illusion of cloth bulging over a teapot, cascading into folds that half hid a silver spoon smudged thick with cake crumbs and berries. I longed to impress him and show my confident facility with substance, weight, light. How with a single slash of purple I could render shadow.

Instead, I made a mess. A horrible, ugly mess, worse than a child's. I sloshed paint, smushing and pooling colors into a soggy green and brown mess.

"Can you see how well I've taught her?" Maria said. There was lightness in her voice, relief that I'd found a way to spring her from the trap.

"My, my, Maria," Huygens bellowed, doubling over. "You have really created a valuable apprentice of your servant."

It hurt to hear him laugh. For her to join in. With each burst of laughter, I wielded the brush with greater fury, creating ever more garish displays of horrible painting. How much I desired to claim my place, for him to recognize my skill. But even more, I desired the life I had with Maria. Untouched. And with each jab and blotch of the paintbrush, I showed her that was what I valued most of all.

"And you, dear Constantijn," Maria said, "must never underestimate the range and value of my artistic possibility and experimentation."

"Well, at least let me buy your wonderful new landscape," he said, speaking of my painting. "It would be an honor, Maria. I'd keep this miracle close. I'd never sell it."

"It's not for sale," she said. "Much as I'd love you to beg. There will be others, I promise."

Without a single word or a side-glance, without a trained monkey's bow, I stood from the wood table, rinsed and patted dry the brushes, and—like the silent servant I'd been since I was a child—hefted the tray of their dirty dishes and went to scrub them in the kitchen sink.

THE NEXT DAY in the studio, a thorny silence spiked between us. "Really, Pieter," I can hear Maria say, "it wasn't nearly as dramatic as you're making it sound."

We spoke, certainly, we spoke. I suppose what I mean to say is that when we spoke, we did so in a different register, like a minuet—formal, courtly, with a stately deference. We had to speak; we were at work on two commissioned pieces for Adam Oortmans and his wife, Petronella de la Court. There were constant decisions to be made. Maria was confident these paintings would yield a third commission, her first flower triptych, which would then garner more patrons on the best canals.

My body kept to my work, but another part of me was tucked far away, safe from the ways Maria might at any moment splinter our life. *Our life*. Really, I wondered, what life was that? Wasn't it all just a way for me to pretend I was more than just simply a servant permitted to wear brocade?

"Linseed or poppy oil?" I asked, beginning to glaze a white peony just past full bloom. It was the painting's sole white flower, wilting and placed dead center in the composition, which made the choice particularly significant. With layers of glazing, I was determined to achieve the translucence of papery petals, wrinkling and thinning as they lost water. The weight of the lead white made the brush movement tricky and the right oil was of genuine importance.

"Or pine? With a mix of clove?" Maria asked in a deferential tone.

"Pine it is." If she said pine, it would be pine. I'd no longer offer countering opinions. Why bother pretending that it meant anything if I chose a glaze? This was her workshop. I would never again pretend it was ours. Yesterday I'd made a fool of myself to protect our secret life. And she would never apologize, never thank me. A thousand small and large humiliations gathered in me and, for the first time, the unthinkable rose within me. That I must put down my brush, leave Maria and the workshop. That I should have slept on the floor in a dirty corner at Rembrandt's and served his mastery. This, of course, was no longer an option. He'd died the year before, penniless, destitute, the creditors itemizing his worldly goods before he'd been shoveled into a rented grave.

And if I left her workshop, what was there for me? What workshop would have me, twenty-four, a girl without references? At best I'd apprentice to a mediocre painter in another city, suffer his groping hands and live out my days preparing pigment for his lifeless work. Or I'd spend my days a maid, high on a ladder or down on my knees. The more I imagined gathering my cloak without so much as a goodbye, the more bitter I became. I rolled the brush in pine oil, but, shivering with anger, I couldn't control my hand, my fingers dirtied with oil. I wiped off my hands, no longer fit to paint. Let me scrub floors. Or better, go to the market begging for lamb bones. Let me do anything rather than remain here in a pretense of working side by side.

"The peony is perfect," she said quietly, after I'd cleaned the brushes as though done for the day, laying them so their tips rested in a shallow well of orange oil. "You've rendered that exact threshold, that difficult moment where it both clings to life and yields to its wither. The whole composition organizes around it. Superb, Pieter."

I continued my preparations to leave, scraping down the palette slab. But there it was: Even as I wanted to resist her compliments, even as I warned myself that she'd spoken only because she'd sensed my insurgency, I was seduced by her praise, and all thoughts of running off to another studio, tamping down my hand to accommodate the shoddy work of a foul-breathing painter seemed an impossible, dreary sentence of death.

"Superb, Pieter, but where can you be going when pine dries so quickly? Won't the flower benefit from further layers?" she asked. We both knew it would, just as we both knew that I couldn't resist her acknowledgment or her prods to surpass myself. After her flattery, she attempted to loosen my tongue with jokes about Huygens. Had I seen the way he'd squealed with delight as I'd flooded the brush with water and paint?

"I thought you'd waste every gob of pigment in the studio." Maria said. "What a holy mess you made."

"A necessary one," I said dryly.

"Indeed, Butterfly, it certainly was."

I managed to keep my guard, withstanding her attempts at our usual banter. What had happened was not funny. I'd suffered deep humiliation to preserve a life we treasured. But what was that life? I was a servant, not her confidante; I was the simple assistant to whom she owed no apology. *This was simply work*, I warned myself as I attended to layers of glazing each petal till the peony glowed with death.

"Do you think the border is sharp enough on this leaf?" she asked.

"It's fine."

"It needs more on the edge by the stem. You agree, don't you?"

"I do."

I continued with terse answers. Her questions sounding increasingly like pleading until she could no longer bear my remove, crying, "Pieter, admit it. Admit you thought I would."

Don't ask, I cautioned myself, even as I was asking, "Would what?"

"Claim it was mine."

Don't speak, I told myself, and this time held to silence.

"I admit that for a moment I considered selling it. Putting a big, big price tag on your little landscape. Worse things could happen than the first sale of yours going to Constantijn Huygens. One day, everyone will want to own a Gerta Pieters. But for now, you're all mine."

"You're right, Maria." My voice flinty.

"I am?"

"The edge of that leaf needs your attention."

"Come see what I've done," Maria said late that same day, the room dissolving into the violet light of dusk. Before I could put my brushes down, she had me by the shoulders, urging me toward her easel. "Do you see?" she asked. Behind me she fidgeted like a restless child eager to be found in a game of hide-and-seek. It took a while until I saw what she clearly meant me to see. Not the three lilies that formed a luminous crown at the top of the bouquet, not any of the dozen flowers—tulip, delphinium, carnation, Siberian iris, columbine—nor was it, in the lower left of the painting, the two ripe peaches resting on the black marble shelf. But there, on one bruised peach, a dark fly sucked the nectar seeping from the newly split skin.

"I am afraid, Butterfly, that I'm the fly," she said and, turning me, leaned in until her forehead pressed against mine. She gently rocked her head, the bony ridge of our skulls rolling against one another, the sensation painful and exquisite. "I can't help it."

"The fly?" *She wants to break me open*, I thought, and though I wasn't sure what it meant, it felt true and urgent. I heard the sharp intake of her breath and felt the heat of her exhalation as her head continued rubbing against mine, disturbing, consequential.

"Here's the fly," she said. Then the wet of her mouth on my neck, a pull, a sucking—soft, then firmer. I was dizzy. A shimmering through me. "A fly feasting on your goodness."

"Isn't a fly best swatted off ripe fruit?" But then her teeth gnawed the fleshy bit of my ear, and low in my belly was a trembling, delicious ache, and I lost all words. The lengths of my arms prickled. The room vibrated. I wanted more. I thought I might be sick.

"I understand what you did, Pieter. For me. For us." She spoke in airy bursts as she troubled my throat, my earlobe. And there it was. An admission. What I'd wanted.

She's begging. Don't trust her. Don't yield, I warned myself, even as my body wanted only to press hard against hers.

"I know how terrible it was to not show your skill to him," she said while the fullness of her lips curved tenderly along my jaw. Her fingers on my neck. A hank of hair knotted in her hand, and I felt a whip of pleasure.

With that, I pushed her away, my hair still snarled in her fingers. I shook free and she stumbled, banging into an easel. The canvas wobbled. I started to lurch toward her to right it, to help her gain her balance, then stopped myself. It seemed then that everything quieted. Settled. The room scumbled in darkness. If only I could keep her there, a few feet from me, I might understand what was happening—though how was it possible that even at a distance, I felt her heat, the rasp of teeth on my skin? I wanted the yank of my hair bound in her fist. I needed her. Her mouth on my throat.

"Pieter," she whispered. Had she ever looked so vulnerable, or gazed at me so openly?

I was unbalanced, vertiginous. "Don't," I managed to say, and watched her face crumple, as if she'd been delivered a terrible blow.

She closed the space between us. Her hand hovered close to my face. "Pieter, please," she said. Lightly, so lightly, she outlined my lips with her finger, then brushing across the seam between my lips, pushed gently. I parted my lips despite myself, and, as she slipped through to my tongue, my whole body pulsed. I bit down. Caught her by the knuckle, my tongue circling, circling the tip of her finger. Someone moaned. Me? Her? Then she was pulling away, her finger released with a reluctant pop. Her brush—she was still holding her paintbrush in the other hand—dropped to the floor, and we looked at one another. Her eyes fixed on me, brimming with tears.

"Oh, Pieter."

Go, I pleaded with myself, *go fast before you fall*. Instead my hands were moving to touch her, to hold her face as I pressed my lips to hers. *Is this what you need?* Who was I challenging? A haze of questions, not one of them as strong as the clear, formidable yearning. I waited for her to reel back, scold me for my advance, for the rough way I held her face between my hands. But there was her mouth meeting mine. The sour of her tongue, unexpected, lashing. *I am kissing her*, I thought. A spectacle of pleasure. *I am kissing Maria*. Unsteady, I was desperate for more. Then, just as suddenly, she stopped. My hands slipped off her. She was trembling. I was trembling. The slight space between us tremulous. Neither of us stepped away. Nor averted our eyes. Around us the room was caped in darkness. Between us a shy familiarity. As if we had always been moving toward this.

She gathered my hands in hers, asked, "Is it what you also want?"

"No," I said, but already it was impossible that I should never again feel that quivering hesitation of her breath before our lips touched. How do I explain this next moment? It was like a waterfall—the steep tumble, rocks and ledges, the eddies and pools, a cascade of all the years with Maria. Of what I hadn't permitted myself to consider. Of what had always been there. And here, now, at this rushing sheer drop, her insistence that I declare my want. As if it mattered as much as her own. Desire ripped through my body; I was flooded, a tide of fury and longing so strong I surrendered to wherever the current pulled. "Yes," I whispered, and drew her tight to me.

We kissed, kissed and kissed deeper, then we were unleashed—slick, wheeling through the studio, braced against table corners. Unlaced, unbuckled, pressed against walls. Our hips gnashed and bucked, skirts twisted, untied. Pins clattered to the floor. Then we were down on knees and hands. We were wave upon delirious wave. Tease of cold. Of breath on skin. We surfaced, ready to drown. Undone, trembling. We slept. Woke inside one another. Brackish sweet of cunt on palm, on face. Hands shoved inside mouths to muffle screams, we screamed. Soon enough it would be known throughout Amsterdam that I painted alongside Maria. We'd lose the private life we'd treasured. It was only a matter of time. Now that particular privacy seemed scant. Why had I ever cared when, tangled and insistent, our bodies claimed for us this greater secret?

WE NEVER MADE a word for what we became. What changed between us was sheer as gauze. As delicate as the whorl of hair at the base of her neck. She'd been my Maria since I was a child, hoping to delight her with the finest ink when I first picked buckthorn and ground it with azurite, preparing shades of green. What servant doesn't know the body of the lady she dresses every day? The mole on her breast. The scar on her hip. Before I'd ever made love to her, I knew her skin better than my own. She'd been my Maria as I'd laced and unlaced her corset, tied the strings of her stockings, during all the nights she was unable to settle when I'd rubbed the small of her back until she slept. Sometimes I was the servant in her bed and sometimes she was the mistress. Sometimes the contrary. Or sometimes, starting as one, we became the other. Mostly we were something altogether different as we arrived together to that puzzling place beyond the boundary of two bodies.

Still, did I ever fully understand what I was for her? Surely many times I thought I did. Surely there were evenings, dozing, exhausted by our exertions, when I fretted I was nothing more to her than another flower which she pulled apart and studied to enrich her craft. She was generous with my worry. Surprised me when she met it with her own. Then we'd hold each other, quieting one another's fears in the darkness—as I am certain many do in their shared bed.

"We don't have to understand it all," she said to me at the end of one tender night, "just protect it."

"From what's outside?" I asked, thinking of abundant danger from the regenten and crowds, who'd happily leave us strung up for birds to peck out our eyes.

"Yes, them. But mostly from ourselves."

NINE

"COME WITH ME," SHE SAID one damp evening, and slipped out the workshop door. I followed her into the courtyard. Shared with the neighboring houses, it was at all hours a ruckus—busy with maids hanging or collecting the family wash, tossing snide or filthy jokes over scrubbed garments. The courtyard was a litter of herbs in buckets, ripe mounds of food waste, and of course animals—welcome and not—scrounging, fighting, birthing.

But this night was oddly quiet. A woolen dusk settled over us. She set her pipe down on a wood bench, motioned for me to do the same, then took both my hands in hers, and we were off, like skaters, rounding the perimeter of the empty courtyard. Lingering under windows like children playing scoundrel, we eavesdropped on our neighbors' conversations. Her face, in the evening glow of house lamps, brimmed with a child's mischievous pleasure. How I loved that face—the extraordinary range of feeling that slipped across it, like weather rustling the sea's surface.

We hid under the cracked-open window of Willem van Aelst's. Inside something crashed. Someone moaned. Then a rolling chain of farts that sent us running away before foul plumes hit us or we were caught cackling and provoked greater wrath. Willem was furious that Maria, once his devoted student who had denied him marriage, was now sought by the best collectors in Amsterdam and all of Europe, her paintings commanding a higher price than his.

"Look," Maria said. We'd rounded back to the front of the windows of our own studio. I turned to her. "Not at me, Pieter," she said, pushing me away. "Look inside." There, on the easels, our two canvases, wet with the day's paint, shone in the lamplight.

"Imagine we are messengers arrived in Amsterdam without knowing who is famous and who is not," she said. "Our only instruction from the king before setting off on our long voyage was to return with one painting, the most superior we could find. And here we have come upon two. Well, which would be chosen?"

"Yours," I declared without hesitation.

"But you haven't really looked yet." She laced her arm through mine.

Around us the evening picked up, the ringing of tin and copper pots, the sour wails of a baby, the *chip chip chip* of an axe on wood. "Get!" a woman shouted. "Get over here!" The rain had turned to icy sleet. Maria shivered and I pulled her close.

Suddenly, I felt afraid to look. To really look. I knew she wouldn't budge, wouldn't go inside, until I did. We stood quietly. At first, I could only pay attention to her trembling and to the fixity of her gaze as she regarded the two unfinished canvases framed in the windows. But when I made myself consider both paintings, despite the near-identical flower choices, composition, and palette, despite the fact that I painted exactly as she painted, I saw that hers was truly the better. A fear unclotted in me.

"Yours is the greater," I said, and in the dark courtyard dared a kiss.

"I know! It really is!" she chirped, as if surprised to have earned a well-deserved ribbon.

I continued, "Only your great painting will be carried home to present to the Royal Emperor of Mughal."

"Well, this is very good for both of us," she said. "I pity the day when that is not the answer. If your painting is ever the worthier, I'll have to send you back to Delft. Off you'll trudge each day to paint little tiles. Vases and plates, if you're lucky." She grabbed her pipe off the bench and skipped in wobbly circles, kicking her heels like a drunk sailor until she stopped in front of me. "My God, I'm frozen, Pieter." She climbed into my arms, her slender legs flopped over mine. I bundled her to me. Arms around my neck, she hugged close, shivering. "Carry me inside, Pieter, and heat water for us to take a bath."

ONCE, I WALKED IN to find her by the window, a book resting in her lap, though her gaze had shifted from its pages. I quietly stood behind her, hoping to uncover what held her rapt attention. Perhaps a flight of swallows or the dewy span of a spiderweb. But I could see nothing out of the ordinary. The mystery of her ignited within me. How well we think we know another. There's the comfort of memories, of completing another's unfinished thought. How often after years of life together, appetites align such that Maria might remark on her craving for cream and figs before I'd unpacked the fresh market figs. But that morning, watching her, I understood that however well I believed I knew her—her hungers and reservations—there was another world within her that would remain forever subterranean, vaporous and impenetrable. I wanted to stand there basking in that unknown. In the marvel of her complete privacy. And, at the same time, I wanted to disturb her, to intrude.

When I touched the soft skin at the nape of her neck, she startled. "Pieter," she said, her face coloring as if she'd been caught having spoken a private thought aloud. "What is it?"

"What did you see?" I asked.

"Nothing, it was nothing."

WHY ARE ALL THE EASY DAYS, the stretch of a simple life, not the real story? I don't have any answer, but I know it to be true. Here's another question I can't answer, for all the years I've asked it. Why do all those good days slurry until they puddle in the mind, when it was this undisturbed span of happiness and health, years without war or plague, years where simply we lived together that were actually the most remarkable? Oh, there were so many good days. Kind days. Grinding malachite. Chasing down indigo and gamboge. I continued to keep the house, to prepare fresh paint, to paint beside her. I continued to lace and unlace her skirts, and we pleased one another in every way a body could imagine. As I'd predicted, Maria's fame continued to spread. We traveled. More grand homes. More spectacular dinners I readied her for. More salons and theater than I can recall. But best were winter nights at home. We drew the curtains against the cold and to shelter what was indoors. Her small frame curled into a chair, feet propped on a heated footrest, reading aloud while I rendered paint for the morning. One night, looking up, her shawl and gown had slipped from her shoulder while she read. She must have felt me looking, a smile curling her lip as she refused to meet my gaze. Such longing coursed through me as I crossed the room to her.

Not that I've done much querying into the private lives of others, but I imagine we were no different from most. How can we explain the unnamable daily delights of life between intimates? The small grudges that, stoked one morning, blaze into fury? Why would we want to? How could an outsider understand the deeper argument when we bickered about a torn stocking? I might try to conjure how one day a tiny phrase repeated at a midday meal exploded into hilarity, and every attempt to right ourselves culminated in soup snorting from noses. But it would make no sense to anyone else how the word *fungi* had us rolling on the floor. I can't explain it. Only that our nonsense was also a pleasure.

Once, before I'd had the chance to fill a bladder with fresh crimson, her hand scooped into the mound and she ran her fingers, thick with paint, down my neck. She instructed me to shed my clothes, or she'd make ruin of my garments. Then her fingers drew vines of pigment from throat to belly. On my stomach an orange carnation bloomed under her fast fingers. "Hold still," she said while each breast became a full flowering. What a sight I was! And soon too, what a sight was she! No surprise little was left of the paint needed for the canvas work.

I promise, I wanted nothing more.

TEN

Jacobus home. Restless, underfoot. Then gone and home again and again and again. I hated holidays. Now he was home once more, grown lean and edged, the last of his baby fat melted off. He was sharp, ribbed, his body cut like an arrow, always flinging himself about, on that edge of childhood where in a moment he'd flip between reckless youth and demanding infant. He couldn't be bothered to go outside to play, instead slamming a ball inside, marking the walls and ceiling, leaving piles of broken crockery or glass in its wake.

"Pick up the pieces," I said, holding out the brush and tin pan.

He looked at me blankly.

"Clean it up." I pushed the pan into his hands.

He let it drop with a bang. "That's your job," he said, and turned away.

I grabbed him by the collar. "You'll do as I say," I said, and added, "when you're in my house."

Then tears. More tears. The claim that I'd pinched him. "My neck," he moaned, returning to his well-worn baby behaviors. The more Maria coddled him, the more the crying escalated. Then it wasn't just that I'd bruised his neck. "My arm," he shrieked, cradling it to his side as if I'd tried to tear it from his body. And the denials. He never bounced a ball inside. Of course he knew better. Why was he always blamed for my clumsy hands? And she said it was her house, he said, pointing at me. But wasn't it his house too?

"Of course, this house is yours, my darling," Maria assured him, cutting me a you-should-know-better look. "And I know Gerta loves you."

"Why can't you love him?" she asked later. "The poor boy lost his mother."

"It's not a question of love," I challenged. "Is he allowed every rudeness because she's dead?"

"If you want to teach him humbleness, it might be good for you to apologize."

"For what?"

"See Gerta, he's right. Casting all the blame without taking your own. He'll learn by our example." As if Maria ever apologized to anyone!

I suggested that the city was the problem, unhealthy and unnatural for a growing boy. Just look at the scamps that roam the streets, causing nothing but trouble. He should be packed off to the countryside, where he'd wear himself out with a slingshot. "The air alone would be good for him," I said, trying to muster concern for his well-being.

"I have no interest in going off to the country," Maria snapped.

When I explained that he might spend a month or two in the house of a distant cousin, who in summer would certainly welcome extra hands to help in the family's gardens, Maria looked at me coldly. "He's my family. You're always eager to have him gone. What has the poor boy done to you?"

Plenty, he's done plenty. But I said nothing and swept up the broken bits of pottery.

I tried to soften my manner with him, but Jacobus sharpened his war against me. One morning on my rounds to empty chamber pots, I found he'd gone about his business as if he had no eyes to mark his aim. I knelt, scrubbing up his mess. And what a mess! I scraped between the floorboards where all matter of foul was wedged. Over the rasp of my brush, I heard laughter. Looking up, I saw the window drapery ruffle, the boy hiding, delighting in watching me clean up his filth. In an instant I was pulling at the drape, beating him about his head with the dirty brush. Even as I knew I'd gone too far, I could not stop. He yelped and shot past me. I stood there, like a madwoman in the window, shaking, holding the brush with its filthy caked bristles aloft for any passerby to see. Soon enough—and I'd known it was coming—Maria marched into the room with Jacobus a step behind, a triumphant grin smeared across his face.

"Have you gone crazy?" she shouted. "What were you thinking?" She pushed him between us. The curls of his hair were clumped with bits of his own shit. He rounded his bony shoulders as if wounded and frightened even as he glared at me, triumphant.

I looked over him and spoke directly to Maria but even as I said how he'd intentionally missed the pot, I knew how it sounded. Knew he'd already spun his woeful story about a cramping belly, no doubt blaming the food I'd set before him. And was it fair that I'd beaten him for an illness he couldn't control? And hadn't he told Maria I wasn't to be trusted?

"Apologize," Maria said, and touched his shoulder. For a moment I let myself hope she expected him to speak. "Apologize," she repeated, glaring at me with an anger that was absolute. "Apologize to my child." I looked at Jacobus, who could barely contain his victory smirk.

"My apology," I said.

"She's lying," he whined.

Maria's eyes narrowed with disappointment. "From the heart," she scolded, as if I were the recalcitrant child.

"I am sorry for my mistake, Jacobus. Perhaps I might fix blackberry bark tea to ease your stomach." My every sugared word a humiliation.

With her arms around Jacobus, Maria prodded, "Now, Jacobus, your turn,"

"But I did nothing wrong." He fell back, crumpling against her body. Oh, the little actor! The indignation in his voice was spectacularly wrought.

"I know, dear son, but we must graciously forgive."

My God, how unbearable it was to suffer Maria in this theater of good and moral mother with her *dear son* and her *we must forgive*.

"Well, I won't have her tea. She's sure to poison me." He turned and hugged Maria, who laughed.

"Don't be silly," she said, "there's nothing to fear. This is only our Gerta, not some cruel woman from a tale." I laughed along, dirty cleaning brush bumping at my side, admiring the boy for the clever idea of poison, one I hadn't thought to consider.

WHEN HE WAS IN OUR HOME, Maria and I were never together at night. She was too busy playing the proper mother. When she wasn't praising his keen mind, she followed him about, sketching his every ball toss and somersault. The more she mussed his hair and pulled him onto her lap like he was still a baby and not a lanky broad-shouldered boy, the hungrier I was to touch her and be touched in return. I practically danced the broom about the rooms to attract her attention. But she had no eyes for me.

Some nights, helping Maria from her clothes, my fingers lingered along her spine, touching her in ways that promised her response. And, despite a few protestations, she turned her mouth to mine. But, suddenly, the footsteps. Wasn't he forever lurking, ready to catch us, to pounce at her slightest yielding to my affections! Then he was pushing wide her bedroom door, wailing like he was five and not thirteen, "I've had a bad dream," rubbing away nonexistent tears.

"Come, come to me." She sprinted across the room and swept him in her arms. "Does this big boy need to sleep in my bed?"

He wiped his face against her shoulder. As they snuggled under her feather blankets, I folded her blouse, tidied the room, and bitterly bade them goodnight.

When he was called back to school at last, I set out to arrange and pack his trunks. She'd spoiled him with gifts—books, maps, ivory carved pens, pearl-festooned buckles—so much so that I could barely latch the trunk.

"Thank you," Maria said when he was gone. "For all you do. It means so much to me."

"Of course," I said. I wanted to ask what he really meant to her. Why all the affection when she might simply have provided an orphan's allowance? But I didn't. Perhaps afraid that what she felt for him now was no longer simply obligation.

AFTER ONE EXCESSIVELY LONG HOLIDAY, Jacobus wrote reporting that when he'd arrived at school, he'd found rotting fruit and meat among his new clothes and books. His books were infested with bugs and his starched linen shirts gummy with caramel. "It must be that horrible maid, Gerta, who's made such a mess of my things," he'd written. Maria and I were in her bed, sweaty and sated, as she read aloud from his letter. "She's out to ruin everything. Please, be watchful of her, my dearest aunt."

Maria found the letter wonderfully amusing. "Yes, we must always suspect that it is the maid stealing caramels and grapes for a semester of school," Maria said as her fingers circled my stomach, playing on my skin with tenderness. "You're quite dangerous, Pieter."

I lifted each of her fingers into my mouth as she read me the rest of his accusations. "It was me," I said, rolling toward her, thrilled with her delight as I detailed all the terrible things I'd done to Jacobus.

"What a wicked imagination you have," she said, straddling me and whipping her hair about my face.

Her nephew, of course, had spoken the truth. I'd cheerfully sent him off with trunks of maggot-riddled meat and rotting fruit sandwiched between his pressed shirts.

"BE WATCHFUL OF HER" was a refrain the nephew warned in his letters, spelling out the old story of the shrewd servant, neckline lowered, breasts plumped to catch the widower's gaze. I took caution, afraid of what he'd piece together of the life between Maria and me. This orphan was a risk; he smelled rotten with danger. It would only get worse as he got older, quick to notice and guess more. I couldn't trust that he wouldn't tell others, herald what he saw. Warn them that I'd fouled Maria. What then would others see when they peered in our house? A leg draped over a leg? A tongue on a breast? A house of two women, painters, who lived a quietly unruly life outside the rules of men? For what rules hadn't we broken?

Yes, I was watchful. Of him. Of everyone. There was too much to be protected.

ELEVEN

1672

"Come, Pieter," Maria called from her bedroom. It was the evening before one of her grand dinners. I was weary, muscle and bone, after scouring markets across town on a quest for the next exotic fruit she might feature; I didn't have strength for a late-night revelation of a banquet display that'd surpass what I'd spent the day creating. Nor could I consider yet another amendment to her planned attire. Already I'd practiced the complicated patterning of Venetian combs and jewels she wanted positioned in her hair.

"Please, Maria, no more tonight." I stomped into her bedroom, prepared to find her pacing. Instead, she lay on her bed in her sleep gown. "Good." I quieted my voice but kept it firm. "It's time to sleep, Maria." Often, when she was too distracted, she needed help getting to sleep. What now? Rub her back? Make a sideways chair of my body for her to fit against? Placing my palms against the soft skin of her temples, I worked small circles. My fingers pressured the brow, the nose, then all the fine points along her skull where I knew how to unwind her worries and excitements. Even her earlobes I riffled between my fingers. In this way, we'd slept many nights right through to morning.

"This isn't why I called you." She pushed my hands away and sat up in bed. I was used to her resistance. Especially nights before these large dinners for distinguished men and women, she had a terrible time settling down, her mind a swirl of possibilities. Already the week had been dizzying, with a sweep of everything we'd hoped for. Not just the triptych. Not just a substantial sale by Huygens. There was the hope of a prominent Amsterdam commission. An onslaught of possible exciting foreign commissions, including one from Emperor Leopold. This particular dinner was to carry the declaration of her larger arrival.

"Is this what's needed?" I slid behind her, reached one hand around to fit between her legs. With the other I combed my fingers up the back of her head, fisted her hair in my hand. Keeping her tight to me this way, my hand pressed and circled. Soon I would have her quickening against me, then she'd settle and sleep.

"No. Get ink," she said, pushing my hand from her. "And there's paper on the table."

"Maria. Enough," I said. I needed to balance firmness with patience, though I wasn't sure I had the strength left to summon either. "No more drawing tonight. You need to rest for your guests."

"Don't!" she hissed as I leaned to huff out the double tapers. "Tonight, you'll draw me." In a single motion she lifted her gown and stretched her pale body back against the length of her pillow.

"Another day," I argued, sliding my knee between her legs.

"No. Now." She rose from the bed, dragging me up alongside her, our purple shadows stretching against the walls as we crossed the room. Leading me to her dressing chair, she handed me ink, brush, a board clipped with papers. "It's time for you to draw me."

She recrossed the room and folded partway onto the bed, one leg hanging so her toes brushed the floor. "Admit it—you've wanted to," she teased, flipping from her stomach to her back. "Show me what you have when I wake."

I waited in the chair as she tossed in bed, her limbs tangling in and out of the sheet. Soon enough, I thought, she'd beckon me back and ask for my hands to shudder the restlessness from her body. But then, with a snort and a jolt of limb, her body stilled. She eased into a light snore.

Even after she'd fallen asleep, I didn't dare dip the pen. I'd drawn flowers and fruit. I'd taken apart garlic, examined the bulbils that grow along the stem. I'd studied the anatomy of pistil and stamen, ovule and seed set. Put my nose and—when I safely could—my tongue to a flower so that its smell, its taste were things my drawing hand understood. But she was right. Of course I wanted to draw Maria. There was no body I'd studied more. I bathed and powdered her and knew the measure of her limbs, the texture of her skin. My hands and tongue had made study of her every fold and plane, but I'd never dared draw her. Now here she was, inviting me to draw her in repose. Could I bring all that I knew to the paper?

I was exhausted, agitated, but through the night, I sketched her as she slept. I drew her arms hatched across her face, the bony instep of her foot. I drew her stillness, her restlessness. The wool blanket bunched between her thighs.

Then morning. A bruised early light bounced off the canal, watery through the curtain. Maria woke and propped herself on her elbow, stared at me and at the scatter of papers on the floor. "What are you doing?" she asked. I lifted a page of quick sketches. The wing of her shoulder, the fine tendons of her neck. Her spine like a rope of amber beads.

"What are you doing?" she repeated, as if she'd no memory of her demand. She pulled on her nightdress, rose from bed, and walked to where I was seated. Heat flushed through me. I hated the speckled stripes of red that she'd see streaking my neck and face. I waited for her finger to trace along the charcoal lines, where, with a smudge, she'd correct the length of an arm, show me where my observation had lapsed in favor of what I assumed should be there. I waited also for praise. *How beautifully you see me, Pieter.* That's what I'd imagined all night. Instead, she knelt, slowly considered each page. Said nothing. A hand curled around the fold of a blanket. The twist of her torso. Her arms flung wide and the fall of her full breasts. She lingered on a drawing of her face in profile. Outside, water slapped as a boat passed. I was suddenly unfathomably tired. I wanted nothing more than to crawl into my own high bed and sleep.

She tidied the drawings into a single pile. "These are quite good, Pieter," she finally said, unfurling from where she'd knelt to stand. Walking back to her bedstead she didn't bother to turn when she said, "Now, go. You'll have missed all the best delphiniums in the market. And, Pieter, I woke thinking rabbits stuffed with fennel and pork will be not enough for tonight's table. See what fowl has come in."

In an instant, my night of drawing had been dismissed and I'd left her room feeling ashamed and small for the praise I coveted. I was late to market. The best flowers would be gone. Out on the streets, the busy rasp of brooms, the other servants long at their chores. I hurried to my bedroom for my boots and hat. Who did I think I was? Always wanting more and more from her. What had I really expected? A compliment for each drawing? Look what she'd already given me. I was in my very own bedroom with tall windows that looked out onto the canal. On my desk the finest paper and brushes. Three pillows stuffed with feather, not reeds or straw. My pillows. My desk. My bed. A life beyond what I had known to imagine. Why was it, with each greater possibility, I insisted on imagining more? I grabbed up two wicker baskets and rushed to find birds at market.

BY EVENING TALL URNS of delphinium and peony lined the hallway. I'd cooked twenty rabbits stuffed with pork, rice, and fig, and twenty herons stuffed with grape and almond. There were tiered trays of pies, savory and sweet. That evening, as I refilled goblets, when the guests grabbed my bottom or pinched the swell of tit, I didn't have to fight an urge to spill wine on their coats. I let each unwanted touch be a reminder of my place in her house.

Late in the night, when the guests were plenty drunk and the arguments had grown loud and dull, I heard the shatter of glass. I hurried out with pan and broom, expecting to find that some man had deemed it essential to punctuate his latest philosophical position with a burst of destruction. Instead, there was Maria, standing on the Chinese lacquered chair, arms lifted above her head, fingers splayed wide. The guests gathered in a loose ring around her. Thousands of shards of red glass, her favorite Italian vase, spread like a shimmering garment on the floor beneath her.

"Oh good, Gerta," she called when she saw me. Her voice was lively, lit, as if the glass shone upward. "How quick." She beckoned me with both arms. "I didn't even need to call for you. Gerta, don't you think it's time I show everyone my latest work?"

I wasn't sure what she expected me to do. To step in and sweep a path so that she could safely get out of the pool of glass or run first to the studio and bring up the finished triptych she wanted to show off?

"I've been hinting to everyone that we have a big secret, Gerta. It's time to properly show them." I felt my legs buckle and I steadied myself with the broom.

"Maria, come on," Huygens shouted. "Not this old trick you dragged me through years ago."

"Just wait." She was practically singing. "I'm full of more tricks than anyone could ever guess."

At her instruction, a chair was brought into the center of the circle of men and women. The next thing I knew, a guest was heaving platters of fresh figs onto the floor and I was hoisted onto the cleared table, still clutching my broom and pan. "Pass the maid," Maria commanded, and the table, with me on it like a roast duck ready to be served, was shifted from the hands of one guest to the next until I was in the center of the clustered guests. Maria ordered that I be set on a chair, the table pulled close. Directly above me, she hovered on the lacquered chair. She scanned the room, certain all her guests were paying attention. She hushed and cut off a wayward group who remained in private conversation. When everyone was corralled to her satisfaction, she began.

"Gerta, my maid, was a mere child, the family's servant, when it occurred to me that she wasn't different from any laborer who, acquainted with soot, nuts, the work of slaughter, might be well suited to prepare ink. I set her to the task. Trust me, she was inept. Very clumsy. Many days I thought it futile, that she was too simple, too dull-witted to be trained. But sometimes there were glimmers, perhaps only lucky mistakes. I persevered, schooling her as you would a stubborn horse until she could assist me in this way. And slowly the glimmers became a more constant show of talent. Yes, her methods were slow and often unorthodox, but scouring bogs and forests, she'd begun making unusual inks. I was pleasantly surprised. I told no one. Instead, I readied her for the next level."

Anger choked in my throat. In her narrative, I was little more than a puppet or show animal. I began to shake so hard the chair skidded forward, the bed of glass crackling beneath.

"But perhaps you are unmoved, thinking that paint preparation is noteworthy but not remarkable for a servant. As we all know, many a young boy has come to the city to apprentice in an artist's workshop. But clearly . . ." Maria paused. "The shapely bottom and breasts I've allowed you to ogle and pet all evening are not those of a farm boy. Behold this lovely girl, my servant since she was seven, raised in the shed. I've schooled so that her hand is steady and exact. Tonight, you will see that I have done the unthinkable—trained a maid who paints as well as a man. Gerta, if you would, please paint a composition of tonight's dining table."

There was an uproar. Rowdy laughter led by the groans of Huygens, who clearly assumed he was being forced to endure the old joke. "Kindly make this quick," he moaned. At some point, the broom and pan I clutched were replaced with charcoal, brushes, a dinner plate ringed with globs of oil paint, and a small pot of linseed. I craned my head to see if Maria would give me a sign. Any private gesture that I was to make a mess, slap paint about like a fool, and make her guests laugh as I'd done for Huygens in her workshop. I would've happily made a comedy of myself. Anything was preferable to this. But Maria kept her gaze outward, a clear refusal to look at me. She loomed above me, her arms outstretched as if still welcoming her guests. With the slightest flare of her nostrils, she signaled to me that I was to obey. With the second flare of her nostrils, I understood. This had been the entire point of the night's banquet.

I felt lightheaded and horribly confused. She'd needed the element of surprise to entertain her guests and patrons, but why blindside me? Clearly, she hadn't trusted me. Hadn't trusted that I wouldn't refuse this cruel exposure. Or couldn't be bothered to tell me or see my reaction. I wanted to resist her. I knew I wouldn't. It was my fault for letting any private happiness cloud my vision. How had I not anticipated that as Maria's work exploded, she'd need to formally establish that her studio was capable of carrying out more commissions? Even with her increased fame, no young men wanted to serve in her workshop. But Maria figured out how to turn that to her advantage. She understood that what people loved most was novelty. And I was novelty.

I closed my eyes and when I opened them, I was ready. With confident strokes, I roughed out platters of mounding fruits, the flower and feather centerpiece I'd assembled all week. I sketched lemongrasses waterfalling over trays of picked-over heron and rabbit carcasses. The room's silence broken only with gasps of *Impossible* and *Is this actually her maid?*

"See how I've taught her to control line and composition," Maria announced. She bent over me. Her hand scuffed the top of my head. "Now paint, Gerta."

As I began to paint the tableau, I remembered the night before. In my eagerness to draw her body, what sleepless trance had I allowed myself to be drawn into so that I forgot that anything Maria offered most often had a second purpose? When she moved among wealthy patrons, I was quick to applaud her ruses, her manipulations. We plotted together for ways she'd ask for more money or gain favor with a dealer. Now I was the one being used. The invitation to draw her sleeping was an apology in advance. Just as her coldness in the morning was a reminder of my position.

More than once in a moment of doubt, I'd asked why of all the interesting men that courted her and even those few women that offered delighting, she would want someone as common as me. She'd scowl and say, "How can you ask that?" as if hurt by the question. But with the men and women watching me as I followed her directions, it seemed that maybe her response was not hurt but surprise. Because the answer to my question was so obvious. With me, she'd always come first. Who else would give her that? What she chose in choosing me was my absolute devotion.

I painted fluently, with precision and not a moment of an apprentice's hesitation. I showed an enviable range in mixing color given the limited palette provided. I performed just as she'd known I would. With each deft stroke, with each subtle blend of color, I indeed made them croon, *Maria*, practically in unison. My skill was proof of her genius. Maria van Oosterwijck, woman painter among men, who'd schooled her maid to paint with a skill that made them gasp. *Clever one*, they congratulated her. *Out of nothing, look what you've created.*

"What else are you hiding, you sly one?" someone shouted, and Maria shouted back, "Isn't it the nature of women to have brilliant skills hidden in plain sight?"

While the room succumbed to banter, I layered transparencies with semiglazes of linseed and smalt. I ribboned a single blade of lemongrass, letting a purple shadow slip beneath. I painted delicate heron bones pyramided in a glass bowl. And when I painted the bones as they refracted through the glass bowl, even Maria cooed with delight. Only Huygens looked angry. He chided, "Once was a joke, but I don't like being fooled twice." As I worked, I rocked. Back and forth. Back and forth. My boots ground the broken vase. I pressed harder against the floor, grinding and fracturing glass under my wood heels.

When she determined that what had been shown to her guests was sufficiently remarkable, she commanded me to stop. "Stand up, Gerta. Take your proper *révérence*." Oh, didn't she enjoy her bit of French! But I couldn't move. I was exhausted. By this future I hadn't chosen. By all the times that I'd be lifted into circles of men and women and commanded to paint and take a bow. "Up," she insisted, tapping her fingers on my head. "Stand." I looked up at her. She was radiant. I stood. Took up the broom and pan and swept the splinters of glass.

LATER, AFTER THE LAST of the guests had congratulated Maria and a few had actually bowed to me as they tumbled out onto the streets, Maria danced, whirling about the kitchen. "Your debut! You were perfect, Pieter." She twirled behind me as I scraped and washed platters. "What a perfect night." The crystal beads sewn at her gown's hem rang like tiny bells. Perfect? As if we'd rehearsed it! My debut? As if together we'd conspired this spectacle! I dipped an alabaster platter into sudsy water and circled with the wet cloth.

"Huygens might have actually pissed into his silk shoes," she said, drawing her finger along the ridge of my ear. "Van Uchelen has asked us over. To see the exact spot where he hopes to hang my painting. And Jan Six offered an invitation. He wants two pieces— one by me and one by you. You'll need new dresses." She flounced my skirt and tickled me. "Beautiful dresses for my assistant." I leaned the platter against the stone sink, hefted a jug of boiled water to rinse it. "Aren't you happy, Pieter? I want you happy, Butterfly. You need to be happy."

"Of course," I made myself say.

She spun me toward her, almost knocking the platter and jug off the counter, then kissed me, childish and insistent. "We're happy," she said between kisses. "You were spectacular. Even I was amazed at what I'd wrought."

I leaned back so that we gazed directly at one another, though what of me could she even see when she was so flushed with the fullness of her night? I was small, inconsequential, and she gleamed.

Under the hanging lamps, her dress shone a deep blue, her thin neck banded by strings of shining crystals.

"Now every one of those Guild men will watch how quickly I'll surpass them. If they hadn't bothered to consider me before, now they won't be able to avoid me."

"You've done that," I said, my eyes holding hers. How well she'd always understood that a woman, considered foremost for loveliness and humbleness, might make use of her invisibility, until she emerged blazing with talent where no one expected. She'd used this night, this show of me, to further catapult her fame. Why should I have expected otherwise? She'd made use of me, but I wondered if I was really so different. Wasn't my invisibility as a servant also a gift, something to use? Maria never suspected that someone who emptied her piss pot, dusted every shelf, dressed her, heard her secrets, prepared her paints, washed the bedding where they made love, that this servant might quietly dream of recognition of her own, of her place among artists.

"I'm happy, Maria," I said. And, strangely, then I was. The bitterness gone. I felt a new edge to my life, like touching the tassel of a curtain that, pulled aside, might reveal a landscape more remarkable than any I'd known. Tonight, I wore a serving uniform. Soon I'd wear a new dress, finer than any I'd ever owned. Soon I'd return with her to the home of Jan Six and not enter through the servant's door.

"What a night!" she said, her voice tousled and sleepy. "You did well, Pieter."

"I've learned everything from you, Maria," I said with tilted reverence.

THE RICH ARE PRONE TO CRAZES. They can't help it. The itch to spend. To acquire. Often couched in curiosity, they fill boats with colorful birds to fly about their houses. Study a single salamander, and soon they possess whole cabinets of leopard frogs, newts, and snakes. Then they hear that a discerning ear and pleasure with music indicates a man's quality, and, within months, there's a dedicated chamber cluttered with lutes, single-stringed instruments hailing from the East, citterns, a rosewood tessellated organ, and an elephant-skin drum from Africa.

For the wealthy, suddenly we, the Van Oosterwijck workshop, the unmarried lady and her servant girl that paints, became the craze.

Our dear Huygens, with his keen mind for opportunity, quickly forgave Maria for making him seem foolish and brokered many sales. Just as the portrait painters convinced the wealthy that pendant wedding paintings were de rigueur, Huygens proposed to this same clientele that it was less intriguing to buy only one painting by Van Oosterwijck when you could hang a second by the servant as well. Both, of course, signed with Maria's name. What could be better, Huygens suggested to prospective owners, than to entertain guests with a game of guessing which was by the lady's hand and which by the maid's? Games, of course, are another diversion of the rich.

Soon we were scheduled out with commissions for the next three years. It seemed a new one came each week. We fell into a sturdy pattern of work and talk. It was comfortable. No, much more than comfortable, both with work and with each other. It was as if, with one less secret to guard, any tumult, any breach had been mended, and we were in better harmony than ever.

At the end of the day, I'd plug two pipes of tobacco, and we'd sit on the stone windowsill ledge to regard our progress. From this vantage—just across the room—mistakes and possibilities we'd overlooked were glaring. What was also clear was that Maria's work was changing. There was greater vibrancy in her paint, a fresh robustness to the compositions, and with each painting, she increasingly departed from her old teachers. Each element, each blossom more entirely hers. No longer polite observations of transience, each vessel with flowers became a portrait, not a still life. Maybe I'm quick to flatter myself, thinking her changes had anything to do with me. But I believe that working by her side, I emboldened her. You could argue all that had changed was that others knew I was in the studio with Maria. But now I understood that the secret had yoked Maria, kept her timid, beholden to Guild men who would not include her. Now the Van Oosterwijck workshop was unlike any other, and this was a freedom and source of strength for her.

PER USUAL, I accompanied Maria when she went to draw at the Hortus Medicus, but now that I was declared a painter, I also drew whatever rare plant Jan Commelin, steward of the gardens, had newly brought to the grounds. I felt proud when he lingered to watch the sureness of my hand as I built tones of highlight and shadow for the waxy thick camellia leaf. So much so that I didn't even mind that, when watching me draw, he directed the compliment to Maria, saying, "I've heard tell of your student, Gerta Pieters, but I didn't really expect you'd schooled her so well." He wasn't the only one. The physicians who studied medicines were as likely to linger and compliment Maria on my drawing as they were to consider the benefits of the jasmine flower.

It wasn't that I'd forgotten how much I'd loved the secrecy of my private painting life with Maria. There is a powerful freedom in having secrets, in controlling what is known to whom. I truly would have kept our whole lives secret, but suddenly I was as rare as the new Chinese tea bush in the garden, and it became clear that this was another power. The freedom to be seen. For my worth to be known. I liked their eyes on my drawings. Yes, it was her they complimented. But it was my name they said as well.

ONE DAY AT THE GARDEN, I heard, "Gerta, Gerta," and looked up to see Luyc, the apothecary, loping toward where we sat with our drawing tablets. "I knew it!" he shouted. "Much as you've denied it since the first day you came into the shop, I've always been certain that you are an artist."

I couldn't answer or meet his eyes. It was odd to see him outside of his shop, and I was embarrassed by his straightforward notice of me. He always had a good word for me at the shop, and I loved to make him shy by offering my own loud praise when the shop was busy. We enjoyed all the funny ways we each found to ruffle one another. An amusing show of respect had become a contained friendship over the years. But his open praise in front of Maria felt somehow indecent.

Maria cleared her throat, waiting for a proper introduction. When I gave none, Luyc bowed, making much celebration of her name and international fame as he introduced himself.

"I own the humble shop which has had the honor of providing you with pigment these many years. Though it is your Gerta, a fierce and discerning customer, who insists there can be nothing but the very best quality for Maria van Oosterwijck."

"I must accompany Gerta to your shop one day. You must think it laziness that I send her in my stead, but I find it hard to leave the workshop once the day begins."

"My shop is hardly worth your distraction. From the heft of your orders, I'm well aware you have no shortage of work to complete."

Maria and Luyc continued charming and flattering one another. I was unable to assemble a single contribution. Finally with a deep bow, Luyc said, "I'll leave you fine artists to your endeavors. I'm off to attend what I hope will be a fractious, come-to-blows discussion on the benefits and vagaries of field mycelium."

Luyc had barely gone when Maria drawled, "That was a revelation. He practically turned inside out over you."

"He was just honored to make your acquaintance."

"Come on, Pieter, I have eyes. The way he looked at your drawings."

"It's your work. He declares you're the best in Amsterdam."

"You've never mentioned that our apothecary has such longing for you."

"I assure you, Luyc is more concerned with mushrooms than me."

"And you? Do you long for him?" Her voice was stiff. It took a moment to realize what seemed incredible. She was jealous.

I stared at Maria with a forthrightness I never dared in public. "Maria, I want no one but you."

"First the apothecary, and then who knows who else will come forward wanting Gerta Pieters, the artistic darling of Amsterdam." She closed her folder of sketches and began packing the vials of ink into her satchel, her face still so vulnerable. How did she not understand that no one else ever mattered? It took every restraint not to pull her close and kiss her right there in the garden of the Hortus Medicus.

Those days, when we were invited out, or sometimes just strolling the canals, we dressed in similar shades, mine always in a hue a few steps down from hers. If Maria wore midnight blue, I wore cornflower. "We are always a statement," she crowed. A walking advertisement for her studio. For this particular visit, Maria wore a dress of tangerine silk brocade. I wore pale peach. Her cloak was forest green; mine, moss.

We climbed the front staircase. Before we even knocked, the great door opened and we were ushered inside the house, Maria's arm looped through mine. We nodded to the doorman and to a young maid, who thanked us when she took our cloaks. I looked down, admiring how the blond light from the open door pooled at my well-shod feet.

"Maria. Gerta," Jan Six boomed. "Welcome, dear friends."

Though I'd been in the house before, of course, I can't be blamed for pausing in my finery and taking an extra moment in that remarkable gallery of pink marble, with its ceiling-to-floor display of gold-framed paintings. Maria, on the other hand, didn't bother to look about. Instead she vaunted forward to gossip with Jan Six. When they were a few steps ahead of me deep in conversation, I twirled twice around in my silk dress before hurrying to catch up behind Maria as they walked side by side through the rooms of his great house. "You'll approve of your placement," Six said to Maria. "At least I hope you will." His voice was earnest, as if he genuinely desired her approval.

"I hope I will, too," Maria said, subduing every trace of the bounding excitement she'd displayed on our walk to his house when she'd bubbled to me, "First one, now two more—that makes three paintings from my studio!" She'd listed every artist of repute with only one or two paintings in Jan Six's collection, tossing off the names as if they'd become mere afterthoughts.

"It's a prime spot, you'll see," Jan Six said. "But first, I'm certain you're curious about my other new acquisitions."

"I am, of course," Maria said, as if making one's way through a bowl of rancid porridge was a requirement before gorging on platters of oysters and elderberry fritters and cream.

I was no stranger to witnessing people's passion for their possessions. I'd seen a merchant bent with reverence over pages of a book written in a language he couldn't understand. The skull of a hummingbird or a rare shell from across the world might invoke rapturous stanzas. But when Jan Six spoke, it was different. He spoke of his acquisitions with great restraint, as if they were under his protection rather than ownership.

Maria endured a portfolio of etchings from Italy and another from France, her foot tapping as she pretended to admire the intricate carving of a jade figurine. But when Jan Six began to lay out on his table a collection of brightly hued watercolors of Caribbean fish, Maria finally burst. "And my paintings will go . . . ?"

"Of course, I've been rude." He laughed. "Forgive me."

He led us directly through three more rooms where there was so much more to admire, and into a large dining room where two flower paintings signed with Maria's name were indeed placed prominently, opposite one another, at the heads of his grand table. We regarded one painting then slowly circled the long table to stop before the second flower painting. We circled the room twice more.

"I enjoy the idea," Jan Six said, "that over the natural course of a meal and conversation, our guests will gaze upon each painting before proclaiming which is Maria's and which is Gerta's."

"And you?" Maria said. "Have you already decided?"

Jan Six looked back and forth, his delight quickly draining. This was an inconsequential game, he'd thought, a merriment between courses. As his eyes went back and forth, he realized that there was more than one way to lose this game.

"Maria," he said, his voice tempered. "I would never presume to make a guess of such gravity until I had long lived with these paintings, which, as you know, will be my daily pleasure for many years. The game, if I can call it that," he continued, now undaunted, "will be how my guests judge and what it reveals about their thinking."

"I'd sleep much better if all my paintings were in the homes of philosophers like you." Maria took his arm. "Now will you show me once more that sloppy portrait by Rembrandt that makes you so very proud?"

Truth be all, she had not a moment of interest in seeing any Rembrandt. This gesture was entirely for me. We'd argued about the painting and, more than once, I'd accused her of letting her assumptions get in the way of truly seeing. But even for the portrait of Jan Six it was hard to leave the dining room, where my painting—yes, signed Maria van Oosterwijck, but still mine—hung. I imagined the important guests, dignitaries from all the world, who'd be entertained in that room. And someone, I dared to imagine, might claim that my canvas was the finer. It was a torrent of feeling, unknown to me before that moment. A messy wave of awe and fear and joy and disbelief that *my* tulips, *my* carnations, *my* butterfly were framed on the wall in that house, which featured so many great artists.

And, perhaps, I also stalled knowing that when I left the dining room, I'd stand again by Rembrandt's portrait and be filled with a sense of unworthiness. Also, terrible pride to have my painting in the same house as his. If my first experience years earlier seeing the

Portrait of Jan Six was a shock, this viewing was no less striking. But it was also a dear return, like seeing again a face you've cherished and craved; when reunited with it, the face is more remarkable because you'd forgotten so many details—the skin's mottled texture, the crooked scar on the chin. And then, there it is, before you again. A little different. Ever dearer.

Of course, I was different as well. Having honed my art, I understood even better the daring as Rembrandt played between rough and smooth brushstrokes. The push and pull. It was so personal. It spoke not just to his mastery but to his complex understanding of his subject. The scarlet cape tossed over one shoulder against the crisp white linen proclaimed, "I understand the balance of this man, Jan Six."

"Gerta," Jan Six said suddenly, the first he'd spoken to me since his initial welcome. "You had some affinity for this painting, if I recall. Now that you yourself are painting, might you help Maria understand what's worthwhile?"

"Yes, Gerta." Maria laughed. "Please, help me."

"Well . . ." I stammered, wishing for a more confident tongue. But neither of them waited for my response nor turned to look at me. They babbled on as they wandered the periphery of the great room.

"Speak up, Gerta," Jan Six said, his voice amused. Maria tittered a shallow laugh. It stung. Though I hadn't entered through the servant's door this time, though one of two paintings he'd dine below every night was mine, I still owned neither my words nor my art. What was required of me here was to fulfill my part in an entertaining parlor game. That was all. I was no different from the maid who had taken my cloak in the front hall and now stood silent in a corner, on hand for any required service.

"Well, just as the flower painter contrasts her perfect flower with a single withered petal to make us aware of our impermanence," I began, striding past Maria and Jan Six to approach the portrait, "do you see how Rembrandt, with these two hands—one perfectly rendered and the other crudely sketched below the glove—says something about the man Jan Six?" I didn't look at them. Instead, I addressed my comments to the young maid, extending my arm to beckon her closer to the painting. She took an awkward step forward, then stopped. The room fell silent. I didn't let my eyes stray though I felt Maria and Jan Six behind me, and I continued. "His mastery in paint"—I pointed just as I'd seen Jan Six point when speaking about his acquisitions—"is that through it, above all else, he conveys emotion." Then I bowed to the girl, who, bewildered by my attentions, once again dropped into a curtsy and slipped quickly from the room.

Jan Six coughed. "Perhaps your maid has attended a few too many lectures as your companion." Now I was *your maid*. No longer Gerta.

"Clearly I've confused her," Maria said. "Let's please go visit your Vermeer so I can cleanse my palate with someone who knows how to paint."

"I WANT TO GO WITH YOU," she said as she watched me fasten my high riding boots. It was late in the evening after we'd returned from Jan Six's.

"It's no place for you." I was quick to answer, not bothering to hide my annoyance. I hadn't been able to stop hearing the scorn in Maria and Jan Six's laughter, their dismissal of me. Anger rose in my throat and I swallowed it down.

"Why then is it a place for you?" she pouted.

Throwing my hands in the air, I said, "Clearly I've confused you. The docks are knives and grabby hands, not a fancy lecture or salon where it's been made clear I was mistaken to imagine I had a place." I fastened the last buckle on my boot and stood.

"Pieter, don't be silly," she said, coming to button my waistcoat. "It was you who lectured the innocent maid and practically frightened her to death. Do I need to remind you that our purpose there was not an exhibition of your brilliance but to review the placement of two Van Oosterwijck paintings?"

"I can't allow you to go," I said. "It's not safe. Who knows if there's even any worth in my going tonight." There'd been rumor of an incoming ship from the East with a grade of lapis never before seen in the city.

"You don't allow or not allow me, Pieter. I want to go, and will," she said. Before I could gather a response, she pulled from a bag on the table a man's linen shirt, which she promptly layered over her bodice. "I want to see for myself all you've described. Anyway, I hoped I'd have more use for this than the costume ball." She stepped into a pair of coral pants, then slipped her arms into a deep green waistcoat and motioned for me to untie her skirts and help her with the buttons. There was no point pretending I could stop her. When I'd finished helping her dress, she reached into the coat's pocket and withdrew a length of cream silk to tie as a cravat at her neck. "Forgive me for being so much better dressed than you, Pieter, but perhaps this wealthy merchant will negotiate a sweeter price than you."

The port at night wasn't a costume ball. Dangerous enough to walk at night as a woman, the danger doubled if one were caught as a woman dressed in male clothes. Her hat, which I pinned in place, was large enough to shadow the delicate angles of her cheeks and chin, which I stubbled with dark paint. But what if someone snatched her hat and her curls tumbled out? If she insisted on coming, I was going to need to ready more than her attire.

"Stand wider," I ordered, pushing her legs apart. "Keep that distance with each step." Just as she'd once schooled me to take the narrow steps of a woman, I instructed her to walk with the lumbering gait of a man.

"I make a fine man." She postured and took a theatrical bow.

I didn't give any sign of approval. "Take off those lady rings." I needed to impose strictness for our safety. "And, truly, stick close to me. The less you say the better, Maria."

"Who is this Maria you speak of? I'm your cousin, Sander, visiting from Delft," she said, and took a second bow.

As I've said before, the port at night is a busy hustle. Men of every hue and tongue haul and swagger, crates strapped to their bodies and woven baskets of live animals balanced on their heads. It's a world that deals in shouts and hushed threats, where what is passed from hand to pocket might be worthy of a gentleman's nod or the slice of a sailor's ear. Some nights the air is rich with the smell of timber. Other nights the salt air stings with spice. After unloading cargo, men off ships are hungry for whatever can be grabbed on land. You learn to recognize the sailors who debark from the grand pepper ships not only by their pungent odor but also by their overstuffed pockets as they toss money toward every pleasure. Meats grill on open fires. Nuts roast. A man opens his mouth and a green speckled snake emerges. Crates are pried open. Brightly dyed Indian fabrics and Chinese fans hawked. Sailors gather around men, showing feats of impossible strength. Others contort into shapes like dough. Men stomp and twirl and sing, accompanied by bizarre instruments that the next day will be the city's latest craze.

Nights waiting for what might arrive, I learned to keep to the shadows or crouch silent by the fires, listening. If you said little, if kept your eyes sharp, you learned a lot. Soon it was easy to nose bravado from truth, to know whether an offer was honest or dirty. But there was no crouching nor listening for Maria. She took to the docks as if she'd arrived at a festival, and there was little I could do to contain her. Impossible to convince her that what might appear simple could, without notice, ignite. That rolling dice might spin into hurtling knives.

"Look," Maria squealed, her voice undisguised, as a dark-skinned man led five ostriches down a ship walkway. I pinched her arm to shut her up. But she pulled away from me and I had to run to keep sight of her as she wound through the crowd.

I stood behind Maria as she joined others shouting, "More, more," as a man, naked but for his turbaned head, squatted over and over, an iron weight inconceivably strapped to his balls while, in his hands, he juggled five flaming sticks.

There was a series of loud booms, and, in the moment I turned to see what was happening, I lost sight of Maria. Didn't see her merchant coral pants. Didn't see the yellow hat with its red plume. This way and that, pushing men aside, I ran. Even as my fear mounted, there was the scalding echo of her voice, *You don't allow or not allow me, Pieter.* I slowed to an amble. She wanted the docks at night? She didn't need my caution? Fine. Let her manage her own good time.

When I finally spotted Maria, she was thicketed deep in a grove of men who were clapping and hooting. In the center, a woman in a sheer red dress tossed scarves, her body curving with each catch, the scarves slithering about her like reptiles. She beckoned to one man, and instantly the cheering crowd parted as, chest puffed, he stepped forward. She wound her scarves tightly about the two of them, so that they proceeded to dance as a single undulating form while the onlookers whooped and yelled. You didn't need to know the many languages to understand what their motley shouts encouraged. I'd seen unspeakable things happen to women at the port while men looked on cheering. I'd seen how quickly performance becomes dispute, how gaiety flips to savagery. More than once, I'd risked a blow by kicking a boatman who'd ripped the apron from a young woman, determined to wrestle off more. But I kept to the outskirts as Maria wedged between and under the shoulders of the men until she stood in the very front ring. "Brava! Brava!" she shouted and stomped and clapped as if she'd landed at the opera. "Brava!" she shouted, her voice theatrically husky.

In a deft move, the Woman in Red flung her partner away, and he tumbled back into the crowd while she again spun in circles, bright scarves floating around her. Then she came to an abrupt stop, her gaze fixed on Maria costumed in her rich merchant garb. The dancer beckoned, her arms luring the merchant to join her for a dance. Without a moment of hesitation, Maria reached out, grabbed hold of a red scarf and began turning herself in it, wrapping close to the woman all while keeping up a bright jig. I stayed at the edge and watched as the two began their intimate dancing, knowing what Maria should have considered, that as the Woman in Red clasped tight, her hands would discover the secret of Maria beneath the merchant's clothes.

What is it about a costume that unleashes behaviors one would never exhibit in daily life? Perhaps Maria was no different from the crewmen, whose families back home wouldn't have recognized the outlandish behaviors of their obedient sons in foreign ports. Under her guise, Maria refused to stand in the shadows, and I could hardly blame her. I knew all too well the relief in being free of what you've always been. Relief to shed all the expectation that drags heavy at the hem of oneself.

At first it actually seemed simple enough. The same scarf dance. The same clapping and stomping from the onlookers. But instead of the Woman in Red releasing Maria back into the crowd and selecting a new partner, the tempo of the dance began to shift, the dancer gyrating with ever greater seduction. "What do you want to see from us?" she called out to the men.

The crowd heated, their demands insistent and rude.

"That's all?" she taunted. "I could give you much more." She arched backward so that her head almost reached the ground, while she held Maria tight to her body.

It was clear to me that the dancer knew that what she had in her hands was a night beyond her usual fare. That she'd tease it out, slowly bending her partner into increasingly suggestive positions, encouraging every lewd call and pelted coins, knowing that for the finale, she'd tear at the merchant's clothes to reveal what she'd felt as soon as she'd taken him in her arms—the shapely body of a woman.

Even with Maria's yellow hat tilting ever more precariously and the painted beard hiding most of her face, I could see her increasing discomfort. Her head twisted left and right. She was looking for me. Expecting me to step in. To rescue her. *You don't allow or not allow me, Pieter*, rang in my ears and I held back. I waited. I reached into my pocket and threw out a coin. Threw out more. Waited as the crowd became a single pulsing animal. Watched Maria's increasing helplessness. I waited. Until I heard it, my name. "Pieter," a whimper from her lips, then louder, "Pieter!" Only then did I elbow through the throng and, taking my knife to the scarves, slit Maria free of the Woman in Red, slapped a last coin in her hand, and dragged Maria through the fevered crowd, refusing to answer when she dared ask, "Where were you?" My only response a sharp "Yes" when for the third time she pleaded for me to bring her home.

IF THERE WERE adventurous nights waiting for ships and days of fancy dress, most nights it was only myself out back, pouring household waste into fermenting pots of Indian yellow or sieving muddy reductions and grinding slabs so that in the morning what was needed in the workshop was on hand. Those nights it was the good quiet of my work, the roosting chickens and the rabbits in their hutch. And when a stray cat yowling in heat slinked near, I pressed a wood muller against her swollen sex to relieve pressure. She rounded my leg, tail raised for more. "I'm temporary relief," I promised. "Soon you'll have a true kater's bone to shut you up."

Other nights I worked amid the neighbors' noisy secrets in our shared courtyard—the hush of lifting skirts and the moan of a man who should have been long under covers with his dowdy wife. Not one of the neighbors liked me. I wouldn't have liked me either, with my taffeta skirts, my lace gloves, and my arm-in-arm strolls down the canal streets with Maria. "Fancy cow," they called me and not in a whisper. Did I care? I'd heard worse. Heard it all. They knew it was best not to speak it to my face. I held a fat purse of their secrets. The egg thief. The merchant who fancied the smooth ass of a boy. The wife who fancied the same one. The swelling waists of maids and what they drank to rid themselves of it.

At the end of each night, I took to lifting a rabbit out of the hutch. After the foul stench from gassing pigments, I bent my head to its neck and shook my nose into its sweet grassy fur. "What a life," I said into the darkness. Hearing its steady breath in return, I envied that the creature never wondered how to live in its body nor worried what it truly was. As I stroked the rabbit, I thought of the uneven gait of the tin-cart man, how when he stepped out on his right leg, he was tall, a robust fellow, but as the twisted left one came forward, his whole body contorted with effort, his cart clanging and jostling unevenly on the cobblestones. Wasn't I a bit like him? One moment turned out in my good clothes, speaking smoothly as a lady, the next expected to be an unsophisticated servant, stumbling in speech and stature. Not exactly a maid but also only a maid. A painter but a secret one. A secret wife of a great painter whom I served so that she did not have to suffer under a husband who'd claim her great skill and her body as his own. I was so many things and none of them. Sometimes it made me unsteady. What did it mean to know my place, or to make my place? And what was our place—Maria's and mine?

I stared in through our studio window and studied the progress of our two paintings while I petted the rabbit free of her jitter. "Which is the one and only painting I'll bring back to the kingdom?" I asked the rabbit. "Which is greater?" Each night, for many nights, as I stared at our two canvases, I told the trusting hare before releasing it back to its hutch that it was Maria's. But in my rivalrous heart sometimes I wished it were mine.

SOMETIME SOON AFTER surviving our night at the docks, Maria offered to employ an additional maid. I refused, insisting that I was perfectly capable of managing the house. "But you aren't managing," Maria said.

"Who do you think made this soup you're lapping up bowl after bowl?" I growled. "Have you ever gone hungry? Put your nose to your clean blouse and tell me if it stinks." I ladled more of the wild mushroom into her bowl. Tore another chunk of bread and slathered it with thick cream the way she liked. "Tell me, Maria, is there something you're lacking?"

"You're up all night in the studio, in the market at dawn, the studio all day. You're cooking, washing, scrubbing floors. You must mind your strength. Oh, Pieter. I'm trying to give you something. Not take something away."

"A meddling maid that I have to teach is your idea of a gift? I don't need a stupid girl underfoot." And why was she worrying about my strength? I was not yet thirty.

"If it's not a gift for you, let it be a gift for me. Why am I the only house on this street with one servant? I'm richer than most of them, yet I live like a common woman." Maria stood from the table. "Pieter, I need the best of you in the workshop. I don't need you to wash my slip."

Could she ever imagine the attention I'd taken since I was a child of seven with her slips and linens? The heated water I scented with chamomile flowers. The care never to scorch her silk stockings. The idea of hands other than mine carelessly or even dutifully scrubbing her stockings hurt me.

"You have to be selfish with your time if you're a painter."

Living with Maria I knew that to be true. But my having the privilege of selfishness, that was a comedy. Still I heard a challenge in her offer. No longer a child, it was time to make a claim—even a small one—for my life as a painter.

"I won't want her to live here with us. I won't have her telling stories about you, about us, in the yard and the rest of the neighborhood flapping their smelly tongues." Maria understood then that she had won. She wore it on her face triumphantly. "And I won't have her eating at the table with us." I waited for Maria to refuse, because, of course, like any Dutch servant, I'd always eaten at the family table.

"She can live and dine with the rabbits if that's your liking. Choose who and what you like, Pieter. The rules are yours. And as for meddling, just snip out her tongue."

Despite myself, I began paying attention to girls on the streets and in the market. Which maids were choosy, smelling melon skins and making sure pears hadn't gone mealy? Which girls minded the family purse, quick to notice when the heavy-handed fish monger threw extra weight on the scale? Which girls dawdled the morning away, making noise with every market boy? And then as if just by allowing myself the thought of employing a maid, my days suddenly became unmanageable. In a single week, I burned the meat pie, let the dye boil over, forgot to chip ice off the front steps so that—had I not been right behind to grab her—Maria might have slipped and broken her wrist.

In the end, I poached a girl from a larger, abundantly staffed house on our canal. Diamanta was a Portuguese Jewess, sturdy and olive-skinned with doleful black eyes. She kept to herself. At first, I wasn't sure she spoke any Dutch, then was pleased to learn she was fluent but not a gab. Meticulous with every chore, she wasted no time with flirting or yapping or trying to make friends with the other maids on the street. When I made my offer to Diamanta's parents, they accepted, clearly happy for a better wage and to have her returning home each night, sleeping safely under their roof. As for the uncommon request that she not take meals with us at the table, they were undisturbed, perhaps relieved that their daughter could maintain their particular food restrictions without any pressure.

Diamanta barely needed instruction, though I was merciless. I wanted her to understand how specifically I ran my household. That, whatever she'd done in another home, my way of folding a kitchen cloth was the only correct way to fold a cloth. Although her cleaning was impeccable, I barraged her with criticism. I wasn't kind. I called her lazy, though each week she wiped down the crystal glasses I often left undusted for a month. I complained all the time to Maria. "Diamanta smells of horseradish," I said when she left the room. When a porcelain bowl slipped from my hands, I pointed at the shards on the floor and blamed the new maid.

I was loath to admit the girl was any help to me at all, although it was obvious she was. I could settle into each day of painting, confident the meal would be ready exactly at the hour I'd instructed. When I rose from the table, I left dirty dishes and cloths, heading straight to the studio to grind ochre. I'd be lying if I claimed to miss polishing silver platters or scrubbing the windowpanes with vinegar water. I went to the shops and to the market to select flowers only when it pleased me. Soon I hardly gave the house much thought. Which I suppose is the key to selfishness. I didn't have to bother with it because someone else was.

TWELVE

CALL ME THE BRAGGART, but who in Amsterdam with means did not eventually own at least one work from Studio Van Oosterwijck? And then well beyond the city. Emperor Leopold of Austria, the Prince of Orange, Cosimo de Medici, the King of England, Louis XIV. The King of Poland bought three paintings. And isn't this what I'd silently vowed? That with my help as her assistant, she'd be feted for her gifts as an artist. Now it was widely claimed that no still-life painter, no painter of vanitas in all of Europe surpassed Maria van Oosterwijck for verisimilitude. Her patrons sent presents in excess of their commissions to show their appreciation. Shell haircombs. Vials of amber and rose perfume. Fine ostrich gloves studded to the elbow with diamonds. A gold and emerald leopard figurine. And yes, an actual baby leopard, a gift Maria politely refused. Philosophers. Composers. Princes. Everyone sought her attention. The finest homes. The Viennese court. Come and stay all of July, wrote Huygens. Always parties and more parties. One year every invitation announced a festive theme, so that I was forever wrapping carmine cloths about our heads and buckling pirate swords to our hips or donning gold-threaded vests and the embroidered slippers of sultans.

Imagine that. I was there too. Invited to their parties and the dinners. As the maid, I'd always accompanied her on trips. But now, Gerta Pieters by name was specifically invited to join Maria. That I was to be by her side, even at dinner tables, became inevitable. I was her moon, Huygens claimed. "If she would rise like she recently is risen it should be nearly gold," he wrote. I was that she! Recently risen. I was that gold! My only rival as a still-life painter, he claimed, was Maria herself!

And before gatherings at our house, she'd say, "Be my good wife tonight," and I'd say, "Gladly," which meant I'd bustle about and make sure the wives were well cared for. Obviously, I was not actually one of them. There would never be a marriage contract or feast. It hardly mattered. Our secret made our happiness sacred. Untouchable. Our privacy like prayer.

How natural life seemed. How easy and full, each day. Maria wanted for nothing. I wanted for nothing. My brocades, my hours painting, a maid who cleaned after me.

Here's the truth. I loved the attention I received so much that my own attention wobbled and I forgot to be wary. I was so charmed by my life as assistant to Maria van Oosterwijck that I was like the drunk guard sprawled at the palace gate singing boozy ditties while any criminal might sashay through with nothing more than a friendly wave or the offering of a tin cup of beer. I never woke thickheaded with the abundant dazzle and praise of those years and counseled my own sobriety. So enamored was I with our life, I never noticed a darker future lurking. But do any of us suspect danger in the coming hour when the prior hours held every goodness an hour might hold?

"So now you're a philosopher too?" Maria would tease if she heard my clumsy way of saying that much as I'd prefer to linger—detail every beautiful canvas, show off the costumes we wore to parties, and recite verses by poets that praised our work—it is more important to tell what happened next. And after that.

BOOK
II

THIRTEEN

1679

IT BEGAN WITH A GLASS. Then a plate. A dropped brooch. Oh, my Maria. What could be glued, I mended. What could not be unbroken, I tossed. Then I dismissed it—anyone might have an accident. But over months, it persisted. A stutter of fingers as Maria fixed pearl clips in her hair. A botched lip stain.

We did not speak of it. Instead, I filled the air between us with rumors of the fishmonger and the baker's wife's infidelity while I retied the fumbled bow of her apron. We took on more commissions. I steeped teas of skullcap and valerian and looked away as she lifted the shaky cup.

Day after day she kept to her work. Seated at her stool, she painted slowly. Then even more slowly with her elbow anchored on her knee. Refused lunch. Refused tea. It was winter, a raw bluster. Ice skims on bucket water. Canals frozen thick. Only when the last corner of light had seeped from the room could I convince her to put down her brushes. I prepared oils of rose, geranium, sandalwood, black pepper, and sage. Slipped tinctures into her bath. Foraged mushrooms. Cowslip. Nettles. Filled her silver pomander with rosemary and bergamot. There were more commissions. I vowed to care for her better still.

ONE NIGHT, as I drew her a bath by the fire, she whispered, "Pieter. Do you think . . . ?" Kneeling beside the tub, I rubbed lavender and rosemary soap on a cloth and washed down her weakened arms, scrubbing in slow circles. "Pieter, what could this . . ." she started again. She turned to me, her face twisted with fear I'd never seen before. I rinsed the sudsy cloth, refused any outward response. I wouldn't allow us any weaknesses. "Sometimes it aches. Sometimes I can't even . . ." She tried to lift an arm from the murky water.

"A terrible damp has climbed into my bones this week," I said. "I'm certain that I've caught something, too."

"Maybe that's all it is, Pieter, something I've also caught," she said. "I'm feverish, yes?"

I put my lips to her cool forehead. "You're warm." I smoothed her wet curls. "You've been pushing yourself, Maria. Much too hard."

"But do you think it's—"

I cut in and, bossy as I could marshal, insisted she go to bed. I eased her from the basin, winding a towel around her slim torso. I dried and creamed her limbs. Rubbed her hands with oils of helichrysum and vetiver. I tucked her in with a heated stone wrapped in flannel and dabbed two drops of frankincense to the roof of her mouth. She called for more layers. More heat. I blanketed her in wool and fur. But as soon as they were bundled over her, she wrestled free, a leg angled out on top.

When she finally fell asleep, I went to the studio, as I had every night for the last two months. I lit the lamps and began to tidy the canvas. I worked very carefully, softening the edge of each flower, clarifying where a petal joined a stem. It was delicate work. Every curled, rolling petal, the violet shadow cast by each leaf vein was rectified. Every flower refined. It wouldn't have been obvious to everyone. But that wasn't the point. She'd never painted for everyone. She painted for the discerning, for those who maintained her work was more realistic than the actual vase of flowers. I watched the decline and saw that she also knew. We said nothing. Both waiting. Like a strained muscle, a crook in the neck, we convinced ourselves it would improve. Instead it deteriorated.

Her failing fingers, her tremoring arms and hands I could not mend. But each night after I soothed her to sleep, I went down to the studio. It's still hard to say this out loud. I corrected Maria's paintings.

Each morning, back at the easel, Maria boasted she was renewed. How pleased she was to be free of whatever had gripped her the day before. I was quick to compliment the rosy color in her cheeks. Morning after morning we repeated the same charade. There was never mention between us of the mended canvases.

I SANDED A WOODEN STICK. At one end of the stick, I wadded a cotton ball wrapped in chamois leather; at the other, I attached a curved piece of hammered tin. It was a mahlstick to give Maria's arm traction. She'd be able to press the ball against the canvas and, holding the stick with her left hand and the curved tin against her chest, rest her painting hand against the stick as she managed a brush.

"What are you doing?" she asked.

"It's a mahlstick to help you." I fitted the curve against my body. "See, it'll stable your—"

"I know what a mahlstick is." She cut me off and, snatching it out of my hands, tossed it across the room. "It's pitiful." With that, her elbow anchored in her left palm, she raised her brush and tried to secure her pinky against the canvas. But her hand would not still. Each furious brushstroke tremulous. She pulled her arm tight to her body to lock it in place. The brush wiggled, jabbed the canvas. Wet paint smeared her fingers. I kept grinding the red ochre. I washed and sieved it and spread it to dry. Said nothing.

"Really, Pieter," she snapped, and threw down a brush loaded with blue. "Who can paint with all your racket?"

BUT THERE WERE other days in that first year, easy days, when her hand was steady, when the paint moved effortlessly once more. What a relief, those days. To work long hours together. Time at the end of the day to sit on our stools, pipes in hand, and admire how she captured the density of the sunflower's dark center, the packed, fused petals. How her layered yellows achieved the brilliance of the flower's rays. While we enjoyed our smoke, it was easy to believe all was restored and our gravest concern was correcting the length of an azure shadow.

"YOU MIGHT AS WELL march up and down the streets of Amsterdam shouting, 'Van Oosterwijck is finished!'" Maria hissed. We were walking, arms laced, as we often did, but now, uncertain when the tremor would appear, she kept her hands piously clasped. Even in the warmest weather, I carried her ermine muff in case her fingers yanked into spasm, and she needed to hide them.

"But your doctor might—" I started.

"Oh, please, hurry for my doctor who happens to be the doctor to every rich merchant, collector, and painter in the city."

"But maybe . . . maybe he has something."

"A fast mouth, that's all he has. How often has he walked into our house and, before he's shed his coat, announced what's down the throats and pants of our neighbors!"

I offered to fetch a doctor from another city or to bring Luyc, the apothecary, to the house. He could be trusted, I promised. Maria refused. Life would continue as it had, she declared. She hadn't come this far for a minor tremble in her hands to take her down. Did she need to point out that many a threadbare, dejected man we passed on the street had once been someone of import strolling the Herengracht? Had I never registered how the city's hunger for ostrich one season became a singular obsession with leopard the next? We had more work than ever and needed to continue seizing our due.

She was right. Of course she was right. And so, she managed her public façade. Accepted invitations, attended salons, concerts, and lectures, always keeping her hands in the pockets the dressmaker had sewn into all her garments. She refused any handshake or kiss with the sly boast that she had too much commissioned work to risk infection. At lavish dinners, even ones at her own home, she refused to eat or drink.

"I've had my share of worldly delicacy and drink," she'd say, encouraging others to keep eating. "Let your company be the sweetness that fills me, not the pastry."

Other times, she'd cast her eyes heavenward, thanking God for what labors he had tasked for her on earth. If anyone privately doubted her show of piousness, no one dared to do so publicly. She'd been cast as the model of virginal devotion for too long, even by those who'd enjoyed many an unruly evening in her company.

"I have so much work," she bragged in a letter refusing festivities in one country home, "I must stay in the studio."

"I miss none of it," she announced to me. I pretended to believe her.

THEN CAME TANTRUMS. Insults hurled. Plates smashed. Then blame. She spun in circles, wanting to accuse. Who had done this to her? And who may have learned her secret? She imagined one man looked at her oddly. Another with pity. How did they know? Surely I'd betrayed her. How could it be otherwise? She tore the silver pomander from her neck. The medicines were bad. The food poison. Was it the fowl? The pig that sickened her? There were days when her fingers locked holding a loaded brush, and she cried out in pain and cursed me as I unbent the rigid clamp of her fingers. Some days by noon, I'd been fired more than once, then by evening, weeping in my arms, she'd have made me promise I'd never abandon her.

For weeks she refused the studio. Then she appeared in her smock, insisting it had all been a nervousness that had lifted at last.

"Look," she held out her trembling hands. "I'm back to myself."

"You're always yourself," I said, as if I'd never been worried.

"Really, Pieter, I have many selves and there are a couple of those selves I'd be happy to give up."

A SILKEN SPRING LIGHT draped through the room. The surprise of Maria, at her easel. The mahlstick I'd made months earlier, which she'd furiously thrown, now anchored against her chest, as

I'd known it eventually would be. One hand secured the stick of the bridge while the other managed her paintbrush. Each stroke was cleaner, steadier than anything she'd achieved in weeks. How many times had I set a path then let her claim the direction? I knew her moods and mind better than I knew my own. For so many years, my own body, my own concerns had been hewed as an echo of hers. Most days I felt my thoughts to be merely an anticipation of her happiness and needs—which only grew more acute as I managed her illness.

"Stop watching over me," she said. "I'm not a child."

I set about preparing my palette, removing the skins that had puckered over the paint during the night, dabbing in bits of poppy oil.

"Every edge was a blur," she said, "but I've fixed them." The messes she spoke of were, of course, my most recent corrections to her murky flowers and leaves, the ones I'd worked on through the night. You might think I would have had to remember my place in the studio to temper my tongue, but I was delighted. This was my Maria returned. Snappish. Refusing to admit fragility. Refusing to acquiesce.

I watched from the corner of my eye as her lips tightened and relaxed in a steady rhythm like a metronome guiding her hand. Small clean strokes, one after another.

"It helps, Pieter," she said, her voice gentle. Still her hand fumbled.

"I'm glad for it."

"Now make me a better one. Fashion it longer so I can brace it between my knees. And a harder wood for the mahlstick. I might want to use both hands."

✦ ✦ ✦

SINCE THERE WAS to be no doctor, I schooled myself in herbs just as I'd once schooled myself in pigments. At the medical school gardens, I wandered behind young physicians as they discussed medicinal plants, then hurried to Luyc's with a list I'd compiled. I waited until the shop was empty of customers, then slipped through the door. At the counter, I mustered a neutral tone, asking Luyc about the various uses of rhubarb, cumin, long pepper, and dragon's blood. What were the benefits of ground coral and antler? With what and how were they best mixed? By the tilt of his head, I watched Luyc diagnose as I spoke.

"Put your hands out," he said.

"I'll do no such thing."

"Put out your hands," he insisted. I held them between us, faking a tremor.

Luyc came out from behind his long wood counter and spoke to a customer who had entered the shop. He weighed and jarred oil of peppermint, then escorted the man to the door and locked it behind him.

"How long?" he asked. When I did not answer, he repeated, "How long has it been going on?"

"Not long," I said. "I'm feeling better each day. It's just lingering a bit."

"Please, Gerta. I'm trying to help. How long has she had the shakes?"

"I'm not sure who you're talking about. It's me who's been ill."

"Gerta, I want to be of use, but I can only be of use if you let me. How long has she had this tremor?"

"A year maybe. Maybe more. It was slow at the start," I said, looking around the shop even though I knew the door was locked. "But now, some days, she has almost no use of her hands. It's moving up her arms. They tingle. They're often numb. Other times too cool or too hot. She won't let me ask for help." I was so relieved to finally speak of the spasms, I answered his every question. Headaches? Fevers? How's her breathing? Are there rashes? Sores? At some point, without ever stopping his questions, all more and more specific—did she sweat? On the neck? The wrist? Was her thinking clear? Her dreams disturbed? What was the color of her urine?—he moved behind the high counter and began pulling out sacks and jars, measuring, grinding, explaining how to create a clay poultice, what drops should go under her tongue, and which dropped in each eye.

"You can't speak of this to anyone," I said as I packed my basket full of medicines.

"You think I've ever shared a word that's transpired between us?"

"No careless chat with the other painters who come in looking for red lake," I repeated, not caring if I insulted his honor.

"I keep all secrets here," Luyc balanced his hands on the scales. "You imagine you're the first to come in with a problem you don't want known? I don't tell you what this man needs to quell his nightmares, or what this woman needs to keep her blood from clumping into pellets."

"Is she dying?" I hadn't allowed myself to ask that question before even in my mind. As soon as I'd said it, I wanted to spool back the words. "She's not dying," I said. "I know it."

"Oh, she'll die. Sure enough." Luyc smiled. "You and I are heading to the dust too. But there's plenty of years in her yet. She's fortunate, Gerta. She has you looking after her. You come here, having done your studies, with a list of herbs most physicians don't know. Who wouldn't be lucky for your loyal attentions?"

. . .

I WISH LUYC WAS RIGHT, that I could make great claims for my care. That I was able to cure Maria or at least harness the illness. Jars of skullcap and ginger tea steeped on the counter. Though Luyc insisted that ingesting Egyptian mummia was not real medicine and refused to carry it in his apothecary, it was easy to procure in the city. I speckled ground tomb skull into tea and, for a few weeks, crumbled more into a paste with molasses, which I spread on Maria's hands at night before wrapping them in cloths. One shopkeeper sold blood and powdered bone, claiming that fresh mummia was more powerful than ancient.

I kept careful note of which ointments and tinctures were tried, which fruit and meat eaten, and if there was a string of good days where Maria—with the help of the new bridge I'd made—could steady a brush, or if after a meal the front of her dress wasn't smeared with dried bits of food, I'd have a surge of confidence. Yes to fish. No to pheasant. Yes to apricots and blueberries. No to cherries and oranges. Then with the pluck of victory, I'd prepare fish stuffed with apricots, spinach, and blueberries. But when the tremor flared again, I'd abandoned these foods, insisting she drink broths of mushroom and of anise and black walnut, deeming the problem was worms, and once cleansed, she'd return to herself. Now I switched the order: By day I wrapped her hands and arms to compress the nerves and at night I unwrapped the cloths for increased flow of blood. The truth is, despite weeks of relief, on the whole the shaking steadily increased.

Over the next months, a new code emerged between us. Maria might speak of weather in our hands, of a damp in our fingers. Always *our* hands, *our* fingers. One day she suggested we rest after our midday meal, and soon, most days we'd lay down then together. I made sure Diamanta was busy outside during those hours. Daylight filtered through the bedroom curtains. The streets eventful with hawking and commerce.

"We've become Italians," Maria said. "Our riposo."

"We could do worse," I said, watching the watery shadows ripple up and down the silk.

She fitted close to me, her chest rising against my back. Her fingers clutched my loosened hair. Sometimes her unbound hands flared, shuddering with spasms. I set a course to our breathing, and while she slept, her fingers would slowly open and still. I abandoned all chores that waited for me and napped beside her. I napped because I was needed. But also because I needed rest. Each night I was awake fixing the edge and wobble of every flower, the highlight on every orange and grape she'd executed during the day.

"LOOK AT WHAT BECOMES of a face," she said. She was holding a hand mirror close to the flame and began stretching her jaw wide, knitting her brow. "It's not just the body, even a good face goes to rubbish." She goosed her cheeks and the skin along her jaw.

"Are you begging for compliments?"

"It's all decline now," she said, her voice laced with contempt. "Even my nose is becoming an old woman's bulb." She was hardly old. She was on the cusp of forty, arguably more beautiful than in youth, even with the trouble in her hands. It was silly, this vanity, her scrutiny of every tiny line. The soft crow's-feet by her eyes only highlighted their alluring green-gray. I kissed her and told her not to be ridiculous, she was a great beauty. Did I need to invite all her admirers over to flirt and compliment? She prodded and smoothed while muttering to herself, "Sow face" and "You lizard bag. How did this happen?" She yanked her skin with disgust.

"I want to pull it all up, like a stocking. Pull and pull and tie all this saggy skin into a tight bun at the top of my head." Finally, I couldn't take another recrimination and grabbed the oval mirror from her grasp.

"You can't understand," she said, and in an instant, I felt the blemish of my ordinariness.

"I'm sure I can't."

"I'm sorry, Pieter. I sound like an ancient shrew."

"Come," I said, and because I really didn't know what else to do, I led her to the bedstead.

"Pieter, that's hardly a solution for everything. Anyway, why would you want me? I'm an old wrinkle."

"Let me show you what the woman I desire looks like." What I'd said was true—though I admit that with years together and the strain of her illness, there were many nights we were glad to lie together in quiet comfort rather than ardor. I pulled back the weighty coverlet and coaxed her down onto the linen sheet. I sat beside the length of her. First, I looked at her as she was—infirm and still magnificent.

"What are you staring at?" she asked, lacing her fingers over her eyes.

"You as you are," I said with quiet authority. "Open your eyes." And when she didn't, I took her hands from her face and restrained them above her head. "Open your eyes. Keep them open." Her eyes fluttered open. She turned her face away from me. I tightened my clasp on her hands. "No, look at me," I insisted, and when she wouldn't, I tugged her hands a little higher until she stared at me. Then I began.

"In the early morning, when you're still drowsy with sleep, I love to put my nose to the crown of your head and inhale that first spicy scent of you." I spoke slowly, only touching her at her wrists, where

I still held her. "Then I draw my mouth down one side of your neck, my lips fitting to trace the slender bone of your clavicle until the tip of my tongue rests in the hollow of your throat." Like that, without touch, with only words, I began to make love to her, never permitting her to turn from my gaze. "I like to lay my cheek against the flat of your ribs as your breasts fall to either side," I said, and then described the hard rise of her nipples between my thumb and finger and the urgent sound at the back of her throat when I pinched tighter. I heard her gasp and felt her struggle against my hold. But I kept her in place and never stopped talking, never stopped the lick of words that rolled and circled and thrust into every soft place.

She twisted and arched beneath my words despite herself, straining for my touch. And when she finally called out, begged for the use of my hands elsewhere, I refused her their efficiency. I wanted to show her that while day to day and night to night we'd grow older and more restful together, that while the landscape of our bodies would tarnish and warp, it was still possible to be cast into new rapture as lovers perpetually finding their way. She cried out for satisfaction by my hands, by my mouth.

"Say it," I commanded.

"Say what?" Her eyes narrowed.

"Say you're beautiful."

"Pieter, stop," she said, shaking her head. "I can't."

"Never," I said. "And you will," and kept on.

A SECOND YEAR PASSED. We made excuses for Jacobus to stay away from home. With each flare of her hands, more deterioration. Then it might, with no discernible cause, mysteriously ease. The hope on her face, those days. She'd make bold declarations, rush to complete unfinished paintings and have me ready new canvases. We were behind on commissions. And when she could work, we worked steadily side by side. But when she couldn't paint, she refused me to step into the workshop. If the illness was volatile, Maria became even more so. Weeks of silence. Weeks keeping to bed or insisting on long walks in the countryside in the hope that fresh air and physical rigor would, as she'd say, clear the jitters from her blood.

MARIA, STANDING AT THE window edge, loosely wrapped in curtain. Her brow furrowed in debate. Her pale eyes dark and seamed. What arguments, what begging, what bargaining rivered across her smooth countenance? I put my hand flat to her brow—in a manner she loved—fitting her snug against the length of me. She tried to shake free. I didn't allow it.

"Pieter," she said. "They've won."

"Who's won? Won what?" I said, immediately regretting the question.

She leaned against me. It was a long time before she spoke. I felt her gathering the effort to say out loud what hurt her to admit.

"It's fine, Maria. This is enough."

"The Guild. Every one of them with their pasted-on smiles and applause who've waited for me to fail," she said, lifting her trembling arm and waving it broadly to the busy street.

"THERE'S NO GOING BACK," she announced one day as we sat down for supper. She placed her hands on the table, which set a glass vibrating so violently I snatched it up to keep it from tipping over.

"Going back where?"

"To our old life. What's the workshop of Maria van Oosterwijck when I can barely hold a spoon most days? I'll shut it."

I set the glass back and pulled her to her feet. "No, Maria," I said. Circling an arm about her waist, I led her to the workshop. It had been weeks since she'd so much as entered the room. Still each day I snuck in to prepare her palette with fresh paints and pots of clear oils. I pointed at an unfinished still life. "This is you. This is your life."

"I don't want to be here," she said. I didn't respond. Instead I hung the apron over her while she murmured, "You don't understand, I can't be here."

"What I understand is that we have work."

As if in reply she held out her hands as evidence. I ignored the gesture and stepped behind her to tie the strings of her apron. "There's work to do."

"Pieter, I can't."

I slipped close so that my body fit against hers and wrapped my arms around her, holding tightly as she tried to pull away. She continued to argue while I refused to engage, her manner becoming increasingly petulant until, at last, her body yielded against mine. My nose burrowed in the lushness of her hair. We breathed together. With each breath I thought, *I'm here. I can make this right.* As one body, I stepped us forward. Guided us to the easel. She pushed against me, but I pressed back harder until we were before the canvas she hadn't touched in a great many weeks. The paint was dry. I lifted her arm and closed her fingers and mine around a paintbrush dipped in fresh paint, then flexed the muscles in my arm to absorb the vibration in hers.

"I can't paint anymore." Her voice was frayed.

"But we can," I said, lifting our hands as one to the unfinished panel.

* * *

OF COURSE, in the end it didn't matter. Not any of it. Medicines. Cheering and insistent words. Not even my will. My love was not enough to make her well. But I wouldn't let us give up. Hadn't she always said that a true artist—even under the most terrible circumstance—will find a way to be an artist? I argued that she was an artist in body and in spirit, and no matter the limitations of either, she couldn't quit. We had a workshop of international renown but how we managed our workshop needn't be known by anyone but us. She wasn't alone. I was here. We'd keep working. What happened in the studio would always be her artistry, her creation.

I'm not sure I convinced her so much as overpowered her with my protests, my own increasingly desperate need to return to the studio—though I never admitted a word of my own need. I carried a comfortable armchair into the studio. Positioned it so the easel was on view.

"You are the artist, Maria van Oosterwijck," I said, putting her apron on and then mine. She sat at a distance, watched, directed. Told me what was needed, and I painted.

FOURTEEN

1682

WHEN HAD IT HAPPENED that the orphan nephew, Jacobus, had gone from a gangly and lumbering boy tripping over his own feet to a graceful and imposing young man? He'd insisted after being kept away the last three years, he must visit his home. Now he was back with us. And he was, it seemed, all too aware of his changes. He strutted through the house. He preened, pausing before every reflective surface as if each mirror and polished goblet should admire his elegance.

Maria was, as always, full of praise. Too full. She gave him kisses, touting the sharp angle of his jaw. She entered rooms extolling how the shirt's muslin hugged the girth of his back. "Look at you," she cooed. "What a man my child has become." What a thing to say to him! Couldn't she see that all her coddling encouraged this vanity? That all this "my child" was nonsense. That a real mother would have taught him his proper place in a room. She was at best a poor surrogate. And he was no longer a child.

He shelved a hand at his hip. "Of course, you'll want to paint me," he said. It riled me how obvious he was. Did he really think he was being clever when she'd sketched him from the first days he'd clipped onto her sister's nipple?

"You know I always want to paint you," Maria said, straightening the collar of his shirt. "If you don't watch out, I'll insist that I draw you today as I did when you were a boy rushing about without a stitch on your bottom." This set them both howling, the nephew throwing off his shirt to strike heroic poses while Maria shouted, "Achilles! Apollo! Hippolytus!" Of course, this was all posture. She'd hidden the tremors and spasms from him as she did from the others.

Given her tremors, I might have welcomed the distraction her nephew provided. Accepted the nephew as a brief diversion from the illness. It gave her an excuse to remove herself from sitting in the chair while I painted in the studio. He was at least a creation she believed she could shape when she'd lost the ability with her hands. But I felt no welcome. Not only for the old reason that he took her from me but because what had begun as a public gesture had changed. She'd clearly come to love him—I could no longer pretend otherwise. It wasn't that she was blind to his selfishness, she seemed to genuinely delight in it. "It's my duty as guardian to help him put all that intelligence to proper use. Then he'll prosper as a good man."

I couldn't understand how she misread his character. A good man? As though rudeness was kindness. As though disdain for others was a virtue. I wasn't fooled. The nephew and I remained wary of one another. We recognized each other—the rot and damage in each of us—as only two orphans can. Knowing too well the other's deprivation made us each greedy, each ambitious for Maria's affections.

My dislike for him and his intrusion in our house was only intensified by his changes. His muscular hands were never still. I'd walk into the room to see this tall creature standing one-legged on a chair juggling Maria's cobalt glasses, tossing them higher and higher, as if daring his aunt to tell him to stop. But Maria, who treasured each expensive acquisition, never said stop. Instead, she giggled as he leaped about the room with her beloved Chinese porcelain sparrow balanced on his head. She was charmed by his reckless gestures. And everything about him was reckless. It took both Diamanta and me to keep the house in order when Jacobus was home. And we barely managed. He was a storm. Every room, every day, was a damage he wrought.

But watching him move through the house was strange. Because even as I distrusted him and wished he wasn't there, I couldn't turn away from him. I'd walk into a room to dust and find him sprawled on the chaise, an arm thrown back so that the new hair in the hollow of his armpit gleamed springy and lush. He was so newly musky. The clothes he shed, changing outfits three or more times a day. All those wet towels he dropped about his room. I fought an urge to press my face in to take a loamy breath. His presence was everywhere. Like cat spray. I was disoriented by him. And yet I was drawn to the trouble like a rash that craves scratching. There, I've said it.

It confused me. I tried to make myself scarce, but wasn't he always calling, "Gerta, Gerta?" Demanding more drinks. More food.

"Gerta," Maria said, enchanted by his appetites, "there's a man in the house now. You're used to feeding small women. Send Diamanta off to buy the whole barnyard."

With Jacobus about, Diamanta's usual downcast expression softened. From the window he sang rhymes while she hung the line with his endless laundry. The neighbor maids clustered around the blushing Diamanta. "Make a rhyme for me, Jacobus," a girl shouted. "I'll wash more than your shirt."

"He's humiliating Diamanta," I said, insisting Maria scold her nephew.

"Take a look, Pieter," Maria said. "Diamanta looks as radiant as that mousy girl might ever look."

I couldn't disagree. Suddenly Diamanta's black hair gleamed as if his attention was a hog-bristle hairbrush that had revived her stringy locks. Each morning, she bounded up the stairs as if she were afraid—having gone home to her parents for the night—she'd missed any of Jacobus's antics. And every day there were antics.

One morning, I found him at the breakfast table naked but for a green satin napkin spread over his lap. "He's an overgrown boy," Maria said when I complained. "He hardly knows what he's doing."

"YOU'D DO WELL to admit you enjoy him." Maria broke the silence one rare morning when she'd joined me in the workshop. "Would it hurt you to ever laugh?"

I kept to the paint. Hurt to ever laugh? Laughing is what Maria and I did so well, our quips quick and searing. Didn't she remember how she'd laughed at my imitation of everyone from Jan Six to Van Aelst, until doubled over, she'd press a palm to keep from wetting her skirts? But with Jacobus about, we could never be certain that anything spoken wasn't overheard. I didn't dare joke with Maria about her nephew's outlandish appetites or that, long past midnight, Jacobus, reeking of God knows where, might enter my room, thrusting a stained shirt in my hands and demanding it clean and pressed by morning. And I was always to sleep in my room. Never a night beside Maria. Never a private kiss when he was in our home.

Even that morning, I turned from the canvas and there was Diamanta in the workshop doorway. "Madam," she said, her voice tremulous because she knew she was forbidden to enter the studio. "Jacobus insists I cook an early meal of the goose you've planned for dinner."

Just as I began to say that he'd have to wait, Maria said, "What a good idea, Diamanta."

I dabbed an ungainly gob of paint on a delicate leaf. What about what I wanted? To be hers, to be hers alone.

"Be sour as pickled plum, Pieter," Maria said, coming behind me, her trembling hand smoothing my hair.

I wouldn't let her soften me with this meager touch, this calling me Pieter, when all week, in front of him, it was Gerta this and Gerta that. I kept my silence and refused to yield to her touches.

"Be as you will. Still, you know it's you who'll paint his portrait," Maria said.

"No!" I sprung from the stool.

"My nephew wants to be painted and I can't. So you will. You'll paint him and me, a double portrait." With effort, she lifted the brush from my hand and plowed it into a mound of carmine. "Look at me. At what I am. He can't know. And it's cruel not to help me." Each time she tried to dredge and thin the loaded brush, it slipped deeper into the mound. Finally, dropping it on the palette, she said, "You'll take care of it."

As I've admitted, I might have been kinder. Without painting, she was lost. She needed him. Needed to be the good benefactor. The good aunt. That was what a double portrait proclaimed. But kindness had never given me much. Work had. With a knife I scraped the excess from the brush. "There are commissions for us to finish. I'm taking care of them," I said, fitting the brush back in her useless grasp. You didn't have to look hard around the studio to see two flower paintings and a vanitas unfinished. "Unless you plan on finishing them yourself, shouldn't they be my priority?"

"The priority is our portrait." She dropped the brush at my feet. "You'll start tomorrow."

I LEFT FOR THE MARKET. Let me wander among the carcasses. Let my only concern be the ripe bloom of cheese. Let my harshness be aimed at the fishmonger who claims his pike is fresh when any fool with a nose smells the ammoniac foul. Oh, beware, cheaters. Take heed, liars. False flatterers, sour goat milkers, swindlers, rotten-fruit farmers—step in my path, and I'll stuff your ears full of my wrath.

Just as I was giving fine broil to one thief of a vendor who thought I didn't have eyes to see the rot and mold on his potatoes, there was a strong arm about my waist and Jacobus in a stunningly refined voice saying, "Good sir, excuse our family maid. We're trying our best to curb the fire of her wanton tongue."

I tried my hardest to push him off, the tensed strength of him up against me, formidable, imposing, vile.

"But still give her your best potatoes. She might be crude in her manners, but she tries to look after my needs," Jacobus said with a wink to the vegetable seller, while his hands pinched and roamed slippery along the fabric of my skirt.

"We'd best be off, Gerta." He steered us through the crowd, holding so fast to me it was as though someone had stitched me to him. "It's good to have some time alone together, isn't it, Gerta?" I remained silent, not knowing how to answer or manage his hands.

Then he relaxed his hold and trotted beside me as I went between stalls. And what was strange was that for a while, it began to seem possible that he was right. That I'd misjudged him. That I'd mistaken his enthusiasm for greed. His honesty for rudeness. When he idled at the stalls, his conversation was well-mannered, deferential.

He bought flowers for the house, a runny cheese for supper, a pair of lambswool slippers for himself, then said, "I'll have a second pair for my maid, who deserves to ease her pretty feet at the end of a long day." I began to consider that perhaps it was my jealousy that kept me from seeing that there was more to him than a petulant child in the clothes of a grown man. That it was the strange triangle between Maria, Jacobus, and me that was the problem.

But just as I reprimanded myself for my distrust and narrow heart, he leaned in. "Gerta, I never appreciated how pretty you are," he said, though he wasn't looking at my face but down at my tits. Then his tongue lapped sloppy on my ear, "You'll like it. Not a single girl's been sorry for the knotty ride I've gifted them." And with one hand pawing apricots while the other kneaded my waist, he hissed, "I like it when the flesh runs juicy when I take a bite." With that he pulled a stone pit out with his teeth and spit it wide, narrowly missing a vendor's ear.

About us, the market kept to its business. The noisy animals and the bloody hang of dead ones and the clink of coins and the thank-yous and the not-the-fatty-end-pieces and his arm tight and pawing as he wandered, dragging us up and down. Going about like we were a sweet and cozy anything. My head cast down, silent. Appalled I'd be recognized. Appalled I'd let down my guard. Appalled because there was also this—the musk and clove of him. Stunning. Close. Disturbingly so. Even as I wanted to wriggle free, I took deep breaths.

"My aunt treats me like I'm still a child in short pants, when, Gerta, you can see I'm well grown." With that he flung me from his side, spinning me out by one hand, then pulling me back in so we stood facing one another. His eyes right on mine. There was a catch in my stomach, an unaccustomed ferment. "She never shares." He bent over me so that his nose rested just where my forehead met my bonnet, then nudged back my cap and thrust his nose into my hair. Drew a long audible intake. "So, I came to find you." I knew I should push him away. That the turn in my stomach should be disgust and not excited unrest. I remained.

"I should be going home," I said. "Maria needs my—"

"No," he interrupted, his lips vibrating against my scalp. "You'll stay. We're having a good time together. Finally, without the old auntie. She shouldn't be allowed the full claim of your sweet flesh." My flesh, her claim? What was it he was saying? "Yes, Gerta, we'll have a good time, or should I let everyone know your sick delight?"

"If you want a midday goose," I said, alarm jolting through me, "let me be on my way before they're all sold." I tried to escape his hold. What did he know?

"I'll have the goose and you," he said. "I'll have the goose and you, and I'll be licking both off my fingers." He seemed enamored with his cleverness.

I tossed my head so it banged against his nose. He shouted and stumbled backward. I needed to run, but before I could take a step, he grabbed me. I pulled to free myself and when he wouldn't let go, I pushed onward, panic strengthening me, pressing me forward, with Jacobus still holding tight. The noise of the market dimmed, and despite the bustle and throng, I knew there was no protection, no help, even if I screamed. I moved and moved until, at the edge of the market, I stopped at the last stall to purchase a goose. I composed myself and aimed questions to the missus.

"Yes, just killed this morning," she promised. "And clover-fed to keep the meat from going stringy." She dangled a goose by its leg, yanked off a feather.

"Not that one," Jacobus intervened. "My girl knows I love my meat good and plump." The woman barely spared us a second glance as she grabbed another bird, slitting down its center to show off the breast. Before I could remark, Jacobus continued, "Don't try to sell off your scrawny birds. Not to me. Those are ancient and dry. Ask my girl. She's done with tasting old hen meat. I've gotten her to prefer a gander that's tender and young." With that, he threw down coins and shoved a fat young goose into my bag.

"A DOUBLE PORTRAIT," Maria announced as we sat to the meal of roasted stuffed goose Diamanta had hastily prepared. "Of you and me." Her voice as sweet as if she were petting his hand. "So, we'll have Gerta paint us."

He spit out the gristle and looked at me while he sucked on a goose leg. "I won't let her paint me," he said. "I want you. You're the best." Maria simply sat, her lips stitched into a tolerant smile as he argued against me first, then tried bargaining. "She can do the easy parts, but I need it to be a true portrait by the great Maria van Oosterwijck." But when he could get no response from her, he finally slunk down, sulking in his chair. "I've changed my mind. I don't want a portrait," he said, and gnawed a crispy bird wing. He pushed about the greens on his plate and licked the grease off each finger. When all that was left of his meal were scattered greens and a litter of bone and tendon, he stormed from the table.

"It will be lovely," Maria called after him. "You'll take the painting back with you."

We heard him bang about upstairs in his bedroom, more doors slamming than there were doors to slam. "I won't have it," he shouted, followed by a clunk where he'd thrown something, perhaps a boot. After more crashing and thudding, he screamed, "That old bitch!"

Maria rolled her eyes at me. I shrugged as if to say, *What did you expect?* and considered telling her about his threat in the market. Then she said, "He makes a lot of noise, but trust me, he wants a painting of us together," and I remembered he was above reproach, and she would make little of my concern.

When he clomped back down the stairs, he was dressed, hat to boot, in the most ostentatious clash of the finest of clothing. He was a garish festival of color. I hoped that he'd storm off into the trouble he was so good at finding in the city at any hour. Instead, with forced softness, he said, "Shall I wear this for our portrait, Auntie?" How had I thought he'd do otherwise? He needed her. He'd scream and stomp, but he wouldn't risk rejecting his benefactor. We were also alike in that way, both beholden to Maria.

"A wonderful choice," Maria said.

"Let's get this done," he said, then swabbed a heel of bread through goose fat and jammed it in his mouth.

FOR THE PORTRAIT, Maria was seated, elegant and formidable in a deep eggplant wool dress, her gloved hands tucked securely under her legs. In her lap lay a white lily. Jacobus stood at her left, one red pant leg mostly hidden behind her chair. He loomed above her in his yellow plumed hat, a blue velvet coat with gold buttons, and a white blouse stitched with emerald thread and pearl clasps. His gloved hand spread wide on Maria's shoulder.

"Gerta, make sure you capture the handsome breadth of his shoulders," Maria instructed while I sketched. "Gerta, too thick with that paint," Maria said, as I underpainted, though she couldn't see the canvas. "More oil."

"She won't get it right," Jacobus sneered. "*You* should be painting me." He fidgeted.

"I'll paint you one day," Maria turned a serene face up to her nephew, "but I'm still waiting for your ultimate moment of strength, intelligence, and beauty."

The more restless he became, the slower and more meticulously I worked. If I had to paint the haughtiness of him, the ownership of his hand on his aunt's shoulder, then I'd make him regret asking for a portrait in the first place. But the trouble was, as I painted there was no turning away from him nor keeping my distance. Painting is like touching. To render the flare and turn of his nostril, I had to touch the dip and curve of cartilage with my eyes. With my brush I shaped the swell of his fleshy mouth, the pressure where the upper and lower lip lightly met, exposing just a hint of their glossy, slick interior. I felt all the varied textures of skin on his cheek, his chin, his ear's helix. How the skin articulated over the bone of his wrist. Even the drape of his pant leg made me consider the leg inside the pants, the force of the hip. I didn't want to look. I kept looking.

After the initial sketching and painting, Maria instructed me to complete the portrait and call them back when I was ready to attend to the finer detail of their faces. As soon as they were gone, I abandoned the painting, turning the panel to the wall. But even with the canvas spun from view, Jacobus was omnipresent. The wood boards beneath and above me vibrated as he jigged through the house, boots knocking and scuffing. Or he was in the yard, pesking after Diamanta, unpinning laundry as she hung it on the line.

"Stop that!" Diamanta trilled with pleasure as he tangled through her drying sheets with dirty hands. She giggled and whooped, whipping him with a damp cotton stocking. It took all my restraint not to wag a finger at the girl as she lapsed on her chores. I would not give him the satisfaction of my concern.

I tried to hide in one of our commissions, to focus on the bulbous tulips, the poppy's puckery crepe, but the rough shape of him roiled through me. With each brushstroke, I felt the smolder of him. His nose inhaling the scent of my scalp. His head bent over me, mouth speaking into my hair. The girth of his neck, the rising knob of throat as he swallowed. In the end, I gave up. Dragged the easel back into the light. I would be done with him. With his image. With the dangerous pull I'd felt when he'd said, *My girl likes young meat.*

As I painted, flies circled the canvas. I swatted them with a rag of linseed oil. Despite the heat, despite the summer air tendrilled with rank canal water and sugared with rotting fruit, I vowed to stay through the night till the portrait was done. Then he'd leave for school with his painting and his well-packed trunks, and I'd be free of the confusion he stirred in me. I'd have our life back. Our home, gentle once more. I'd show Maria every kindness. Every affection. I'd try new unguents, medicines. I'd make her whole.

I worked deep into the night. I remembered standing before the large portrait of Jan Six and also the brutal last self-portraits up those rickety stairs in the master Rembrandt's house all those years ago. My brushwork quickened. Turned rough. Paint, thick and slashed. Smudged with linseed oil. I painted with my fingers.

Another fly landed on the canvas. It twisted, legs sinking deeper till it was stuck in a blue ribbon of paint. I jabbed with my brush, bent the brush hairs hard against the canvas, burying the fly in Jacobus's azure coat.

EVEN NOW I QUESTION how I could have really been so lost in brushwork—so deep inside that particular dream when everything narrows, wedded to the paintbrush—that I didn't hear the door open. Maybe I believed it was my own dream of the boot step and the candle's flicker. Maybe I was not lost at all.

But then, behind me—grab and scrape, rough fingers and the soured, boozy tongue—wasn't anything I'd conjured. Jacobus pulled me toward him, his mouth heavy against mine. "Look at me in your painting. Ravishingly handsome," he slurred, less words than beer-thick hiss. He bound me to him with an arm, while he squeezed my buttocks. I wanted to push him off but I was no stranger to the hands of men for whom the slightest wrestle was an invitation of force. I'd been lucky more than wily in the past. Once I'd pelted and drenched a drunk man with a bucket of milk. Another time two African sailors beat a man who'd pressed me into a doorway. What force could I show now? I had nothing for protection. Only the slender paintbrush in my hand.

"You're handsome indeed." My voice strained, attempting flattery as a weapon. "Come stand beside the portrait so we can see if I've done you justice."

"You've done enough looking at me in paint. You'll like this more," he said, the press of him stubborn against my backside. He swatted at my skirt. "I'd like my try at you. Seems she thinks you're plenty pleasing."

I tried to arch away from him, but he held tight and I toppled forward, grabbing the armchair where Maria had sat for the portrait. Before I could right myself, he levered one hand on my back as the other yanked the fabric of my skirts. I felt a rush of cold then his damp hand slapped the flesh of my ass. A rip of cloth and his fingers fumbled at the cleft of my cunt then, with a stab, he pushed his hand inside. I screamed, twisting out of his hold so that I was upright and facing him. I tried to duck and twist away but couldn't get around the looming bulk of him.

"Don't scream, Gerta. We agreed we both favor young goose."

"I'm having monthly blood." Undeterred, Jacobus grabbed my hand and pressed it against his prick.

"Blood's easier and smoother than spit," he said. "They won't much approve of her habits or buy her pretty paintings when they hear about her nasty interests, will they?" He slid our hands against his stiffness. His mouth a damp weight on my throat. "Just share with me a little of that wet you so freely give my old auntie, and I won't tell your secret."

For Maria's sake, for our sake, I knew I should let him have his rut against the plaster wall. But, as he loosened his hold to shove away my skirt, his prick attempting its way in, my arm jerked free, and without hesitation, I'd jabbed the paintbrush in the direction of his face. The end of the wood barrel quilled into something soft, jellied. I twisted and pushed. Jacobus shrieked and reeled backward, his face clutched in his hands. I'd struck his eye, though how deep or blinding I didn't know. He dropped to the floor, mewling.

I stood above him. My arm raised. I wielded the paintbrush like a dagger. If it had been a knife, I might have stabbed him and continued striking until he was no longer a living threat. Anger and terror coursed through me. But how can I explain? Strange as it was, stewed with revulsion and rage, I had another feeling, as well. An odd, gentle feeling seeing him bunched in the corner—crying, drunk, pathetic. I took a candle and knelt to survey the damage. Pried his hands from his face. The eye was already filling with blood and swelling shut, though I was certain he'd not lose it. "Let me tend to this properly," I said.

The calm of my voice surprised me. As if I were listening to another woman. As if it wasn't my own voice. I was unruffled, my legs steady, while inside my body I screamed and shook.

"Come," I heard myself say. And, as though he were just a naughty child who'd overstepped his play, he let me gather him to his feet and steer him to his bedroom.

"Let me," I said. Relishing being the one in control, I undressed him and eased his naked body down on the mattress. I tendered his eye with a compress, then an ointment of sieved carrot, sweet marjoram, chamomile, and clay. Finally, three droplets of opium under his tongue for pain and sleep.

When I was done, I curled in a ball on the corner chair, wave after wave of panic tremoring through my chest and stomach. The bitterness in my mouth rose and I swallowed it back. Just as my breath settled, another torrent would flatten me, and I rocked and rocked into a tighter ball. In the dark I sought to compose myself, gather back what might be gathered, soothe myself by considering all he hadn't done. He'd not gotten the full bounty he'd come for. I'd suffered the violation of hands and mouth but not the damage he might have wrought. If these were lies I used to lessen the harm, who'd deny me? Let excuses be the tonic I sipped to ease if not cure the affliction. To allow me to claim: I am still here, unruined, myself.

All the while, in the shadowy dark, I regarded him. I'd never seen a man fully naked. The sculpted length of torso. Muscle and rib. The smooth of stomach down to where his soft prick nested. I didn't stay to watch over him and make certain he didn't scratch his eye in his drunken sleep. Or to make sure he didn't wake and stumble from bed to find me.

No. More than once, I walked over to the bed to shove his arm or jostle his leg. I rolled him on his side and bent his leg as if he were running. I rolled him further to view his muscular buttock and thigh. That is, I manipulated his body as I saw fit. Then I gathered up my chalk and paper and began to draw.

GRAY LIGHT SIEVED through the studio before the last of the lit tallows were gone. The streets came awake with the wheels knocking and farmers hawking their fresh goods. I hadn't slept. Whisk of broom, crackling in the fire grate, copper pots clanging. I mapped the dawn sounds of Diamanta's chores in the kitchen. I heard her pause in the doorway, surely glancing down the hall in anticipation of me entering with my storm of daily instructions. I stayed where I was. When Maria called for me, as she did each morning, I neither went to help with dressing nor called out to correct Diamanta when she explained I'd left for the markets before she'd even arrived. I needed Maria to find me.

"THERE YOU ARE. Have you been here all night?" She walked to the window ledge where I sat, as we had so many mornings when we looked at the previous day's effort and prepared for the new day's work.

"Oh!" she said as she looked at the portrait, then again like a distant echo, "Oh."

Maria's form on the canvas was refined. Her dress gleamed a rich brown purple, barely a shade removed from the deep black of the background. The nephew rose behind her, beautiful and monstrous, all texture and color, an excessive, unkempt bouquet. The scarlet of his fitted pant leg curved like a glossy petal of tulip. The indigo jacket, the lustrous gold buttons, the velvet and metal invited touch. The pearls sewn into the white pleats of his starched ruff shone like wet seeds caught on each fold. His fingers were fleshy and pink, the tips meaty, gelatinous. Each fingernail caught.

I'd painted only the first rough gestures of Maria's face though I could have painted it blindfolded. But where the nephew's face should have been, loosely tacked to the canvas was a drawing of a bulbous rotting cabbage.

Maria rose and walked to the canvas. She unhinged the drawing and let it fall to the floor. If she was surprised by the paper hidden under the first—this one featuring the snout and pronged ears of a pig or, after she'd tossed the pig face, the drawing of rabid, red-eyed dog's face—she said nothing. It was only when Maria had torn off all three papers and came to her nephew's finished face painted smoothly on the canvas—innocent, calm, beatific—that she roared with unbounded amusement, "Saint Jacob finally revealed!"

She picked up the cabbage, pig, and dog from where the papers had drifted throughout the studio and lay them in a row on the table. "Pieter, with this degree of honesty, our studio would be bankrupt if we were known for portraits instead of still lifes."

She lowered into the chair and, without any need for assistance, resumed her pose, her face tilted and partly turned. I realized she'd assumed the very position she'd taken for her friend Vaillant's portrait of her. "Now I'm ready for your pitiless interpretation of me," she mumbled through a closed lip smirk. "Or will you spare me?"

"I always spare you." As I spoke, fright flashed through my legs and I grabbed the easel frame to keep from falling. How was it possible that Maria had no idea what had happened in this very studio just hours before? Was there no lingering scent of his awfulness? No stench of my embarrassment, anger, and fear? I wanted—in a rush—to tell her everything. But I knew I'd say nothing rather than hear the excuse she'd make on his behalf. Besides, hadn't I walked with him in the market? And hadn't I leaned my cheek to his chest? I walked over and untucked her hands from where she'd lodged them under her thighs and fitted the lily between her rigid fingers.

"Be quick roughing that part. What if he walks in and sees?" she said, nodding at the flower shaking in her grasp. I was quick, though if you look carefully at the finished portrait, you'll see the dusting of orange pollen feathered on her purple skirt.

IT WAS LATE in the afternoon when Jacobus finally shambled downstairs. "It's nothing," I heard him say as Diamanta and Maria flocked about in a fluster of concern. From their fretting, I deduced he had fashioned an eye patch to cover the damage I'd inflicted.

"Just a poke," he said. "A low branch snapped back at me." Was I imagining that he spoke loudly as if to make certain I heard him? Was he testing? Fearful? Did he even remember?

I listened to the drag of a chair and across the kitchen floor imagined him sagged over the table, still half drunk, arm propping him up while with cheerful, childish flutterings, Diamanta tried to please him with dish after dish.

"Where's Gerta?" he asked.

"Doing the final glazes," Maria said. "I'm quite surprised by the portrait."

"She's finished?" he snarled. "She's done my face?"

"You'll be pleased."

"I want this eye patch in the painting. It looks more impressive than the trifle it took to get it."

Maria laughed until she realized he was serious. "You won't," she insisted. "You can't."

"But I can and I will," he demanded. "I'll hang this painting in my room and there will be stories to tell."

"But Jacobus, you are most beautifully revealed by Gerta. There won't be a need for me to ever do a different portrait." Her voice brought me back to those easy nights when, after a long day, we'd relaxed in the courtyard smoking pipes and looked through the windows to judge our paintings. Always it had been hers that I'd announced superior, always hers I'd vowed to carry back to the king in a distant land. And though I'd never thought it would come to pass, hadn't I wanted at least once to look through the window and see that I'd surpassed her? But hearing the quiver in her voice, I understood there would be no more nights outside. The game had changed. Now any assurance that an art dealer would present her paintings to the count, the prince, the pope, was a different assurance altogether.

"At least come see the painting before you get stuck on some foolish idea." As I listened to Maria trying to reason with her nephew, I dipped the brush in raw umber and crudely fashioned a strap angled over his smooth brow and a rough-painted scarlet eye patch over his eye.

When I heard Jacobus's chair scrape the floorboards, I stood back so that when they entered the studio they'd have an unimpaired view of their double portrait. The nephew's beauty stunted by the coarsely painted patch. The artist's fingers too tightly grasping the lily flower. And, in the corner, the canvas signed with Maria's initials.

I WISH THAT WAS the nasty end. That whatever anger or fear resided inside me, had been buried into the canvas alongside a dead fly. But what was worse was the shadowy creature that remained. At night behind the shut door of my bedroom, it was not the memory of the violent push of his hands that made me startle up in my bed. It was his cool skin under my hands in the hours I'd sketched him while he slept in his room. It was my eyes running the length of his drugged, sleeping body, and the paper where I drew the blade of his hip bone, his arm thrown above his head and the taut tendons of his calf down to the arch of his foot. The drawings of him, stashed in a folder beneath my bed, burned through the mattress until I pulled them out and, dizzy with a frightening insistence, I looked at them over and over until the dark of night had burnished to the steel of dawn. I couldn't align my anger at his hands with my desire for them. I was vile.

The next day the house slanted. I was unsteady, but no one noticed. Maria had given herself over entirely to Jacobus for what few days he remained in the city. There were lunches and visits. Concerts. Packages delivered throughout the day were a map of their excursions through the city. I was glad for the hours they were out of the house. I returned to a painting in the studio, but found myself fidgety, unable to find my rhythm. I soaked hulls for ink. Ground stones for fresh paint. I made Diamanta scrub floors that were already vinegar cleaned. I washed the fine china and every glass, and stood on the walnut table to clean each beveled crystal of the chandelier. Then I went out to the hutch and lay down in the bedding. The rabbits nuzzled close, stepping over me, nosing and poking. I took one in my lap. Breathed in the sweet behind the ears. With a bit of damp cotton, cleaned the ink-dark wax from her glands. Then another rabbit and another. I couldn't lose myself in the work even as I felt lost. Why had Maria insisted that I paint her with Jacobus? Anger and darkness rushed through me. His power. Hers. What was ever mine?

I stood up. A sleepy rabbit dropped from me. I toed it with my boot. Its narrow face tilted, stunned. I gave it a little kick and quit the hutch, not bothering to whisk straw off my apron.

LATE IN THE DAY, I heard them mounting the front stairs. They came as one through the door to the kitchen as I was slitting a skinned rabbit. A second rabbit lay gutted and ready on the table. I cut the cavity and in a single steady motion, tilted the carcass, and pulled down to bucket the intestines and organs. I set aside the lungs and heart. Then separated the legs, the belly, the ribs, and neck. In one strike of the cleaver, I split the breastbone.

"A knife suits you, Gerta," Jacobus barked. "But I thought you were too good for the kitchen these days." I sliced the tenderloins off the spine.

"Come." Maria tugged at Jacobus. She knew better than to ask why it was me at work in the kitchen rather than Diamanta. "Stop your pestering, Jacobus. Let's take these last hours together looking at the maps I've bought you. Then we'll have a fine meal before you leave me in the morning."

Dinner was a feast. Rabbit, herring, cod with raisins and juniper berries, pineapple, pomegranates, and marzipan. I held nothing back. The table was set with Lyon silk cloth and laid with the good porcelain plates and gold-rimmed glasses. The whole room garlanded with flower wreaths. The portrait of Maria and Jacobus had been carried in from the studio and other paintings rearranged so that, for this one night, it hung on the dining wall. To round out the celebration I insisted Diamanta dine with us and went so far as to offer her a swipe of stain for her full lips.

Maria was in great form, toasting her nephew, promising him that he would accompany her when she traveled to Rome to deliver a finished painting. There were bottles of French wine uncorked. And French songs. Diamanta sang a glum Portuguese song, which she explained was the cry of a woman beseeching her lover to return by the full moon or else she would die of loneliness.

"Who could blame a young man for running away if these sad notes are the best the girl had to offer?" Maria teased. "Jacobus, teach her a beer-hall song that can hold any man's attention."

Diamanta's cheeks turned as red as her lips when Jacobus pulled her from her seat, dancing her around the table, singing bawdy lyrics, and carrying on with his arms clenched about her waist.

I served. Filled glasses. Laughed when the others did. And kept my countenance neat.

. . .

LATER THAT NIGHT I walked like a sleepwalker, yet I was not asleep. Though I wish I could tell you that I had been. His door was ajar. I turned to start back down the hallway then pivoted, my hand gripped the metal latch on his bedroom door. When he coughed, the sound scraped down my spine and without waiting for any sign of his sleep, I pushed open the door. The room was pale, flame from bridge lamps slicing through the windows. He hadn't bothered to close the curtains. His room, cleaned each day, was upended, the cupboard doors open, every garment tossed onto the floor. He slept, stretched out on his back, his sleep shirt bunched high on his chest.

My nightdress glowed milky as I stepped into the room. I watched my bare feet as they crossed a band of yellow light until I stood over him. Listening. To the gurgle clotting in his throat. To the rasp of his legs against the sheet. His eye patch had shifted, the swollen, discolored skin revealed.

I could have still left his room. Instead, without ever taking my eyes from his face, I eased my body over his. He made a slight huff at my weight, but his eyes never opened. I moved on him, brushing and pressing myself against him, until I felt him rise and slipped him inside. At first I moved very slowly, keeping him ever so slightly fitted just inside me. Every time he arched up to press deeper or tried to flip me, I pushed him back in place and refused his hastening.

Tracked only my own urgency. When I was ready, I ground down against him. I wanted to take my time hurting him, wanted to strip him of something that was his. I took his rough and preen, his haughty beauty, his threat and power. I rode deeper into darkness, until I was darkness, and damage, crave, and hurt. In silence the demon within me seethed: dam broken, crops flooded, cities in ruin. I was the nail-studded club, the iron-spiked caltrop strewn on battlefield. I was the plunderer; taking, I took back. Until there was nothing more of him to want. And in him, there was her, Maria, and I took that too and, in bitterness, owned her nephew as she never would. I spun on him to face away. Pulled his legs up and apart. And without mercy, rocked forward and rammed his ass with two dry crossed-knuckled fingers. Then from below me, somewhere, a cry, an urgent shudder and release.

When I stood from the bed, his legs, his penis, his stomach were smeary with my dark blood. I had not lied the other night when I'd told him it was my month's time. I lifted my eyes to his face. He stared at me through his one good eye. Who can say what he saw.

"So, you like to ride? Lucky for you, I'm not afraid to be ridden nor pierced," he jeered and tried to yank me back down. I leaned over him. He lessened his grip, his lips parting, expecting a kiss. Instead I braced my arms on the bed and hovered just above his face. Looked hard at him. Did not look away. I would not allow myself to ever. Ever again.

"You were right about one thing," I said. "Blood's easier for a rut." Then I spit hard across his open mouth.

THE NEXT MORNING, he departed.

"Doesn't the house seem lonely without him?" Maria asked. "Even Diamanta is back to her sad-eyed brooding." We looked out the window to where, slump shouldered, Diamanta fastened his washed bedsheets to the line. I might have called her in and told her the sheets had already been bleached and scrubbed; I'd washed and rinsed them till the faintest tinge was gone and there was no sign of my plunder. But the smell—his and mine, blood and seed—was in my nose. I couldn't be cleansed of it.

"Even you got used to him, it seems," Maria said. "Admit it." I continued to massage her arms with an ointment of ground coral and cumin, though I could get no stillness in her limbs. She'd refused all treatments while her nephew had visited and had taken such care to hide her hands while he was in the house that I hadn't seen how much farther the palsy had gone up her arm. Her hands were twisted; finger by finger I tried to ease them straight.

"Admit it, Pieter." Maria's voice was teasing. "You'll miss the plod of his big feet stumbling down to the kitchen and the sight of him unclothed and unembarrassed as a babe." I worked my fingers along the length of her arm, digging in where the tendons sewed to the bone. She exhaled deeply. "Oh Pieter, I've needed this." She placed her other hand on top of mine. I slipped my hand on top of hers to quiet the tremble, and together we rubbed down her quaking arm. "I've needed you."

She said it so simply. But what was simple anymore? Without the distraction of Jacobus, new questions tumbled through me. Why hadn't I gone straight to Maria when he'd threatened to expose his aunt as a deviant? Had I really assumed that she wouldn't have believed me? But why would anyone believe me when, carried by my own two feet, I'd gone to his bed myself? Her nephew. The unparsed quarreled within me. What kind of woman was I that I'd desired the very person who'd violated me? What was my heart and what my revenge? Everywhere I turned, all I found for certain was my own vileness, jealousy, and yearning coiled within.

"I've needed you," Maria repeated.

I wanted to be worthy of her again, to singularly desire her. But the house had been sullied. By him. By me. Despite my revulsion, I found myself touching the carved back of the chair where'd he sat or lifting to my mouth the cup he'd filled and refilled. Nights, curled beside her, I dreamed Jacobus stormed the room with a band of long-beaked officials who, declaiming our indecency, pecked out our eyes. Or I woke in a sweat after dreaming I'd burned Jacobus in his bed. Other nights as her lips grazed my throat, I had to swallow back my urgency to call out his name. Before Jacobus, it had only ever been Maria, my desire for her as natural as air.

"I've missed you too." I kneaded the flesh between her thumb and palm.

Outside, Diamanta hummed the melancholy tune she'd sung at the last dinner with Jacobus. She too was filled with longing. Which of us, I wondered, doesn't have private hungers? Maybe none of us ever give ourselves fully to another and mostly only belong to our own unruly appetites. Maybe what I wanted most was not the cup of her smooth breast or the plank of his stomach, so much as to feel my own raw desire.

A STRANGE EXPRESSION, ISN'T IT? "Life went back to normal." I suppose it's truer to say that I resumed the shape of our old life. Before dawn I haggled with merchants over stones and plants, and back home, began the day's preparation of paint. I prodded and scolded Diamanta, then went upstairs to help Maria dress. When she was ready, she came down to the workshop as she had for so many years. With a shaking hand, Maria poked and tested the viscosity of each mound of paint on the palette, requesting additions of oil or gum thickener. Then she sat on her cushioned chair and each day oversaw the commissions while I sat on her stool at the easel and painted.

"I need to watch the burnt sienna under my shadow," Maria might say, as I worked the many delicate blossoms of a carnation. "My edge is too soft on the broken leaf," she'd say, and then, "I'm not finding the full volume."

My shadow. My edge. I kept my eyes on the canvas as she spoke. "Too heavy," she'd direct, and I softened my application. If she sounded critical, it's because painting is a critical art; with each stroke comes the chance to sharpen, augment, revise. It must have dearly troubled Maria that she could no longer steady a brush. So many years establishing her place among painters, and now, if she attempted to draw a carnation, the charcoal zagged across the linen like a child's crude mark. As I sat on her stool before her easel, it seemed fair that she judge my skill harshly. She who was renowned for composition, for the balance of her arrangements, for the harmony of her color and verisimilitude.

We live in the shape, the likeness of truth, don't we? Rose, lily of the valley, tulip, each only a brief bloom. And the butterfly that alights and then is gone. But in a painting, everything endures and does so by the artist's truth. The purpose of my life had become to make possible an artistic life she could no longer accomplish alone. My hand had become hers. Her verisimilitude.

At the base of a cobalt vase, I painted a reflection of the studio windows, the mullions, the milky afternoon light and the silhouetted shape of the artist standing before her easel. I gave her permanence. I was mostly not myself but Maria. *I am you*, I said with each flick of the brush. All day, in this likeness, we painted.

IF I'VE MADE MYSELF sound steadfast and generous caring for the range of Maria's limitations, I wasn't always. Many days the noise rattling my head was worse than ungrateful. I was exhausted by the demands of her illness. Gone was any luxury of my doing one thing at a time. Gone was having a moment's rest before my name was again called. It was hard to shape constant kindness when her demands piled so high I felt buried. Not that she'd ever unbuttoned her own dress. Or washed the dirt sticky between her toes. But now I ground and mulled for paint and also for her daily tinctures and salves. And many meals I spooned broth to her lips before I fed myself.

"You can't leave me shivering like this," she reprimanded, when I came to where she sat in the bath's cooled water. "I called and called for you. You stranded me."

To see her chilled, unable to hoist herself from the tub without my help should have cracked my heart. And sometimes, yes, it did. Other times there was only a rain of silent rebuttals and none of them were *I'm sorry*. Truth is, it was worse than that. I'd linger after finishing the rendering of a shadow one leaf cast over another leaf. I'd hear her shout and shrill my name while I slowly filled and tamped down tobacco in a pipe, charred the pack with the first match strike, then took my time burning through the bowl. And even when it was finished and shaken free of ash, I'd stay, admiring the canvas, and not bound the stairs two at a time. Let me go a step further in honesty: I didn't bound the stairs only because I resented her dependency, but also because I was enjoying the precision of my line and color, reveling in my skill. Yes, she'd schooled and shaped me, but with each completed commission, it became harder to yield the credit entirely to her. If Maria had been the finest still-life painter, who was better now than me?

It's not that I was never sorry. I was plenty sorry. Sorry for her. Sorry I couldn't make her better. Sorry for the anger it brewed in her. Sorry for myself as her caregiver. And sorry, too, that my skill would never be celebrated as my own. And sorry if that makes me look selfish. But if you've never cared enduringly for another, than I can't suppose you know the ways love can also be stingy and mean.

FIFTEEN

WEEKS OF MUSHROOM-GRAY DRIZZLE. My mind a mist of gray. Unseasonal winds. A chill run up my legs had set me unwell. A boiled wool cap kept my head warm, but I remained poorly with such queasiness each time I swallowed. I took to changing into Pieter's trousers in the studio, vest and coat and a scarf doubled around my throat. Still, I was not free of the chill. We had commissions to finish. There was no time for me to rest, so I kept to my work.

Soon enough, I was spied through the window by a neighbor's maid, and word broadcast through the canals that our workshop had a new assistant. A young man no less. No shortage of maids stopped by. Some with warm cakes and swan eggs. Others with odd requests from our storage and shelves in the kitchen. Our poor Diamanta was horribly confused, having no idea what the other maids were talking about when they asked after the new man. She'd never heard Maria call me Pieter, nor seen me in my man's garments. I'd trained her so severely that she never dared enter the workshop, so she had no idea what others had seen through the window.

"Just thank them for the cakes and give them extra of whatever grain they claim to need," I instructed. She was serving our midday meal. I'd rolled up my pants and slipped back into my dress and smock. I picked at my bowl of cod bisque.

"But is there a new assistant?" she asked.

"Diamanta, you're a smart girl." I pushed a spoon of fish and beans into my mouth but the flavor was somehow revolting. "Wouldn't you know if there was someone new in the house?"

As soon as I'd sent Diamanta from the room, Maria asked, "Wouldn't it be simpler to tell her it's warmer to work in pants?" Nothing was simple. Diamanta was a quiet girl and never the nasty gossip, but she also didn't know how to lie. Imagine the rumors that would abound about the maid-turned-painter who dressed in men's clothes in the home of the unmarried lady painter. Enough stories loomed over our house thanks to Maria's refusal of old Willem van Aelst and every other reasonable offer of marriage.

The next morning, I was back in skirt and apron, sipping warm beer to quell the damp in my bones. My mouth was slick with sour saliva. A cloud of exhaustion hovered. I wanted nothing more than to yield, to curl in a corner and nap. I drank the herbs I prepared daily for Maria. Were my hands also beginning to shake? I listened in the market for rumors of new fevers taking the city.

IT WAS ONLY AFTER WEEKS of drinking herbs, of muddling through each day as if aboard a ship mired in fog, that I bounded up in the bed in the middle of one night. Gray speckled through seams in the bed curtains. Maria repositioned, her body cleaved to my hip, but she did not wake. How had it taken me this long to recognize in myself what I would have recognized immediately in any animal in the shed?

The room spun. I counted and recounted the weeks since my blood had stained Jacobus's cock. I'd ridden him with fury and furious pleasure, marked him with my mess as I'd taken my revenge. I'd been so confident that given my monthly release, there could be no consequences. Now revenge was his once more.

Maria's cheek nestled against the folds of my sleep gown. I stroked her head. I who'd seen a goat buck blubber and snort in the few seconds it takes to sex a doe, I who'd watched the claw of mating turtles, who'd slathered a cow to grease the bull's entry, I should have laughed at my romantic foolishness. Now, inside me, her nephew's child. That is what I thought as she snored. Not my child. Hers. My body grew something that already belonged more to her than to me.

"What is it?" Maria asked, her voice rose-sweet and sleepy.

What if I confessed that inside me was a child, a child of her blood? Maybe it'd make her happy, an offspring of her family, the child that she and I could never have together. But that would be a hollow offering to make palatable the unpalatable. It sickened me. This was Jacobus's child taking form inside me, his foul. But it was worse—it was my foul. My betrayal of Maria, of our life, of the world she'd brought me into when she'd first taken me to Utrecht.

"It's only a fool shouting on the canal. Go back to your dreams."

She eased her leg under mine and her breath deepened.

BY DAWN, I was across town, in a warren of dank streets I'd had little reason to traffic before. The early morning's damp darkness pressed down. Whatever sun might eventually break would appear a weak tea stain. I wound my way through the already choked streets. Women tossed night water, food, all matter of waste into the canal. Carts maneuvered around pig and dog. The dress I wore was plain hemp, like any simple girl. Wasn't that what I was? Whatever finery I'd come to believe was my daily cloth felt shredded. Nothing was my due.

Turning a corner, I came upon the gable stone I was seeking with a scissor and knife carved into it. I walked past the small house and went twice around a square of blocks, practicing the story I'd tell. Even before I knocked, I heard grunts and laments from the other side of the barber surgeon's door.

"Come in. Be quick." A tiny woman grabbed me by the arm, practically slamming the door before I was inside.

"The barber?" I stammered.

"Well, you can see it's not the bread shop," the woman said, her mouth gaping wide. Looking down into her maw, I could see the few chipped and brown teeth she still possessed. The shop's ceiling was hung heavy with pots, the room's scent thickly layered with the pong of antiseptic, mildew, metal, and blood. A moan issued from one corner of the narrow room and then, as if in response, a piercing cry from the opposite corner. All through the room people were draped in sheets, and seated on low stools, the barber surgeons, each with his tool and bucket, bent over an outstretched limb.

"I need bloodletting."

"Sure you're not wanting a loaf of rye?" And again, that wide toothless chortle. Then her face clamped shut, suspicious. "What ails? The barbers have no time."

"My husband has sent me, hoping that with a letting, I'll be fit for a child. I'm having trouble." I conjured my face innocent, as if this invented husband understood what I couldn't. Especially my own woman body.

"Tell him for a child you need his prick not the scalpel." Laughter ballooned through the room. "Best for you to run home and announce there's a barber ready to offer that service if your husband's prick's a flop."

"Dropsy." I plowed ahead, as if I didn't understand the merriment that shook through these miserable souls. "Bloat." I kept my voice soft, almost a whisper, as if referring to my female body was unbearable. "Retention of the monthly blood. My husband says, the vein of the mother should be bled."

"Isn't this husband of yours an expert," she said. "Get out."

"Pardon?" The room stilled, only the steady run of fluids plinking like syrup into buckets.

"You think you're the first to show up angel-faced with a whore-child stuck in your womb?"

"My husband says—" I began again but she cut me off. Jabbed at my belly.

"If the barber risked his life for every nightgirl's unwanted end from a toss under a bridge, he'd be dragged to jail more days than there are in a week." Her hands firm on my stomach, she shoved me backward. "Get out, whore!"

Nightgirl. Whore. I stumbled. Reeled down the street. I, who'd cavorted in the highest company, with my closet of dresses edged in Spanish lace, was now nothing more than an unmarried wench with a child in her belly. The streets tipped precariously. There was no hiding my disgrace—not from that woman, not from Maria. Carts lurched close then wheeled away. Passersby leered. A slit goat strung up outside a butcher's shop drained blood into a basin, a bowl of innards glistening beside it. A street dog hunched—shit coiling from it—and growled as I hurried past. But where and what was I rushing toward?

Every day since childhood, hadn't it had been my daily job to make one thing into another? Nut into ink. Stone into viscous paint.

The chicken I clucked to as I scattered melon scraps became the stew I spooned into bowls. Even myself, a constant transformation—girl child to boy, servant to budding girl, woman to man to woman, maid to painter to lover—every shift managed to an end. For Maria. For our future. Now all was mangled and I, the mangler. Even if I was brave enough to tell Maria, I couldn't point a finger at Jacobus without tarnishing her name. Besides, which finger could I point since it was my own feet that had taken me down the dark hall to him? My own feet. My own snaggled pride. When did I, that child who had owned nothing, become a woman who believed she owned anything—even her feet or her pride?

The tin sky pressed down, embossed on the canal. The wake behind a barge rippled out like knives. I stood close to the canal, leaning until I saw my reflection in the dull water. I stepped away and then returned to the edge. How easy it would be to lean. Fall in. Be done. Tomorrow, I'd be fished out, bloated and beyond saving.

"Gerta, Gerta, so good, so very good to see you." A familiar bellowing voice as arms encircled me in a kindly hug. "What luck that I should see you my first morning back in the city. May I walk with you?"

Beaming down at me was Constantijn Huygens, crisply beruffled, his once-dark curls now a frizzle of gray. There was no moment to register how strange it was to see him in this working neighborhood, nor to ascertain how to answer his greeting. I was so troubled, so entirely dislocated with myself that there was little chance I could find words. But that didn't matter; he'd already taken my arm in his and set us walking. "I, too, love the early morning, Gerta. To walk unnoticed. And in a hidden neighborhood. All too soon, the streets will be one pleasantry after the next. No time to savor one's own thoughts."

He guided me down one street after another, keeping up a lively one-way conversation, pointing out curiosity after curiosity—a shop owner's misworded sign, a whimsical punning gable stone, the mounting symphony of church and cart and horse bells. "You're surprised to see me here in this neighborhood, Gerta? But why are you here? What secret potion or pigment are you hunting?" Again, he didn't wait for an answer. I let myself be carried along as Huygens spoke about his recent travels, about certain appointments and his most recent book translations. He barraged me with questions. Did I speak Italian? Had I ever grafted fruit trees? When I didn't answer, he continued, taking my silence as a challenge to defend his philosophy on the scientific benefits of grafting, as if I questioned or opposed his ideas. As if I'd ever dare to oppose Huygens. Still, nothing in his tone condescended. He spoke with me as fluently as if he were speaking with Maria.

"Gerta." He abruptly stopped walking. We were on a bridge. A narrow boat passed under. "It is quite fortuitous that I've seen you this morning without Maria." I felt his direct gaze, but I didn't lift mine to meet it. "There are two important things I'd like to discuss. I think it best, if you can do me this favor, to keep this chance meeting confidential, though I would never want to put you in the position of betraying Maria."

Betray Maria? How was it that he'd gleaned my circumstance? Perhaps he'd seen me leave the barber. Had he noticed me close to pitching myself into the thick water? Perhaps my desperation was that obvious.

"Gerta, Gerta, not to worry." Huygens chuckled. "My requests are actually quite simple." In a knot, I could make sense of nothing.

"I would like, no, I would love to have in my private collection a Gerta Pieters's painting. I thought it better to ask you directly and privately, since we both certainly recall Maria's rather secretive and squeamish response to my praising a certain landscape in the studio years ago that I now understand was yours. I would like one of your extraordinary original compositions. Perhaps one of your still lifes with landscape that are distinct and strangely personal."

I said nothing—how could I have expected this turn? *Extraordinary! Original!* Then Huygens rushed to add, "For purchase, of course. That is what I mean. I wish to purchase one of your paintings, Gerta. Would that be possible?"

It might be that I answered, "Yes," or perhaps, "I'd be honored, sir." Truly, I have no memory of what words I managed to stammer.

"Well, then it's a deal," Huygens burst, his enthusiasm daunting. "I only hope my next request is as simply managed." Huygens pivoted us off the bridge through a maze of backstreets, avoiding any of the larger squares or newer canal streets where he was certain to encounter those who'd want to greet him. Soon his circuitous route brought us close to Maria's house. Oddly, the streets looked unchanged, while my life had flipped twice over—from painter to pregnant whore back to painter. And not only as assistant to Maria van Oosterwijck, but as an artist soon to be in the collection of the esteemed Constantijn Huygens in my own right! "She must go," I heard Huygens say. "She's said no over and over. I need the aid of your encouragement."

"Who?" I mumbled. "Where?"

"Gerta, you haven't been listening. Maria, of course. To London."

"No. She can't do that!"

"My, my! Suddenly such big opinions, Gerta." Huygens's tone was amused. "And why would that be?"

How to answer? I couldn't speak about the constant shake of her hands, the numbness that had crept beyond her elbow, the way she'd stopped attending dinners where there'd be glasses and spoons to lift to her lips.

"This is an important commission she's garnered, and, when it's completed, she must deliver it herself," Huygens insisted. "She'll be invited to stay a few months, a year or two perhaps. Our Dutch painters have greatly benefited from these court appointments."

"She requires solitude. She's renounced festivities."

"Ridiculous! That's just her latest posture. Who loves a fete more than Maria?"

"She's changed," I said. "She wants only to concentrate on her work without distractions."

"Dear Gerta, I am most confident that you'll find a way, as you always have, to help Maria understand that this will be a crowning achievement in her career." Then before I could protest further, Huygens bowed and with a quick step turned, his cane clicking as he made his way down the street.

MIDDAY, I WAS AT LUYC'S apothecary ready to unroll a lengthy list of pigments and herbs from my apron pocket.

"Oh Gerta, it brightens my day to see you. I hope I can only make you as happy today." Luyc slung his lanky frame over the counter as his hands reached to take mine. "Maybe I'll make you happy enough to finally wed me." We'd nurtured this playful affection for years and if his was notably greater than mine, he appeared content for the genuine friendship I offered.

"You think I'd marry for a bit of decent azurite?" I worked to keep up our usual banter. Though it wasn't easy to manage a lie with Luyc.

"Never! I hold you in the highest esteem." He winked. "But for the red bugs I think you'd do anything. It's the cochineal I've got today. Some of the finest red I've ever seen."

"You know red's my weak spot," I managed. "Might truly be worth a marriage."

"Gerta." All pretense dropped from his voice. "If I had a life with you, I would try to offer you much more than red." Such kindness. It was moving. Forgive me if for a moment I considered it then. To marry him. Have the child. I knew that I could tell him the truth. He would accept me unredeemed. No one else would be the wiser. I would be the apothecary's wife, carrying, each day, a basket of the best pigment to Maria's studio. He was a thoughtful and decent man, who'd certainly permit me to work outside his shop so long as I returned nightly to untie his apron and rub oil on his long feet. I wished I could return the frankness of his affection. That I could take the good life he would have given me, honest and respectable. One I wasn't worthy of.

I forced a smile. "But before our festivities begin, Luyc, I must carry this lengthy list back to the workshop." I took the list from my pocket, pushing it across the counter.

"Let's hurry then," he said. "What's on your list?"

Juggled in with the regular list of pigment for the studio and the weekly charcoal and herbs for Maria's tremor were myrrh, black hellebore, syrup of artemisia, pennyroyal, and rue, all herbs that I'd gleaned were good for doing what needed to be done. I'd added clove, yarrow, and sugar to the list hoping to confuse him.

"That's a powerful mix of medicine, Gerta." His eyes narrowed. He was not confused. "I must ask you—"

"Must you?" I interrupted. I worked to keep my face straightforward and unsoured. Of course, he wasn't confused. He knew every possible use of each root, herb, and leaf in his shop.

"Yes, I really do need to ask." His look was so direct it hurt. "Gerta, these medicines are extreme. These medicines. What need have you?"

"Is that good courting? Asking without any discretion about my monthly difficulties?" I tilted my head modestly toward the patrons behind me, then forced myself to hold his eyes. "Especially in front of strangers."

His face reddened. "You've spoken with a doctor, Gerta." It was not clear if he was asking a question or giving himself permission to sell me the potent herbs.

I clasped my hands and stayed utterly still while he opened canisters and drawers, then wrapped and bottled my full order. When the counter was covered with packages, he stopped and looked at me again with such a jumble of kindness and worry that I was afraid I might yield to tears and, in a rush, confess everything.

"Gerta, if anything happened to you, I could never forgive my—"

I cut him off. "Your care is always appreciated, Luyc." I reached out and touched his stubbled face before gathering all the parcels and hurrying from his shop.

"Well, look at that. Suddenly there's pep to you again, Pieter," Maria said. How right she was. All afternoon I went about my business brisk and light-footed. I felt almost giddy. What the surgeon barber had refused, I'd do myself and be rid of this terrible mistake.

All day I kept to tasks. Priming canvas. Precipitating alum. Putting the studio into order. When, from her chair, Maria instructed me to darken the petals of the nasturtium, I mixed umber in the yellow lake and did not argue that this would certainly unbalance the composition. I would not veer or confuse my place again. When Diamanta scorched the hem of my blouse, I did not scold. Instead, I said, "Mistakes happen." Diamanta, stunned by the novelty of my kindness, repeated her apology more profusely each time we crossed paths throughout the day.

Finally, day done. Diamanta sent home to her family with lemon and thyme cakes. Extra valerian slipped in Maria's tea so that she'd sleep soundly. Curtains drawn taut about the house, kitchen fire stoked and ablaze. I began. Every parcel unwrapped, every leaf, flower, and stalk boiled and steeped, ground, then distilled for drink and unguent, pessary and plaster. I was no stranger to expulsion. I'd purged the bent wombs of sheep and goat. I made purgatives to swallow, to press on my pelvis, and a clyster to push deep inside. There were enough mixtures to empty the wombs of a gaggle of port wenches. I'd use them all if necessary.

I set about preparing my bedroom, carrying rolls of heavy muslin to cover the bed and floor. I brought in empty tin pails and others brimming with water. Standing in the room, I looked at my carved rosewood bedstead, the walnut desk where I'd tutored myself to draw and paint. How extraordinary this room had once been to me, a room I'd believed people on the street gazed up at with envy. Over the years, it had become a room I barely noticed. Now the polished wood gleamed under the candelabra's glow, and I saw that this room was not where I belonged on this night. Perhaps I'd never truly belonged there. My presence, my pregnancy was a stain on the room. I gathered all my preparations and went downstairs. Like a goat, my place was out in the shed on a bed of straw with rabbits and roosting chickens as my judges.

Did I ever, for a minute, really consider the other life? The life with a child. The life where she was born. The life where he was born. The child conceived of me but also of Maria's blood. A child as close to the one we might have made if we, Maria and I, could have made our own.

What if I had gone to Maria then and confessed my transgression? Might we have together shaped a story avoiding arrest or scandal, or slipped from town to raise the child in another city?

Of course. Of course I considered it. I was no different than any woman with child, wanted or not, in her belly; I considered everything. Saw possible futures down one lit path and another and another and another. With each step, I lived a lifetime with this child. Every simple joy. The day I heard my son's voice lifting in imitation of a reed warbler. My daughter's clever rhyme. And also sorrow. I lived the countless ways a mother fears the unforeseen. Hours fretting an unbroken fever or worse, a child lost to drowning, pox, or some horror I hadn't yet considered that occurs on a perfectly ordinary day. With each step, I was also no different from the woman whose husband cannot feed another mouth for reasons earnest or derelict, or the woman alone, taken in by false promise. I suffered my choice, even as I understood it was mine to withstand whatever grief would befall me. To foist my circumstance on Maria was wrong. To abandon her, unthinkable. Or be judged by her and forsaken. My path, imperfect as all paths, had been chosen.

Those who judge me will want to know if, on that final stair, I paused again. Reconsidered going back to my beautiful room and carrying my filled womb to fruition, trusting with faith that all would be well. I didn't. I knew better.

I WAITED IN THE SHED'S DARK and eventually it began. Nausea. Low ache and belly grip. Cramps rolling through me with a jagged escalation. Vomit. My body was studded with pain while above, the chickens snorted and cooed asleep in the rafters.

. . .

WILL IT MAKE IT less wrong to know in the dark queasy hours how much medicine was needed? If I took one strong purgative or twenty?

ON THE DIRT FLOOR writhing, bleating, a rag stuffed in my mouth to gag the cries. Intestines wrung, shit- and piss-covered, scoured, rasped, lips blistered and bleeding. I squatted. Lurched between the hutches. Dizzy, I braced against the shed wall. A fresh seizure bent me hard over a drying rack, hoping pressure would yield relief. Contraction after contraction. More sweats. Ringing in my ears. Uncontrollable shivering. Then I was tearing at my clothes, the heat surging. No *me* to me left.

DAWN CRACKED THROUGH the wood slats and stirred the crepuscular rabbits. A single ostrich doe, pink, puckered, and scratching for her mount, stared at me, unmoved.

SUDDENLY, a heavy pudding of blood began pooling. Then more. It issued forth in knots, the muslin cloth clotted crimson. More blood. More shit. I clawed the soaked reddened straw until the ferrous reek bloomed.

"**GERTA, GERTA.**" The chickens marked their questions in the dirt. They clawed my skin.

⁂

"Gerta? Gerta?" I pushed off their accusations, but my arms couldn't move. Body turned inside out. The expulsions muscular.

"Gerta." The chickens pecked, but their gold eyes became Diamanta's sad black ones. And when they clucked, "What have you done?" it was in Diamanta's worried voice. Her hands holding the cool wet cloth, her arms that lifted the body that was no longer my body. I tried to tell her to go, to leave me alone, but a burning torched up my legs, splitting open my belly. A rush of liquid, torrential. Then I heard someone calling out for her mother and understood it was me.

SIXTEEN

I WOKE IN AN UNFAMILIAR BED with a woman in a red scarf beside me. Her hand cool on my forehead. The tang of mint as she leaned over to wash my neck, my chest. Where was I? How much time had passed since I'd closed myself in with the animals? The woman seemed vaguely familiar. Did she know what I had done? My many wrongs. Get out. I had to get out. She firmly held my body, soothing down my arms, speaking in an unknown tongue, her voice insistent and yet gentle.

"I have to go." I pushed against her grip. But had no strength and fell back.

I DIDN'T WANT to open my eyes. I opened my eyes. The same red scarf. The same concerned face. But peering over the woman's black-shawled shoulder was Diamanta, offering a thin smile, and I remembered Diamanta's hands lowering me into a wheelbarrow, covering me with blankets, and the unbearable wobble as she'd steered the cart over the paving stone streets.

"Gerta, we weren't certain you'd live," Diamanta said. "Mamãe says you're better but still very weak." My face must have shown terror. Diamanta whispered, "It has passed. You are empty."

"Diamanta." What a terrible risk she had taken bringing me to her home. Surely she knew she and her mother could both be arrested for helping me. "Diamanta," I tried again, wanting to ask why she had shown me such kindness when I had shown her so little. Beside Diamanta her mother began to speak.

"Mamãe says you must stop talking while you sleep. You never stop. You've lost blood. Mamãe says right now the mouth isn't for words, only for eating."

"I must go," I said. "Maria needs—"

"No. Maria says she will come to you when she's ready."

"She knows—" I didn't finish the sentence nor ask Diamanta what else Maria had said. *When she is ready*. Would she ever be ready? And when she was ready, how would I answer the obvious question, who had gotten me with child?

BUT I WAS NOT BETTER. I rose out of a delirium, then sank back in. Restless with fever and dreams, I cried out in terror. Red- and gold-eyed chickens stared at me. "Hush," a gentle voice said. Luyc, kneeling by my bed. Was he a dream? An angel? His hand cupping my face.

"I'm sorry," I mumbled. I couldn't bear for him to know what I'd done. Nor stand the worry that etched his face. Maybe he wasn't really there. Then droplets on my tongue. Burning cold down my throat.

"Three times a day," I heard him say. "She'll live."

. . .

BY DAY, installed outdoors in a low chair, wrapped in shawls and blankets, I slept, woke, and slept again to the lilt of Diamanta's mother, Ximenes, singing in Portuguese. To build back my blood, Ximenes brought me broths of bone and greens. Warm beets, dried apricots. And always three times a day the droplets that burned cool. She circled her hands on my stomach, pressing to release the buildup of air, all the time nodding her head, muttering in Portuguese.

"I'm sorry, Ximenes," I said. She wouldn't look me in the eye. She gathered the empty bowl and spoon and went indoors.

WEEKS PASSED LIKE THIS. Then a month. Maybe two. Mornings, Diamanta left for work at Maria's house. In and out of sleep all day, I dreamed of home, of myself replaced—Diamanta buttoning the crystal buttons of Maria's blouse, easing stockings above her knees. In some dreams, I stood silent by the kitchen fire while Diamanta sat at the table, her hair elegantly pinned, sipping wine and gossiping with Maria. If I tried to speak, it came out a donkey's bray and the two of them giggled and fell toward one another. At night when Diamanta returned to her parents' home, hair tucked under her plain bonnet, she neither smelled of wine nor seemed capable of giggling. She was, as usual, serious and contained. I questioned her care of the house. Had she remembered to polish the silver cups, the spring washing of curtains? Despite her kindness to me, despite her mother's broths, I tried to find any detail she'd neglected. I refrained from asking the only question that mattered. *Is she ready yet?*

One night, after I'd finished my interrogation of how she maintained the house, Diamanta pulled one of my young rabbits from inside her woolen cloak. She placed it on my chest. "I thought this would bring you comfort."

I held the rabbit close. It sniffed, chewed the hem of my sleeve. When it rubbed its teeth and purred against me, despite every effort, I began to cry.

I GREW STRONGER. Maria did not come.

FIRST USING BITS OF charred wood on paper Diamanta brought to me, I began to recover my hand. I sketched Ximenes hanging the laundry. Ximenes braiding loaves of egg bread. I sketched Diamanta and her three sisters while they prepared the table for family dinner. I sketched the clothed table dotted with low bowls, Sabbath candlesticks, and a wine cup in Diamanta's father's hands as he prayed. I sketched the things that filled the house with its unique sounds—the wicker cage of mourning doves, the wood creak on the stair landing—and, like a child, I practiced and scripted *copo*, *vela*, *escadaria*, *mamãe*, under my drawings.

STILL SHE DID NOT come for me.

I DREW THE POTS OF THYME, flowering chive, and rosemary clustered in the door of Ximenes's kitchen.

STILL SHE DID NOT call me to her.

* * *

I DREAMED OF MARIA alone in the workshop: She stands from her stool, a brush unsteady in her hand. She attempts to fasten the paintbrush to the mahlstick I'd made for her but hasn't the strength to position it. The wood handle flops wildly till it drops to the floor. Then I dreamed a studio apprentice, a young man, carefully adding oil to the paint he mulls. Then Maria alone in her bed, trying with one hand to sooth her spasming arm. Or Maria in her bed, her body tangled with someone who isn't me.

DIAMANTA'S SISTERS CALLED the rabbit Orelhinhas, "little ears" in Portuguese, though its ears were long and slender. Ximenes teased, "It is time for this fat Orelhinhas," and dangled the rabbit above her stove pot, the sisters shouting, "Não, Mamãe, não!"

I WAS NO STRANGER to shops run by Portuguese Jews. They owned many of the best in the city. And Maria had sold paintings to more than one wealthy Jewish merchant. But though our ports and streets welcomed a colorful fan of people from far worlds, in Ximenes's kitchen, I learned how little I understood of others' lives. Here, every dish, each preparation bore meaning and followed laws I didn't know. Ximenes cut the nerve on the beef leg before cooking, then salted and soaked the meat because, according to Jewish law, animal blood was forbidden. On Fridays, I helped Ximenes cook a dish that in Portugal her family had been forced to hide on threat of death. We are a strange creature—humans—that a dish of lamb neck, eggs, chickpeas, dates, garlic, cinnamon, mint, and turmeric might send a person to her death.

Now, in Amsterdam, no longer hiding, the women of Diamanta's family came veiled to their table to light candles and lift cloth and bless bread. In their home, I abided by their customs. I wore the lace veil, fumbled and mispronounced prayers. I, who understood a hidden life, prayed as a Jew with Jews. All that answered was a hollow soreness, the sin I'd sown in my body. Yet sometimes, in that crowded, happy house, if only for an hour, I forgot why I was there.

DAYS AND WEEKS, slowly strength in my limbs. Time slipped—weeks, a month, months. I was allowed to help in the garden, the kitchen. I slipped the skin from roasted beets. Mended stockings. One evening, before we'd eaten, with a curt command in Portuguese, Ximenes gathered her daughters.

"Follow us," Diamanta said, offering me a cloak and bonnet.

"Where?" I asked, but she didn't answer.

It was nasty outside, a biting icy rain, a night when no one would step out unless it was essential. The rain sliced against my cloak. My soaked-through shoes slipped on the cobblestones. I had not gone beyond the courtyard since I'd found myself at Ximenes and Benedito's home, and I wanted desperately to turn back to the warmth and safety. As if she sensed my reluctance, Diamanta reached for my hand.

"Where are we going?" I asked, looking down at her fingers laced with mine. My inclination was to pull my hand from hers. Instead, I reached to hold the hand of the younger sister who walked on my other side.

"To the mikveh," Diamanta said, and realizing I hadn't understood what she'd said, she added, "Our baths."

I was happy to arrive at a narrow unmarked building where I followed the others inside. My drenched outerwear was taken from me. Singly we turned down a steep staircase and came into a room so dimly lit that at first glance I thought it was empty. The walls and floor were stone. As my eyes adjusted, I saw in the center of the room was a dark shape, a rectangular opening dug into the stone floor.

She called it a bath, but this is a grave, I thought. *They have brought me to my grave.* I felt relief, not fear.

"Hang your clothes," she said. "We'll fill the bath."

Looking around I realized that what I'd assumed was the steady sound of the rain outside was water funneling through wood pipes that ran along one wall. The pipes emptied into a wood barrel and the girls began bucketing water from the barrel into the opening Diamanta claimed was a bath.

"Hang your clothes," Diamanta repeated as she poured, nodding to hooks in the stone wall. "Unfasten all clips from your hair. Then you'll douse. This is where we come to cleanse impurities. From monthly blood. From fluids of childbirth and . . ." Here she paused, her face wrinkling with discomfort.

"If it's impurities this redeems," I said, "then I'm less in need of a douse than a full submersion."

"You'll go under three times," she answered, without acknowledging my attempt at a joke.

As I undressed, the sisters continued their collecting, some buckets poured directly into the opening and others brought to a small fire Ximenes had started. Ximenes exchanged each bucket with one she'd heated that was then emptied into the bath. When my clothes were off, Ximenes motioned me to the fire. I hurried over eager to get warm. The heat from the fire coursed, traveling the length of my body, and I felt a tingling of the hairs on my arms and legs. Ximenes held my chin with one hand and pushed at my lips with the other, prodding me to open my mouth.

"She wants to make sure there's no food, no strings of meat stuck in your teeth," Diamanta explained as her mother rubbed a cloth over each tooth. "You must be rid of all food, clothes, every single pin in your hair."

When Ximenes was satisfied, she guided me to the tub and gestured for me to descend. There were three steps. I entered and was told to sit. The water was barely tepid; my skin puckered like a newly plucked bird. The women began to chant and Diamanta motioned for me to submerge. I went under. *Let me be done*, I thought as I lay flat against the stone base. I'd done so many unthinkable things. Maria wasn't coming for me. Why would she?

I resisted coming up, holding my breath until I could no longer defy the urgency to breathe and emerged gasping. When I was steady, Diamanta asked, "Are you ready?" I nodded. The women again recited prayers. Again, I dipped. I felt a darkness wash over me. I touched my belly, that place where a life had begun within me. A terrible sorrow stirred through my body. Above me, muted voices floated.

On my third submersion, just before going under, I thought, *I'm ready*, then slid down against the rough stones. *I'm ready to be forgiven*, and yielded into the darkness.

THE NEXT DAY, I sat beside a small oval mirror. I turned my face to one side, then the other, keeping my eyes trained on the tinted glass. How many times had I checked my hair in a mirror to adjust a stray curl, or paused at the front door mirror to make certain that all was tidy and composed before stepping outside? Now in an ill-fitting borrowed dress, my hair roughly knotted at the back of my neck, I regarded myself, taking in my countenance without fidgeting to correct how others might see me. I had no idea where I would go. No idea what my life offered next. I regarded my reflection and sketched the uncertainty that looked back at me. In that house I drew my own face for the very first time.

SEVENTEEN

WHEN SHE CAME, she did so abruptly, without dispatch. She filled the doorway, stunning the noisy household to silence. Diamanta bundled her sisters from the room. Ximenes carried forward a chair, cushioned with a pillow embroidered with forget-me-nots. But Maria did not sit. Silent, imposing, she remained framed in the doorway.

"Look at you," she said, though she wouldn't look at me. Her eyes scanned the kitchen. "You're very comfortable here, it seems."

I saw the room as she must. Meager and cramped. Plants overflowing from rafter nails, feathers loosed and floating free of bird cages, jars jammed on shelves. A cluttered family home that I should have detested.

"Maria," I started, but the shake of her head was a whip to silence.

"You're comfortable here and obviously have been in the other squalid stalls you apparently frequent," she said. "Who knows what mess you enjoy? Obviously, I did not. Do not. Whatever fine taste you cultivated with me over the years, clearly vulgar appetites appeal more to your palate." And with that, she turned and was gone.

FIVE DAYS LATER, she again loomed in the doorway. Same recriminations. Same scorn. What was her purpose? To make sure that I understood all I'd lost? Should I have pushed back? Dropped to my knees with apology? Or spoken Jacobus's name to silence Maria? This was my chance to summon the courage to spit out his name. My chance to say that it was for our life I took the risk. That it was for her good standing that I'd gambled my life in cleansing my womb.

But then I imagined her confrontation with Jacobus and the relish with which he'd describe how I stole into his room and attacked him while he innocently slept. *Dearest Aunt*, he'd say, his lips fixed in that awful pouting smirk, *haven't I repeatedly warned you this maid is a devious one? When I refused her lusty advances, she forced herself on me and tried to blind me.* And wouldn't that also be true?

No, beyond the mikveh's cleansing, I needed to face Maria, her anguish. To withstand her lashing. Her cleansing by chill and fire. To fall to my knees and speak her nephew's name would only be a greater cruelty, one she didn't deserve. I'd never speak his name, nor invent a rogue sailor who'd snatched me on a dark street. I'd commit to silence, wherever it led. That would be my penance.

SHE SPAT OUT NAMES. The fishmonger? The hairy cobbler? Luyc? She wasn't a fool. She'd seen the way he looked at me. And did I think she hadn't noticed the smile I gave to the pepper merchant? She wasn't a fool. What had I wanted? A bigger home? A wealthy husband? Or was it just pitiful hunger for the plug of a man's stiff tail?

THE NEXT TIME MARIA CAME, she breached the doorway. She struck a determined path to the wall where the sisters had tacked my many drawings of them carding wool, sewing, peeling turnips. There were studies of endive and frilly-leaved lettuces. Ximenes scrubbing the chipped stone floor. Her husband, eyes closed, hands lifted for blessing. Maria took her time regarding each drawing but lingered longest before my single self-portrait.

"You think that because I brought you to the best homes, sat you beside me at the finest tables, you're irreplaceable?" Maria said without turning to me. "There's a lesson I must have forgotten to teach you when I took you from my father's home. Nothing's irreplaceable. Not the most beautiful porcelain teacup. Not the rarest emerald. Not even a good fuck in one's bed, Pieter."

What I heard above all else then, above the statement that I was replaceable, was that she'd called me Pieter. And at the sound of my name, the name she alone called me, I went and stood beside her. She didn't back away.

How had I not noticed before that, despite her blue wool cloak and matching spring muff, she was misbuttoned, her face rouge and lip stain botched? Diamanta wasn't fastening buttons each morning. No one else was helping her. Under her good cloak was certainly the slip dress I'd sewn that required no fastening.

Maria turned toward me with the self-portrait she'd torn off the wall. "You still have your hand." She'd claimed nothing was irreplaceable, but for her I was. She wouldn't allow anyone else to see her infirmity. There was no new apprentice in the studio. No fresh painting had occurred. The pending commissions had not been started. Perhaps my crime was less pregnancy than that I'd risked my life, a life she needed to sustain her work as a painter.

However salty her insults, my task, I understood then, was to conjure the return to her, because, while she needed me, it was impossible for her to invite me back.

"Have you seen Huygens?" I asked abruptly.

Maria's countenance ruffled. "Huygens?" She turned to me, perplexed. Truth be all, I surprised myself. I'd completely forgotten my strange meeting with him on the street near the barber surgeon till that moment.

"He's counseled me," I continued, "that you must deliver your completed painting to the royal court of England."

"When did you meet with Huygens?" She sounded horrified as she rounded the question. "What have you to do with Huygens? Was it him?"

I had to hold back laughter at the absurdity. "I've nothing to do with Huygens. He merely encountered me on the street and begged me to convince you to make the trip to deliver your painting."

"I've told him I have no interest in such trips. He can go on my behalf. He'll be knighted again, and double knighting will become de rigueur for every Dutchman worth a coin."

"I told him you wouldn't go."

"That's stunning. Now you're speaking on my behalf! Who cares what you've said! I should go to London. Maybe now is exactly the moment," she countered, just as I'd wagered she would.

"Then you've finished the commission?" This question hurt to ask. She couldn't lift a brush. She twisted in a circle like someone with a foot caught in a trap before she rushed back to the door.

"If you'll allow me," I said before she stepped outside, "I'd like to clean the workshop tomorrow."

Maria paused in the open doorway. "You could have come to me then, Pieter." Her voice trembled when she spoke. "You can always come to me."

IT WAS PIETER who went to the studio the next day. Pieter, in wool pants and vest, no longer caring what rumors neighbors spun. I went back to my humblest beginning, a scrappy boy who kept to his tasks. It was Pieter who scraped palettes. Who scoured floors and washed windows with vinegar. There was no task too menial. Pieter cleaned the studio but didn't lift a brush to an unfinished still life I ached to finish. Pieter didn't sit at the table for a meal nor run upstairs to Gerta's bedroom, with its fine furniture and wardrobe filled with splendid dresses. Here was a Pieter of work, of letting Gerta remain banished.

For a week, I cleaned the studio. Kept to myself while Maria chatted with Diamanta in the kitchen. At the end of the day, Maria entered the workshop to point out what I'd missed and what needed my attention the next day. Then I said goodnight and returned to the noisy house of Ximenes and Benedito. At their doorstep, I slipped on a skirt and took my chair at their family table.

ONE EVENING, after I'd buttoned my overcoat, Maria said, "While you're here, you might as well brush my hair." My pulse quickened. I forced myself not to throw down my coat and run to her. I kept every movement natural, gathering various hair utensils, as if there'd been no interruption to our usual routine. I stood behind her and unpinned her tresses. With fingers dipped in lavender oil, I began to open the densely matted locks, untouched, it seemed, since I'd been gone. When they finally loosened into curls, I slowly combed, untangling, careful not to snag or tear.

I worked in segments until her hair was smooth and the teeth of the comb moved easily against her scalp with a pressure I knew she liked. Then with the brush, I started at the nape of her neck as I had since she was a girl. And as it had since she was a girl, her breath softened to the rhythm of my strokes. Her hair was flecked gray now, a shock of it at the temples. This was new. I went slowly, one hundred strokes before I pinned her hair as though she were to attend a formal dinner. I handed Maria her horn and silver mirror.

"I think we're ready." She smiled approvingly at her reflection. "Painting begins tomorrow."

I ARRIVED EARLY and by candlelight organized the palette. We began as we'd left off months before. Maria in her painting chair while I stood before a panel, untouched all the months I'd been away. Other than her instructions, we were silent.

I returned the next day. And the next. Each day I stayed later, missing Ximenes's dinners, stumbling down icy streets to the house for a few hours of sleep before slipping out the door again, well before dawn to ready the studio for the day's work. When the final layers of paint and glazing were dry, I turned to the panel prepared for the still life commissioned by the English queen.

"Have you thought about the composition? Which flowers you'll include?" I rummaged through the cabinet, sifting through bits of charcoal and chalk for a strong but thin piece to use in sketching the design.

I AM YOU

"Not at all. I'm giving up the commission. It's an embarrassment to be so late."

"You've never given up a commission," I said.

"Nor had I ever been abandoned."

"I'm here now."

"I won't risk you leaving another canvas wet on the easel." She stood from her chair, and went to wrap her shawl about her shoulders but her hands couldn't quite manage it, the shawl slipping off her arm and dragging on the floor.

I went to her and knelt. "I'm here, Maria," I said, gathering the fringe of her wool wrap in my hands. "I'm not going anywhere." I embraced her legs.

"What are you going to do next? Wash my feet and beg for forgiveness?" she scoffed. I held my tongue to keep from saying I'd been washing her feet my whole life. The way I'd once freely teased her no longer had a place between us. "Fine, Pieter. If you're so desperate to restore yourself into my good graces, we'll give the queen her painting. I want the whole bouquet on the edge of demise, the vase precariously perched on the edge of a shelf, the flowers wilting toward death. But before any of that, start by draping this shawl around me."

I DREW ENDLESS preparatory renderings until, once she was at last satisfied with a composition, she had me fix the paper to the panel and follow with pouncing, a technique of poking small holes in the drawing and sifting chalk onto the canvas. We generally preferred the immediacy of sketching loosely on the panel, when with the simple smudge of charcoal we could correct or augment before we went on to dead-coloring. Clearly, she was trying to impress that we were no longer in the realm of the usual. That nothing was loose anymore, and maybe would never be again.

But each day Maria eased and asked more of me, and soon I returned almost to the full range of life in the workshop and the house—roasting chunks of cobalt mixed with liquefied glass then poured in cold baths to shatter before I ground them rough for smalt, paring her toenails and shaping the fingernails of her vibrating hands, sitting for meals at her table while Diamanta served us. At some point she asked me to change out of men's clothes, and, wearing a skirt, I held her arm for spring walks under showers of white elm blossoms.

I can't remember which exact day I returned to live in the house, or when I reclaimed my room, though I can say I never again felt that the room was mine. Still, I was grateful. To resume daily errands; to paint; to prepare Maria's tonics, tea, and salves; and when she asked—and she did!—to help with her dressing and bathing. Those first baths it hurt to see how she'd suffered in my absence, her hands so unable to manage that she'd forsaken bathing. Her skin was dirty, scabbed over with dry patches. I wanted to look away. But this was the woman who insisted that the job of an artist was to look, and to do so without judgment. That you must never draw the idea of a flower but observe each specific bloom, honor the torn petal, and the hint of purple dabbed on a leaf's underside. How could I not regard her in her filth and decay? I did my best, scrubbing and oiling her skin till it was somewhat restored.

And, yes, at some point I returned to her bed. What there was between us under the canopy was practiced and quiet. How could it have been otherwise? Though I wanted—as much as I'd always wanted, and, despite everything, will forever want—to put myself fevered to the salt of her, fingers pressed to her depth, the abandon, the freedom between us had broken. Still, we slept close and well.

The painting progressed slowly. She wasn't satisfied. After six months of working, she had us start over. And months later, a third time, altering some of the original choices and then, when she was still discontent, altering them again. While Maria had once been ready to abandon the commission, she became increasingly determined and committed to its excellence, its endurance. "It's not just for this queen. She may well be gone before we've finished. These queens seem to last a minute on their thrones before the next assumes the crown. This painting is for the pleasure of every queen to come," she said, insisting more than usual that every distinct area of painting I worked on, what is called the opmaken, be shaped, every boundary distinct before going to the next.

"This painting should challenge our patience and faith," she declared when I said the paint was dry enough for the next glaze. "This is not a *dry enough* affair where glazes then go muddy and cracked," she said. She called the canvas her elegy. And when I asked, "An elegy for whom?" she looked down at her hands bound in herb-soaked cloth and said, "Isn't it obvious?"

I WAS SO GRATEFUL to resume something like our old life, to be back in the studio, that it took all those many months, almost a full year, though I don't know how that was possible, to see what was missing. One day, as Maria detailed which colors were required for the day's palette, I glanced up from where I was mulling oil into pigment to ask if we'd need yellow lake and, with a start realized what, in my determination to reestablish our life, I hadn't seen. All my original work in the studio was gone.

By which I mean that every still life, every landscape that had been the work of my eye and hand alone, every painting not done in the name of the studio—work not signed, or initialed, or commissioned for Maria van Oosterwijck—was gone. It didn't seem possible. How was it possible? I scoured the workshop. Nothing. Nothing signed by Gerta Pieters was left. All that remained were the canvases, in various states of completion, that I'd painted for Maria. Where I'd been her hand. Signed her name.

And then, as with a misplaced ring, glove, or gate key, I searched again. Methodically untying every portfolio, in search of the hundreds of flower studies, insect studies, sketches of Maria I'd drawn over the years. I pulled canvases from the racks. Unrolled untacked paintings. Went to every corner of the workshop where she might have shoved my work out of sight. I staggered through the workshop, unraveled, unable to sit or find footing, my throat parched as if I'd been shouting.

All the while Maria sat in her chair watching me. She never said a word. Did I scream? Did I grab her by the shoulders and shake her? Did I demand, where were my paintings, all the years of my own work? I didn't. I didn't say a word. I can't even say that I was furious. My body felt as if it'd been beaten. My mind was exhausted, battered. But how to explain this—there was also a layer of relief. As though I'd been waiting for further execution of justice. Maybe this was it. The final punishment I'd needed. I'd never accounted for my crimes. She didn't know the extent of my betrayals. If she'd known she might never have allowed me into her home again, might have had me banished, tossed me to the street. She'd taken me back. Certainly, this was kinder punishment than the Spinhuis, the detention house for women, where, with a word of my crime against the unborn, Maria might have had me locked, imprisoned, spinning garments for the rest of my days.

Eventually I went back to the mortar, added four drops of oil, and continued mulling the malachite, careful to keep it coarse so the green wouldn't go brown.

"I BURNED THEM," she announced at dinner. Her hands jerked as she tried to cut her meat. I took the knife from her shaking hand. "At first, I lit the paintings one by one," she said. "But that was awful. It was painful to watch and so slow." She sounded confessional. No timbre of gloat. No triumph. "But then it became a different terrible, that large, awful blaze of the mounted pile." I slid the knife against the grain, meat slipping wet off the bone. "Everything changes," she continued, apologetic. "You know this, Pieter. Look." She held up her aggrieved hands. "Everything transforms. Not always as we wish."

I couldn't accept that burning my drawings and paintings was transformation. Still, I nodded.

She fumbled the bowl close. The stewed meat now cut and shredded for easy spooning. Meat dribbled off the spoon onto her sleeve's silk cuff. "I've lost so much," she said. She leaned in, slurped from the juddering spoon. She wanted to equal the scales.

Feel pity, I thought, looking at her mouth smeary with grease. But I couldn't conjure a grain of pity. Any remorse I'd felt hours before in the studio had broiled to anger. And devastation. Our scales had never been equal. Whatever I might have pretended. Over and over, I'd been reminded of this. And she'd destroyed the one thing I'd had that had ever felt truly mine.

"Who am I?" she said. "Who am I?" She looked genuinely misplaced. "Tell me."

"You're Maria van Oosterwijck," I responded flatly.

"No, Pieter. You're Maria van Oosterwijck."

"It's your paintings that hang in the best homes and palaces. With your name, your initials," I said. "You're Maria van Oosterwijck." Even as I insisted she was wrong, it was also true. Many times standing at the easel, my feet planted in her wide stance, my body bending with the brush as she once had, the boundary of my person dropped away and I felt more Maria than I did myself.

"Look at these hands." Holding out her hands, gravy shook from her trembling fingers. "I can't even sign my name. You had everything. My hand became your hand. My paintings and yours. And a baby. And you abandoned me. And I have nothing."

The range of feelings I felt was dizzying. Just as I'd grasp one feeling, and with my whole body brimming with anger want to shout for her to look around at every painting I painted for her fame, she'd say, "I have nothing," and I'd see those useless hands. Then in an instant, whatever pity I felt spun to bitterness. "I'm sorry," I said, furious but still apologizing.

"Everything was yours. Even my love," she said. "And you were no more constant than a street cat."

Love? Had she ever in all these years together said she loved me? Had she ever given me that certainty of expression? I wasn't sure I believed it now, even as I ached to take her hands and one by one kiss each trembling finger clean.

"Who is he?" she demanded.

I'd been waiting for this. Still I hadn't prepared an answer. "He's no one," I said.

"You'd risk our life for no one? Don't belittle me."

With every strength I possessed, I fought to keep my resolve. It was hard not to finally be done with it and blurt out, "Jacobus." But I didn't. Even if she actually believed me, if I could convince her of his ill intentions, he'd become yet another of her losses. Impossible to unravel the knotted skeins of protecting Maria, of fury—and the tangle of fury at her, at me, at Jacobus.

"Or did you finally get a little too curious about what the swing of a man's prick offered? How did it go?" She chewed, and I watched the meat pulse down her throat. "Just tell me who he is."

She persisted, shouting accusations and names. I said nothing. "My hands were gone. You were gone. It was your turn to lose something," she said, her voice icy. "Now you have. All that beautiful work. And it was beautiful. Frightening to watch it burn. You should know, the charcoal you sketch with in the studio is all that remains of your paintings."

I took up a dinner cloth, wiped grease from the knife blade and from her fingers. Left a smear of meat fat on her parted lips.

IN THE NEXT MONTHS, a careful patience crept between us. We were no strangers to patience. Or to the consequences of rushing. Years together in the studio had taught us that with each dip of the brush there's a temptation to hurry, wet into wet, and risk muddying the rose. What I knew best was labor, the steady accumulation of days that makes a future, so I busied myself with fitting strips of lead into clay jars. I bedded horse dung in a narrow shed and stacked the jars tightly atop trays filled with vinegar, then bolted the door. It'd be months before I'd unlock it again and pull cakes of lead white ready for a rich warm paint from the reek. The promise of time. The promise of what good comes of dung. Maria and I might've even laughed at that. But we weren't yet laughing. Instead, we kept to the work. Work sustained us. How many times over the years had patience smoothed our foul angers? Been its own apology? But at odd moments, maybe bending to buckle my shoe, I'd recall an early painting or a simple study of field grasses, and sorrow would gust through me so that I would have to flatten my palms against the floor to keep me from shouting, "You burned that too!" Other times drawing, a nub of charcoal in my grasp, I tried to feel which painting of mine it came from, and I could conjure nothing, feel nothing. Not loss. Not fury. Not love.

EIGHTEEN

1685, December

T HEN, AS ALWAYS, HE INTRUDED. A new letter from Jacobus. Maria read aloud while I worked in thin layers of glaze on the panel for England. Then she read it again, stopping to extol her nephew's every turn of phrase. She was so proud, so very proud of the good and busy life he detailed. He'd returned from his travels and, with the connections he'd made, set up in the village of Uitdam, where he was an occasional minister. Wasn't it kind the way he wrote about his aunt's goodness and patience? He'd furnished a room for her in his house. And not for visits. *Come live with me, dear Aunt.* Imagine that! Wasn't it kind that he worried if she'd approve of the tapestries he'd hung?

"He can afford kindness," I flashed. "You paid for the travels, the tapestries, and his house!"

"Pieter, when did you become so humorless?" she scolded, and returned to the letter filled with boasts of his prosperous and virtuous life. "You're so unkind. He even offers you a room. Listen, he writes, *There's even a bed for that too-proud-for-her-bodice maid of yours.*" Maria laughed as if this was an old family joke.

Images of Jacobus loomed before me. Drunk, menacing. His thick hands pressed against me. Would I never be rid of him? Once again disrupting, once again endangering what fragile peace Maria and I had assembled.

"Always good to hear that your nephew has become a pillar of the community," I said, and stippled the browned torn edges of a carnation petal.

MORE AND MORE, as weeks passed, Maria dreamed of us joining Jacobus. "Maybe it is time to leave," she said. "The great years of Amsterdam are finished anyway." Had I considered that the city's fetid waters were to blame for her hands? Didn't I find the crowds increasingly belligerent and crude? She'd never planned to stay so long in the city, she claimed.

"What would you do in his little village?"

"I'll retire. Live a quiet life."

"You told me you'd never stop painting." Once I'd spoken, I recognized how callous I sounded, standing in front of her canvas while she sat in a chair, spasming, numb to the elbows, watching me paint. All she'd ever wanted was to paint. Yes, she'd wanted great fame and great wealth. And she'd achieved both. But the everyday work, the spiritual process of moving from sketch, to composition, to execution—the relationship of colors, the precision of a brush of two hairs, the textured veins on a leaf—that was what she'd lived for. Now, years since she had held a brush, who was she? Still, I persisted. "You, happy in a quiet life by the sea?" I said. "Impossible."

But was I truly concerned with Maria or was it my own position that worried me? She'd been in hiding for so long, said no to so many invitations that the invitations had stopped. She lived a reclusive, practically monastic life to veil her illness. At her nephew's, she could gracefully retreat, assume her place as the proud aunt and not the crippled artist. But in his house, what would I be? Without her workshop I'd no longer be her apprentice; there would be no commissions for me to paint. In Amsterdam I had only to leave the house to be reminded that while I was servant to Maria van Oosterwijck, I was also known to be her assistant. Among vendors, I was distinguished from other maids who came with their baskets. Small deferences were shown—a finer cut of meat, a wrapped package of goat tongue and bones slipped into my basket, a warm buttercake kept aside for me. And it wasn't only at the market. On every canal, I was greeted by men and women of high standing who owned paintings from our studio.

More than once, laden with full baskets, I was stopped by Jan Six. He'd inquire after Maria but after the formalities were over, he'd linger. "Gerta, without Maria here today to boss us both," he'd joke, "perhaps I'll convince you to tell me which of my two paintings was painted by you. If you won't betray her with talk, just nod your head when I guess correctly." He'd reach into a basket for an apple and bite straight in without bothering to rub it against his jacket. Once he asked directly, "How are you, Gerta Pieters?" and waited for me to reply. Maybe the pitiful joke is that a maid claims any trifle shown to her as stature. Laugh all you want but I've not met anyone—maid or mistress—entirely free of desiring another's regard.

"You'll be bored in a week playing the doting aunt," I insisted the next time Maria argued that we should take residence with Jacobus. "You'll need more." Did I believe this to be true? How often do we convince another something's good for them when, in truth, the benefit is not for them but for ourselves? How many times had Maria done that with me?

"Look how welcoming Jacobus is, Pieter, how far he's come from those funny childhood accusations. Remember when he thought you'd put rotten meat in his school trunks? What's your resistance?" she asked.

I'd done my best to seal all that had transpired away in a box. He no longer swept through my nightmares or my desires. Nor did I find myself, while walking down the street, raging at him and conjuring terrible circumstances for his downfall. Jacobus couldn't be trusted. He wasn't a good man. But just as he couldn't be trusted, when it came to him, I didn't trust myself. My own darkness emerged. For everyone's safety we couldn't live under the same roof.

THE CANE TAPPED ONCE, twice against the door, which I opened to the sight of Huygens, imposing—though shrunken and frail with age—impeccable, and somehow dry, despite days of a wintry March drizzle. "You look wonderfully surprised," he said, laughing. I felt my face redden. Seeing him returned me to that terrible morning when I'd last encountered him. I'd been despondent, pregnant, stumbling down the streets, leaning over the canal imagining my end. "I wish I had this astonishing effect on everyone." He handed me his cloak. "I'm afraid most think I'm an old bore."

"However old and doddering you are, Gerta's clearly quite taken with you. She's spoken of your private meetings," Maria said, turning to me, her voice barbed.

"I hope she hasn't divulged all our secrets," Huygens said, delighted to be invited into playful repartee. "And, however brutal you are about my quickening tilt toward the grave, you, in contrast, are always a vision, Maria!" With tremendous effort, he kneeled before Maria, who was seated in her red velvet chair, gowned in layers of red silk. She didn't offer him her hand. "You're the only woman worthy of what agony I'll suffer tomorrow for this ancient body bowing before you on the floor. Let alone if I'll ever be able to stand up."

"Gerta, no doubt, likes to get you up." She laughed at her pun. "She seems to be an expert at helping men get up. Let me watch you help him now, Gerta."

Barely registering her sting, I was lost recalling that morning when Huygens, unaware of my despair moments from my end, had walked beside me declaring his interest in buying my painting. He'd made it possible to imagine a future, to imagine staying alive.

"Gerta," Maria insisted.

By the time I lumbered across the room, Huygens had struggled to his hands and knees. Hanging on to Maria's chair, like a crab, he squatted and dragged himself to his feet. "No, no. I'm fine. For a decrepit man, I still manage." He brushed off his jacket. "Though I wouldn't refuse joining you for a meal, Maria."

I left to prepare his plate, as Maria claimed she'd already eaten.

"Nothing grand," Huygens called after me. "This old stomach can't enjoy what it used to, I'm afraid."

I returned with a board heaped with apricot, fig, quince, and cheese, sliced pheasant, a mug of scallop chowder, and a thick triangle of mushroom pie.

"No, no, no, and oh, how you will make me suffer tonight," Huygens said, showing no restraint. He slurped down spoons of fat scallops without the bother of a single chew. Bits of pheasant hung from his lips while he and Maria argued as they loved to with one another, jousting tiny points of difference. After scraping the last juices from his platter with crusts of bread, Huygens wiped his mouth. "Now for the true nourishment of my visit. I imagine, Maria, that you must be close to finished on your still life for the English court."

"Indeed. Better than that. Signed and the paint nearly dried," Maria said. "Gerta, bring up the painting."

THE ROOM WAS ALTERED when I returned from the workshop; a somber weight pressed as if a storm were imminent. Huygens paced while Maria sat stubbornly erect, arms pinned in her lap.

"Gerta agrees," Huygens said when he saw me. "Tell her, Gerta."

Uncertain what I was being pulled into, I placed the finished canvas on the easel. Huygens moved very close, then stepped back, creating distance. Right, back, left, he moved in a slow box step, as if to assess from all angles. His gnarled fingers doing that fluttery evaluation I'd watched over the many years he'd visited the studio. I kept to one side as he regarded the painting I'd just completed and signed with Maria's name.

"Maria." His voice was solemn. Dread mounded in my throat. He must have recognized the lesser hand of this painting. "Maria," he continued, "how could you not want to march this to England yourself? It's as spectacular as anything you've ever painted."

"It certainly isn't," Maria spat. "Have you lost all judgment?"

"Stay on for a year as a court painter. It will change everything for you, Maria," he said. "Think of what life at court did for Van Dyck."

"Why should I want changing?"

"Less stubbornness might help."

"It's stubbornness that's delivered me here."

"You're impossible."

"I'm worse than impossible. That's why it's better for you to present me as you have before. Explain that I'm an unpleasant recluse. I won't be a court monkey sitting on the shoulder of the queen."

Huygens doubled over with pleasure at the image of elegant Maria as a monkey. "Here's to my stubborn dear Maria." He poured himself another glass of the Austrian wine. "Though I'd rather drink any day to you swinging from the chandelier by your simian tail."

"But Maria must go to England." It was out of my mouth before I'd reckoned what I'd done. At once, both shouted my name.

"Gerta!" Maria scowled.

"Gerta!" Huygens crowed.

"You must go," I repeated. "You won't be the court monkey. You could never be, because I'm the monkey." I'd never dared speak this forcefully in the company of anyone visiting Maria. But daring was necessary. England was necessary. The very diverting path I'd been unable to conjure on my own. If she could be convinced that there was more fame, more money to be made, she could be convinced to stay in England. We'd live there and paint; Jacobus kept at a distance. "A painter in the court is not a novelty," I continued. "But Maria van Oosterwijck, who taught her maid to paint, that's novelty worthy of poetry by the great Constantijn Huygens, knighted in the English court."

Huygens's enthusiastic recognition of his verse gave me strength to continue. "We'll arrive in London bearing the commissioned painting. Maria will be honored, though she'll decline all festivities. When invited to paint in the court she'll again decline, claiming painting too sacred, too private for her to be observed in public. In her place she'll offer a sight never before witnessed in the court, a lowly maid trained to paint as well as any painter in England. Then a competition. Their best still-life painter against Maria van Oosterwijck's maid."

"Gerta." Huygens threw up his hands. "A wonderful plan! Genius. It will draw tremendous attention."

"Attention for whom?" Maria was furious. "Gerta seems to have plenty already."

"Don't be ridiculous." He laughed. "Not Gerta." As if attention to me was indeed preposterous. "It is all you, of course, lovely Maria. It will be just as you amazed us years ago in your home." Huygens's hands arced through the air like a conductor conjuring a score. "Continue, Gerta."

I took a breath as a musician might two beats before the flute enters the final movement. "You'll explain to the assembled how you took a servant from the yard and transformed her." Even to my ears, the unfolding began to sound wonderful, and I continued, my voice increasingly lively. "Perhaps rumor of this has made its way to England but, impossible to fathom, they've shaken it off as ridiculous gossip. Still, they're curious. The lady painter so great she taught a servant to paint. Then you begin the boast. Like an after-dinner bonbon. 'My maid,' you'll declaim, 'once painted a prince's favorite hound.' And to add to the entertainment, you'll drop your voice to a whisper, 'Though I won't name names, she once painted the gnarled feet and rucked ingrown toenails of a certain Dutch merchant.' And then, before their eyes, you'll instruct me. You'll correct me. It will take more than one day. And when they see the finished canvas, the best of England will understand what your genius has wrought."

I hated each fantastic word from my mouth. I hated the whole convincing plan even as I carefully described it. It was not lost on me that I, who had painted the still life before us on the easel, the painting that would hang in the royal court, would be only known there as her trick. But the urgency of keeping far from Jacobus mattered more.

"And what if you're not better than the English painter?" Maria slashed. "What if he wins?"

"Not an option."

"Why bother?"

"Your fame, your worth," I said, "will be further distinguished having done what no one has before."

"Most impressive." Huygens applauded. He stood from the table with the help of his cane. "You've even taught Gerta to think like the bright woman of commerce you've always been!" With that Huygens bowed to Maria. Then to me. He collected his cloak and scarf and haltingly made his way from the house.

IT WAS SURPRISING how quickly and wholly her mind turned to England. Maybe it shouldn't have been strange knowing Maria's appetite for recognition and wealth. After all, hadn't that been my gamble? Still, I was confounded by how instantly all talk of moving to Jacobus's home evaporated. London became everything. Within a week, I was waiting at the port for bolts of silk and satin and ushering the dressmaker up the stairs for new garments.

"London isn't ready for me," Maria announced, as the seamstress pinned the linen ties that would be sewn to her sleeves so her arms could be fastened to the dress bodice.

"London is where I need to be," she announced, with the same adamancy as when she once claimed she need never leave Amsterdam to be famous across the world. "Huygens barely has a breath left in him, and whom else can I entrust to deliver the paintings?"

I might have reminded her of the various dealers who'd sold and ferried her paintings to France and Poland and Austria. Instead, I folded gowns, packed twenty pairs of shoes, wrapped each of her fifty pearl hair clips in a separate cotton cloth. Packed trunk after trunk, which promised months, if not years, in England.

"The staging must be brilliant," Maria exclaimed. "At the start of London, you'll dress the part of the modest servant. But after I perform your transformation, you'll need fine clothes, Pieter."

For every dress the seamstress sewed for her, Maria insisted on a companion dress for me. "Oh, they won't know what to make of us, Pieter," she said, and giggled. Actually giggled. That was the other strange thing. The restraint and accusation in her tone with me was gone. In its place, the old playfulness. The old affection. I wished I could have met her playfulness with my own. Wasn't it what I longed for, to return to the companionship of our old life? But in burning my paintings, she'd made clear that the true companionship I'd once longed for had never existed and never would. I was a servant. At best, a workshop assistant. That was all. Having created this monkey exhibition of me in London, I refused to pretend otherwise.

Yet she persisted. She cooed at the back of my neck. She gifted me a butterfly pendant, given to her by a duke enthralled with a commission. "For you, my butterfly," she said, fastening the gold and diamond chain about my neck.

But despite my resistance, I was wooed by her excitement, by the eager flush of her cheeks, by seeing the old enthusiasm flicker in her eyes. I couldn't help how good it felt to watch her delight, her determination that her entry into the London court be perfect. I, who as a child only wanted to be her Aleppo, still craved her happiness and laughed to hear her scold the cobbler over an uneven seam in her new leather shoes. "I won't let the Dutch be judged in London by your clumsy hand," she said, kicking the shoe off her foot with such gusto that it sailed through the air narrowly missing the cobbler's head.

Every day between fittings and packing, she insisted we practice our presentation for the court, and every day it became more elaborate. "I must lead them on with twists and turns," she said, deciding to begin with the story of my childhood years as Pieter, brought into the family as a servant boy, whom she taught to make gall and walnut ink finer than any imported. "But it turned out our servant was not what he seemed to be," Maria would announce, and we practiced my shift from boy to maid. How the court must be made to gasp when I undid the belted trousers, and—behold!—below the cast-off pants and shirt, a linen skirt and bodice. She'd entertain them showing how she uncreased my boyish manner for a maid's sweeter step and tongue.

"When it comes time to learn paint, at first, you're all thumbs. Hardly able to hold a brush," she said. She had me practice being clumsy, incapable of drawing a straight line. "It won't be easy to teach someone as limited as you appear," she said. "But, behold, through my constant and vigilant adjustments, you begin to show a grasp of dimension, color, tone." How she loved repeating the theater of that word. "'Behold, ladies and lords, how I've created what all say is impossible, a female servant equal to any male apprentice in any painter's studio.' They'll be terribly stirred. 'Impossible,' they'll shout."

We practiced how I'd slip away while she bantered with the audience, provoking them and challenging them to bring forward any court painter whom they thought could best her maid in a painting. She'd rile them up until it wasn't her but someone in the audience who'd shout that the competition must have a prize for the winning artist. Maria practiced standing from her chair to declare, "If I lose, I'll forfeit my commission on this painting. If I win, the queen will commission a second painting at a higher price."

Then she'd call for me as they laughed and twittered, and I'd emerge, transformed. Looking every bit the lady in a beautiful gown, a dress not quite identical to Maria's but—as we had done years ago—in a slightly less brilliant a shade than Maria's, the ruby and sapphire butterfly pendant glittering against my pale throat. No longer boy or scrub maid, I'd look the equal of every lady in court attendance.

"Here," Maria would announce as I took my place before a well-primed canvas. "Here is Gerta Pieters, my creation."

"I WAS BESIDE MYSELF." Luyc was somber as he filled my order. I'd avoided his shop since my return, going to lesser apothecaries for herbs and pigment. I couldn't bear facing another person whose trust I'd misused. Especially a man as true and good as Luyc. Had I dreamed of him or had he actually come to Diamanta's house, kneeling beside me with medicine and risking himself further? Yet the order of pigment, herbs, and medicines needed for London was extensive. And quality couldn't be compromised. On the way to Luyc's shop, I practiced how I'd apologize, acknowledging the danger I'd put him in, knowing he could have been arrested and charged with helping me lose the baby.

When he saw me open the door, he rushed from behind the counter. "Gerta, Gerta." He embraced me, practically dancing me around his crowded shop. "It's so good to see you, Gerta." He pulled back and regarded me. "You look well."

I started to speak but all my practiced apologies jumbled and fell away at his open and caring face. His genuine affection. "It's been a long time, Luyc," I said, the best I could do.

"When that sad-eyed girl came in your stead, terrible thoughts plagued me, Gerta. I felt responsible. I was responsible. I had no choice but to ask. To determine your whereabouts. At first, she claimed you'd gone to care for your sick uncle—"

"It's good to be back," I jumped in, happy at least not to lie. "But my return is brief. We are going to England and might stay there."

Luyc shook his head. "But I knew what she said wasn't true. There was no sick uncle," he said. "I insisted she bring me to you. I knew what I'd packed in your parcel. If anything had happened to you, Gerta, I would have—"

"But here I am," I interrupted. I tried to resume our old games. "I couldn't stay away from you, Luyc, but if I don't return to the workshop with this order, I'll be tossed to the streets and might show up on your doorstep." Then, forgive me, I actually winked.

But he refused to return my foolishness and turned to my order, opening jars and canisters, weighing, and wrapping leaves and pigments. While tying a string bow around a bag of herbs, his eyes steadied on me. "Gerta, I'd open my door to you under any circumstance. Always." The shame I felt then was more complete than any before in my life. That he knew. Who I was. What I was. That he didn't shun me or castigate me for what I'd done nor how I'd implicated him. I didn't deserve his kindness.

"I'm sorry, Luyc," I said, and forced myself to meet his earnest gaze. There was so much I wanted to say, but all I mustered was a pitiful "Truly sorry."

"I am always above anything your friend," he declared. "You must understand," he continued, somber, refusing diversion, "I would take you in under any circumstance."

"Luyc, I'm not worthy of your—" I began to cry and, gathering my parcels, hastened to the door, the shop bells ringing as I pulled it with force.

"THE SPASMS HAVE BEEN particularly violent," she said. It was after her sponge bath. I rubbed her arms with rosehip cream. She stilled my hand against her leg. "They wake me," she said. "Come to bed."

"I have so much to get ready for London."

"At least settle me. When I'm asleep, you'll go back to work."

I helped her to her bed. She asked that a taper be left to burn so that she could watch our shadows against the wall as she arched against my humming mouth. "Even our shadows have gotten older," she said. It was tender. Once released, she slept.

I eased from the bed to continue packing. From the wardrobe I pulled cuffs and collars to wrap in tissue. I packed earrings, rings, crowns of gold filagree into a wood box inlaid with bone. As I sorted and packed, I rehearsed the performance we'd practiced for days. "Here is Gerta Pieters," Maria was to say as I took my stance before the easel, slowly tying a painting apron over my fine blue gown. "Here is Gerta Pieters, my creation," she'd say. With arms bound to her dress, she would give a faint nod in my direction, then I'd curtsy deeply to the king and queen.

My creation. I cringed each time she practiced the line. At what point was I my own creation? At what point was I creating her? But as I packed her combs, I reminded myself that going to London served me, was due to my fear of Jacobus. I promised myself when she called me her creation, I'd tie the apron bow with genuine reverence and lift the brush as she commanded.

Sorting through shawls, I selected a crimson wool square and her beautiful blue Chinese silk decorated with cranes, their white wings raised in a whoosh of embroidered flight. I wrapped both elbow- and wrist-length gloves. There was a stray red leather glove that would match well with the red shawl. I knelt, rummaging for its mate in the wardrobe. In the far corner, my hands felt a bit of fabric—not leather, perhaps the muslin hem of a discarded skirt. When I tugged, it stayed stubbornly in the wood slats. I tugged harder until the slat dislodged. Still, it took both hands to yank the muslin and, after much struggle, I lifted out of the cupboard a small wrapped package.

Before I'd even finished unwrapping it, I'd realized what was inside. It was a painting on a wood panel. I also knew, before I'd peeled back the flap of fabric, that it was mine. That very first painting that Huygens had celebrated, believing it to be Maria's. I wish I knew the words to describe what moved through my body seeing that small painting. At learning that she had not destroyed everything. That though she'd set aflame all my work, she'd saved this, my first real painting. That day, so many years before, when she'd encouraged me to paint the landscape as I saw it and she'd said it was like nothing she could render. I began to cry. I held the panel in one hand, traced with a finger the one tree on the horizon, the faint red in the leaves. Clouds gathered over the field, cooling the greens. A perfect spring day, though dabs of purple massing at one corner suggested a coming storm.

And then I saw that in the lower corner, with a jagged, smudged hand—at best a child's blocky scrawl—Maria had signed her own name. I touched the signature. She'd claimed my landscape. How desperate. How sad. And spiteful. And enraging. Once devotion had defined me. To let her shine had been my only desire. That boy, Pieter, that young woman, Gerta, would have quickly taken a brush to smooth and refine Maria's signature on my panel. But I was no longer that child, that singularly faithful young woman. As a child when I saw the daytime sky go dark, I thought the world was ending. Nothing ended. The scientists say it is as simple as the moon coming between the earth and sun. A solar eclipse. Was her illness the eclipse that that had come between us? What it took from her, it gave me. If that sounds cruel, wasn't all of it cruel.

If I'd never become an artist, I don't know how I would have made sense of the turns a life takes. No doubt, I'd have found a good enough way learning my lessons from the garden and barn. But I'd become someone else, a painter who sat at the best tables in Amsterdam listening to conversations about lenses that scoped great distances. It wasn't only that my hand had changed, or the way I observed shadow and light. All of me had changed. Hadn't I, like the butterfly in its final stage of transformation, become an imago? Of course, none of it would have been possible without Maria. Without her, in what coarse manner would I understand myself, I cannot say. I think I may have been kinder.

Sitting on her bedroom floor, Maria asleep in her bed, such confused sorrow, such love and bitterness coursed through me. I cried then for us both. For all that had been taken from her. For what had been taken from me. For what could never be repaired. *Oh, Maria! Oh, Maria!*

"Pieter." Maria stirred as if she heard me.

I slipped the painting back in the folds of cloth. "Go back to sleep."

"It's a mistake going to England," she said. "They'll see what I've become."

I went to the bedstead to quiet her and tell her it would all be fine. But I couldn't speak. I couldn't make myself tell her anything was fine.

"Touch me. My hands." She pushed herself up and made room for me to sit on the bed beside her. I took one hand between mine and pressed, trying to warm and circulate the blood. Then finger by finger, I kneaded, working my way down each knuckle.

"Some drops will help."

"Useless, Pieter. They're numb and useless." She said this often, and I was always quick to say, "We have my hands. My hands are yours." But it wasn't true. My hands weren't enough for her. How could I have ever thought they would be? Whatever they'd done, my hands were my own. The painting, across the room and hidden in muslin, was a lurking terrible presence. It demanded something of me, though I wasn't sure what it was.

"You're crying?" Maria said, and with great effort lifted her free hand to my face.

"I'm so sorry, Maria," I said, knowing I'd give her more drops, stay with her until she slept. "I should have done better."

"Just look at me." She laughed. "I might have done better too."

WHEN SHE SLEPT AGAIN, I wrapped myself in her shawl of flying cranes, took the painting, and made my way down the unlit hall to my bedroom. I slid the wrapped panel into a pillow casing and hid it in my trunk. Then went downstairs to the workshop.

When the mind is askew, there comes a chance for clarity while holding an instrument of precision. Through the night I put myself wholly to a small square painting. My brush was fast and rough. And, though it was an arrangement of flowers set on a table by a window opening on a watery landscape, it might as well have been a portrait of all the love and grief, the knowing and confusion, all the blunt and difficult weathers that stormed within our life together and, too, the calm that steadied and kept us rooted. I painted all the apologies we owed one another, as any two who have lived side by side owe. I painted the life we'd secured and its unknotting. I painted all that I didn't know and couldn't say and the future I finally understood we wouldn't have.

BEFORE THE BRIDGE lamps had been tamped down, I was out walking with determination to the house where Constantijn Huygens took his lodging when he visited Amsterdam. It was not yet dawn when I called on him. Huygens emerged, his coat misbuttoned over his sleep gown. "Gerta, what's going on? Is Maria unwell?" He lumbered down the stairs, his legs stockingless and shoes unbuckled.

"You asked to purchase an original painting," I said, propping the landscape, its paint still wet, on a step.

"Gerta? Is this necessary at this hour? My promise to buy a painting will be just as good at noon."

"Here is one that is fresh, still wet, and I think worthy." I set my price without room for him to bargain. I sounded firm, though I was frightened to speak to him so directly. Despite having been roused in the night, Huygens's inevitable curiosity and appetite for that which was superior drew him close to the small canvas. He peered at it steadily, tsking, smacking his lips as one might upon tasting a good dish of food.

"It's not signed," he said.

"I wanted to do so before your eyes," I said. "So there would be no doubt that this is *my* painting in your collection." From my satchel, I pulled a brush and a small pot of paint. "I've chosen this blue, from lapis. It's traveled a long distance, as have I."

And with that I dipped the brush and signed my own name.

NINETEEN

WE LEFT FOR LONDON WITH our many trunks. Setting out on a clear day, we were encouraged that we might avoid the vagaries of weather that can beset even a simple voyage. Our ship was pleasant, and while on board Maria insisted that we continue practicing what she'd playfully begun to call The Ultimate Act. With every tweak, the story became more elaborate. In her telling my childhood was stark, my only companions the rabbits. I was practically feral until she began to shape me. "It has to be dramatic. The more tragic your beginning, the more astonishing your transformation," she said, though it was clear that she soon began to believe each embellishment.

At first, I was able to keep Maria from inviting the captain and his crew to be our audience by insisting they were loose-tongued, unreliable rogues, that we didn't want rumor of our extravaganza to precede us. But when Maria learned that the captain was not only an admirer of her paintings but an owner of a Maria van Oosterwijck vanitas, bought right off the parlor wall from a captain who was in his debt for reasons he refused to disclose, the flattery was so intoxicating to Maria that she pulled the captain aside to tell him we had something secret and spectacular to show him.

"Are you trustworthy?" Maria asked, in a bright, flirtatious tone I hadn't heard in many years.

"You've trusted me with your lives aboard my ship, need I say more?" the captain said, ushering us into his private quarters.

Luckily, if I dare call what happened next lucky, there was no chance to show him The Ultimate Act. The wind abruptly shifted. The waters lifted and churned violently. The ship hit a trough that sent us lurching. I sprang forward, catching Maria just before she smashed face-first into the captain's walnut desk.

"Please, stay here," the captain said, and rushed out, slamming the door behind him just as the ship struck another sea trough.

There is nothing delicate about a storm at sea, and, within moments, Maria and I were on our knees, managing rather poorly. I held tight to Maria, knowing that without the use of her hands she was unable to protect herself as the ship plunged and pitched. We couldn't hear one another over the unceasing bang of wind and the crack of wood. I managed to find a rope and bind us together but, before I could knot us to an unmoving post, we were thrown around the cabin as one, my hands protecting both of our heads as we were slammed about. At one point, I grabbed hold of a leg of the captain's desk, hoping to keep us in place. Then the ship listed and continued tilting and tilting, so it seemed we'd surely capsize, and I lost my purchase on the desk's wood leg. We slid across the floor, heaving this way and that until we slammed against the captain's bedstead. Somehow I got us up and into the captain's bed. And then, as suddenly as the storm began, it passed. All was quiet. Despite the new calm, I still felt the roiling, and even the gentlest rocking of the boat had us both retching, soiling the captain's wool blankets.

Soon the door opened, and the captain said in a lighthearted voice, "It is indeed surprising and spectacular to find two ladies in my bed. As I was saying, you've trusted me with your lives, so let me assure you there is no further reason for worry."

But I knew he was wrong. I had reason to worry. For while the ship groaned and we were tossed across his room as if we were no more substantial than a piece of crumpled paper, I understood that I'd been terribly wrong and this grave weather was a sign of what was to come. I'd tricked and convinced Maria into coming to London all because I couldn't imagine anything worse than living under Jacobus's roof. How narrow my vision! This sudden storm was a reminder that there are always horrific unknowns, that even when I thought I'd solved a problem, there was everything else I hadn't prepared for.

The captain lifted the filthy blankets from the bed, assuring us that all was now well. Anyway, he robustly declared, it was known among the seafaring that a few rough swells at sea augurs a steady foot and good business on land. The rest of our trip, he proclaimed, would be placid. But, again, I knew this was a false assurance. Any stillness or calm was momentary. Worse, it lulled one into imagining that safety could last. In my hurry to avoid Jacobus, I'd only looked at what I was running from. Confronted with danger, I'd believed I'd wrested control. But crashing about the room, it was obvious there was no control, and I'd never truly had any. Whatever London I thought we'd set sail for was probably not the London we would find. I was unsteady. The storm's damage wouldn't quit just because we saw land.

WHO KNOWS FROM WHICH fantastic sea tale the captain yanked that omen, but I never found a single placid or steady foot in London. I was always lurching and wobbling, a nausea that never quit sat thick in my throat. I can still hardly stand to speak of that place. It is as if by just saying the word *London*, I'm thrown, pitched unsteadily back without any relief that time affords. Instead, I'm afraid that when I recount our days in that grimy city, it will unspool topsy-turvy, without the gentling benefits of recalling the past. But since it was my insistence that brought us to London, I will try my very best to keep sturdy.

WE STUMBLED DOWN the ship's plank, bits of dried vomit speckled on our clothes. The sooty dockyard air provided no relief. I held Maria as she leaned over the ropes to throw up into the filthy port waters. Then I too was heaving, splattering skirt and shoes. Luckily, I was past caring about the upkeep of our appearances. We managed to make it to the crowded pier. But without a moment to catch our breaths, to stand on land without the continuous sea's rocking, we were hurried into carriages and jostled through the crowded city's bumpy streets.

THEN, FINALLY, THE PALACE. And fresh clothes. And a suite of lavishly appointed rooms, the spindles of the bed wrapped in gold leaf, though, before we'd spent even one night, I was on my knees, giving each room of our apartment a vigorous scrubbing. No need to detail what matter of grime I scoured, but one wondered what passed for a maid in that palace. The first evening we declined a banquet and took a light meal in our rooms. At least for Maria, the food stayed down and there was something of a night's sleep.

How else to speak of the palace? Grand, goodness yes. It seemed there was always some courtier squirrelling close, hand cupped conspiratorially over his mouth, saying, "More than a thousand rooms," as if we didn't have eyes to see. There were mazes, tennis courts, and so many banquet halls and private dining rooms that I lost count, and well-tended gardens resplendent with notable blooms.

Our first morning I brought us to one garden, hoping that the flowers would steady and restore us. The variety of familiar roses did bring comfort. And there were many exotics that required further attention. But we had no time to reflect because too soon Maria was flocked by court artists, avid to be seen sketching beside the new Dutch painter. On the spot, I invented the story that Maria no longer drew or painted in open air. That she preferred to sit in reverent contemplation before the perfect works of God. I explained how, despite many who claimed that Maria's still lifes were the equal of any of God's natural arrangements, she worked only in private so as not to flaunt her skill before the Great Master. When a clutch of painters walked off in a huff, snipping, "Well, aren't you fancy," I was so pleased with the effect of my argument that I revealed to those remaining the straps that bound Maria's arms to her dress. I proudly declared in a public act of deference and contrition—her hair shirt, if you will—that she only released her hands when painting alone in the studio.

When the other artists finally scampered off, yipping and biting among themselves like a thwarted band of jackals, I turned to Maria, expecting to have a good laugh at my cleverness. Instead, she looked sickened and said, "This is exactly why I didn't want to come to London."

"We'll walk the gardens at night," I suggested. "And if anyone bothers us, I'll claim these are our perfume strolls, where in darkness, by scent alone, you refine your understanding of color." I admit I continued to feel buoyed by my quick management of our first morning's problems, hopeful that the turbulence of the seas had finally quelled. Perhaps I'd been unduly frightened by the storm and overestimated our instability. As I escorted Maria back indoors, I felt a renewed resolve that I could take care of Maria and manage our larger purpose in London.

AND MANAGE I DID, though the palace in its grandeur was not easy. Vast, hall after reeking hall mobbed with stinking, sneering courtiers, who only momentarily halted their biting gossip to bow and kiss a hand when a duke passed. All day it seemed they roamed the halls in their mildewed finery, hoping for a better hand to kiss, or to be invited into a better hive of courtiers. From morning to night, in every corridor and hall, they snatched morsels from platters of meat. Eating well past satiation, the nobles paused on staircases to vomit in metal vats, then wandered out to play racket games in the gardens. I watched while a courtier scarcely bothered to step away from a conversation to relieve himself against a wall, his waste drenching the hem of a tapestry, then pooling on the stone floor.

The staff at the palace was considerable and, at every turn, we met grooms and masters, cofferers and clerks, each introduction more pompous than the next. Trying to keep Maria's spirits lofted amidst the throngs of staff and lords, I called myself her Mistress of Wardrobe, her Groom of the Stirrup, her Treasurer of the Household, and at night, as we lay under our packed-feather blankets, I held her close and called myself her Principal Mistress.

It also became clear that there was to be no wandering the gardens at night because, although Maria was loath to attend the palace dinners, as honored guests we were unable to avoid night after night of interminable banquets. At least in the eating chambers there was less of the untidy, rude behavior that the nobles displayed as they wandered the palace. Here napkins stretched in their laps as they picked at abundant servings of mutton, cheese pies, and venison. Here they pretended to barely have an appetite for the servings of roasted pig glazed with mixed fruit, the salt-crusted porpoises, the platters of pheasant, lark, and plover with creamed almonds. Here their conversation was formal, without a dab of the backstabbing blather they'd relished when they'd mingled in the corridors.

"Can't I leave yet?" Maria asked within moments of our being seated each night. But because she hadn't been told when her commissioned painting was to be presented to the king and the queen consort, we had to endure endless courses and entertainment, all the while she cursed and complained into my ear.

At every dinner, jesters circled the hall, squirming onto the laps of lords and ladies, trying to provoke the guests with lewd songs. They popped out from under the table, one wriggling between my legs to pluck a songbird from my plate, sucking lasciviously on the tiny feet while the bells on his fool's cap jingled like warbling birds. Maria, of course, declined to eat in public, sitting stiff-backed in her chair. The linen straps that tethered the violent shaking of her arms had abraded her wrists raw. I hid meat in my skirts to feed her later in the privacy of our bedchamber.

"Do you think we're being held captive?" Maria said after the fifth day without an invitation to present the commissioned painting.

"Shall I offer a ransom payment?" she said on the sixth day.

At one dinner, it was announced that we were to be visited by a world-renowned guest. Into the banquet hall stomped an elephant ridden by a man of such tiny proportions he seemed a mere toddler. In his hands he wielded a polished sword. The crowd bellowed with laughter as the little man slid down the trunk of the great beast. "Here," shouted the man, "from Ceylon is La Bella, a descendant of the famous Hansken, a creature once showcased throughout Europe and known for her superior intelligence." With that, the elephant trumpeted, squawked, and with her agile trunk lifted the tiny cap off the man's head and settled it atop her own. Then La Bella plucked the sword from the man and, practically prancing on her stout legs, marched in circles, brandishing the sword while he frantically chased behind trying to reclaim his weapon. Once the sword was back in hand, the man commanded La Bella to perform trick after trick. With choreographed heavy steps, she obediently executed each stunt and took her final bow with the small man balanced on one arm upside down on her trunk. What must it take each night for this creature of massive strength and intelligence to restrain from flipping and crushing this foolish man, then storming the crowd, her trunk whipping the open mouths of women and men?

IN THOSE FIRST DAYS, the queen was only a rumor. We heard she was pregnant again. That she was tipsy with grief, mourning another lost infant. That she'd taken healing refuge with an order of French nuns. That she'd sequestered herself in her private apartments. We heard she'd miscarried. That there was a sickly baby. That she was barren, her insides permanently twisted. That the devil festered in her womb. We were brought to see her three coronation crowns, "proof" one duke offered, but we did not know proof of what.

The king, however, was everywhere, though mostly we saw only the tasseled back of his jacket as he hastened down passages, a swarm of attendants in tow, or the glint off the polish of his boots as he rode off to the Royal Woods on the back of an Arabian, accompanied by a retinue of huntsmen on Jennets and Barbaries. Wherever he went, chatter followed. Had we seen the face of his latest mistress? Clearly chosen for something lovelier than her sharp face, which was best used to slice bread. Did we know how he prayed? That his daughters were no longer welcome at the court? That he showed signs of insanity? Or that—according to his Groom of the Stool—the king was robustly healthy?

ONE AFTERNOON, having ventured outdoors, we pivoted in the opposite direction of the boisterous cheering and swearing, eager to avoid yet another occasion of the betting that filled the days and nights of the courtiers at Whitehall. Everything was a betting opportunity, from dice to lawn races. We'd watched more than enough high-stakes tennis and bowling games though it seemed more attention was spent in antics of rubbing elbows than engaging in the sport. Gambling, seemingly a court obsession, was not only for the men. Maria had refused multiple invitations to sit with women for board games or cards. "I'm here to collect money, not give money away," Maria said each time. And each time she was met with winks and promises of discretion.

That afternoon, we wandered away from whatever hoopla was occurring in the interior gardens and made our way across the lawns to the fields that led to the stables. "At least the animals won't be idiots," Maria said.

"I'm afraid I must disagree," said a voice behind us. "I've one stallion as foolish as most of these lords."

We spun around and there, alone, striding through the tall grass, was the king. Everything about him was formidable—his long legs sheathed in red satin, the blue cape that waved like a lake behind him, and the tresses of auburn hair that bounced with his every step.

"Though I'll admit even my most truculent horse is smarter and more loyal than all of the stinkers who think my rather prominent nose is clogged to their foul oaths." He tipped his head back and let out a wallop of unbounded laughter.

Maria rebounded, curtsying. "Well, having seen you ride circles around your cock-eyed flatterers, it's clear you know how to rein both horse and courtier without much spur."

"Oh, you are delightful," offered the king, as if he were the first to ever notice Maria's wit. "I'd offer to take your hand to escort you to the stable, but the gossip is your hands are too sacred for human touch. I hardly blame you. With all the dirty habits that abound here, you and I, painter and king, have much to protect." He strode forth and, without looking back, called out, "I'll have the Master of the Horse give you a proper tour."

ON THE TWELFTH DAY, we were taken from what bit of solitude we'd found in our chambers, collected into carriages, and told we were off to a special London sight that would take our breath away. I insisted that we hardly needed that as we'd spent these last days just trying to regain an even breath. But the nobles who accompanied paid no heed. They were too busy telling us that while baiting was officially outlawed, we would soon see that the pleasures of the Beargarden still flourished as a public secret. Today would be a day to remember, we were promised. We should allow, we were cautioned, that though we might find the sport a bit rude, any spatter of blood and bone that landed on us was a bit of a badge and part of the pleasure we wouldn't soon forget.

Once there, we were instructed to our seats, the front row, of course—only the best, unobstructed view for esteemed guests such as ourselves. Despite whatever law existed forbidding baiting, the stadium around us bulged. As the hawkers sold their greasy pies and nuts, as the crowd chucked oyster shells at one another and chanted for blood long before the mangy, muzzled beast was dragged into the pit, I began to feel queasy.

Once in a pepper merchant's home, I had seen a hallway filled with preserved animals—local and exotic birds, crocodiles and marmots, foxes, and wild boar. As we walked down the hallway, the merchant named each creature, less scientifically and more as if they were family pets. To enter the salon, we had to pass under a tremendous brown bear reared up on its hind legs, teeth bared as if ready to attack. It was a truly awesome sight. Noble and terrifying. "You're welcome to touch my bear," the pepper merchant had announced and reached out his hand to rub the bear's snout. *Such self-aggrandizement*, I'd thought as I ducked under the bear's long claws. *How vain and cruel of him to display the power of an animal he's ruthlessly killed.*

The poor bear dragged into the pit was a pitiful creature, hardly noble—its shaggy coat matted, worn thin to bald in patches. Its eyes rheumy and dull. Though I wanted to look away now, I promised myself that whatever happened in the stadium, however, it shook me, I wouldn't look away. It would be my duty to bear witness and honor this decrepit bear torn from its life in the wild.

I NEITHER LOOKED away nor flinched when it took three men to drag in the bear, then a fourth who held the bear down while one of its hind legs was lashed to a thick metal stake. The crowd was on their feet. "Kill! Kill!" they shouted, as one man yanked off the muzzle. The bear roared and strained against his tether. His foot stomped at the end of the rope, then, turning in circles, bit at the stake. All the while, the men taunted the creature, pulling live vermin from their pockets to whip at him while they shouted to the audience. How close would they dare go? Their hats brimmed with bet coins. One man danced in and—just as the bear swiped at his coat—another thrashed the poor creature with a nail-studded whip so that the bear bellowed, twisting hard against its chains.

And I did not look away when—with a trumpeting of horns—a pack of great muscular mastiffs were unleashed in a cloud of dirt. The dogs moved as if they were a single vicious monster and the men darted in all directions, jumping the rails into the stands to avoid their furious gnashing. One man lingered, dangling off the railing, wagging his ass this way and that, and, in an instant, a dog leaped, tearing his pants so that, to the delight of the crowd, he scrambled bare-butted over the fence. The pack of dogs vaulted, teeth bared. Then they froze and—as if they'd just caught the scent—together turned and set upon the chained bear. The bear roared and huffed. It clawed frantically to keep the dogs off. It swatted pitifully with its free legs. With each rip of animal flesh, the joy in the crowd rose. The excitement feverish.

Beside me, Maria began to weep. "Close your eyes," I whispered and took her hand into my lap.

Just then a man leaned out over the pit, opened a sack, and dropped a tiny dog onto the dirt. Was it an accident, someone's darling pet layered in a fluffy pink skirt, a tiara fastened on its tiny skull? A cry of worry rang through the crowd.

"What?" Maria cried out, her eyes still squeezed shut.

"It's nothing," I said, petting her hand as the little dog turned in frenzied circles, yapping wildly, then, without pause, drove headfirst among the mastiffs. The crowd hollered with laughter to see the costumed little dog nipping at their legs, the great mastiffs squealing. The little dog pressed forward past them, and, with a high-pitched yip, ran circles around the bear, who, like the mastiffs, first seemed confused by the fevered momentum of the tiny animal. Then, all of a sudden, with a single stomp, the bear pinned the dog and was soon whipping it in the air like a pink pinwheel. The creature's pitiful shrieks filled the stadium. With a furious shake of the bear's head, and a clack and release of its jaws, the dog was aloft, sailing over the mound of snarling mastiffs. When it landed, the pack abandoned the bear and, in a swirl as though performing a choreographed dance, set upon the tiny creature. The applause and stomping of feet were thunderous.

Maria moaned though her eyes remained closed. I pulled her close to me, wishing for cotton bits to wedge in her ears. "Hum," I said. "Make your own noise in your head."

The bear roared, rearing up on his hind legs. He tugged and tugged at the stake. "Break it!" the audience cheered as the metal stake wobbled in the dirt. The mastiffs, their faces coated in fur and spittle—one with a torn paw in its maw—turned in a fluid motion, stampeding the bear. As they passed, tendrils of drool and blood lashed the spectators. Saliva thinned in my mouth. Bile rose and I swallowed it back. I started to use my sleeve to wipe Maria's face and mine but let my hand drop back to hold hers. She was humming, a steady drone. The clapping again swelled. I understood then that we had only moved from a storm at sea to a human squall.

"It's almost done," I said, trying to sound steady. Whatever order human laws impose, our appetite for violence is poorly governed indeed—men pitted against men, against women in the name of honor and greed, and still it is never enough. Dogs trained. The pitiful bear. The air itself bloody. There was no escape.

THAT VERY NIGHT, we were summoned to the queen consort's private dining room. Of the many things we'd been told about her struggles in providing an heir, no one had bothered to mention that she was a young, olive-skin beauty in a court of pale-haired, pallid women, who chalked their skin whiter still. "I'm so excited to meet you," she said, her voice vivid, bearing none of the sorrows of fertility and infant deaths which we knew she'd endured. Her fingers toyed with the pearls of her choker, which shone against her long neck. The low drape of her gown's ruffled décolletage showed off the polished skin of her shoulders and chest. She showed no mark of the frailty or illness that we'd been told was her constant state. Instead, bouncy black ringlets framed her face, and beneath a thick whip of eyebrow, her black eyes shone. I couldn't help but consider what pigments I'd mix to match the warm undertones of her skin.

We approached her through a retinue of her ladies of the bedchamber, Maria curtsied, and I curtsied as if her shadow. Behind the queen, Maria's commissioned painting, which had been taken from us as soon as we'd debarked from the ship, leaned on an ornately carved easel. "Maria," the queen practically purred, "the loveliest of all names, if I say so myself. Though they've made me just another English bore by calling me Mary. But please, please, you'll call me Maria."

"With pleasure, Maria," Maria said conspiratorially, offering a second curtsy that I again echoed.

"I'm sorry to have been reclusive," the queen said, and I watched her ladies' heads bobble, as if stunned to hear the queen apologize. "I've been looking forward to meeting you, but first needed to spend some days alone with this painting."

"I hope you've found it welcome company," Maria said.

The queen didn't answer but rose from her chair. The orange silk brocade of her dress fell to the ground in a watery rustle. The queen lifted the painting from where it rested on the rosewood stand and held it close to her face. Looking up, she said, "Nothing in this palace, not any other painting in the royal collection, moves me more than this. I've commissioned many, but none have touched me as your bouquet has. How did you understand so deeply my predicament? My soul?" She closed her eyes, put the painting to her face and inhaled deeply. When she opened her eyes, she vowed that she could smell the distinct fragrance of each flower. "In a life filled with only fleeting joy, how can I ever thank you, Maria, for such enduring beauty?" Her finger traced the outline of a fading rose, then lingered over Maria's signature and date on the canvas. Before Maria could answer, the queen insisted that it be given a place on the wall in this dining room so that she might gaze upon it nightly. "Maybe one evening, looking at this canvas I'll see a petal fall from a flower and drift to the ledge," the queen said, as if she genuinely believed that might one day occur.

After sufficient oohing and ahhing over each flower, particularly the roses in their various states of bloom and decay, and after a rather free and even contentious debate between the queen and Maria concerning the two butterflies in the painting and the nature of Christ's resurrection according to Catholics and Protestants, Maria announced that she had something else miraculous to demonstrate for the pleasure of the queen, the king and their entire court. "I am certain you will be amazed, Maria," Maria said and an audible gasp issued from the Ladies of the Bedchamber at the audacity of using the queen's name unbidden. But the queen simply winked conspiratorially at Maria as if they were already bosom friends.

"I long for amazement," the queen said. "My life has been . . ." Quiet fell over the room. The years of loss after loss of babies and pregnancies was, all of a sudden, sharply etched across her face. Her head lady shuffled to the queen's side as if to catch her should she faint or perhaps to block further aggravation from Maria. But the queen regained her color and swatted her aside. "Tell me, what will this amazement be?"

"No, no, I shan't tell," Maria said, flashing the toying cadence that had intrigued many over the years.

"You must answer the queen," snapped the queen's lady.

"But if I tell her now, how will I pleasure her then?" asked Maria, and the queen applauded like a child.

"Oh, you're too much fun, Maria. I'm already more entertained than I've been in ages. How pleasant it is to be teased. Your reveal will be tomorrow night, though even that seems an unbearable wait."

"That isn't possible," flustered the queen's lady, who had taken an obvious dislike to the presumptuous manner with which Maria spoke to the queen—as if they were common friends. "They'll never be able to ready the hall at such short notice."

"Ridiculous," proclaimed the queen. "What does it take? A couple of candles and a few platters of plovers and larks?"

Despite the ongoing protestations of the queen's lady, it was agreed that on the following evening Maria would present her surprise before the queen and king and an audience of nobles in the palace's largest hall.

BACK AT OUR ACCOMMODATIONS, Maria was exuberant, fidgety, insisting sleep was not an option. "Did you see her swoon when she smelled the canvas? We were practically transported to a perfumery with all the floral notes she claimed she inhaled." Maria swirled about the room. All the endless waiting, the terrible entertainment endured and, worst of all, the extreme depravity of the Beargarden, was worth it now that the queen had praised her painting. "And isn't it fortuitous that we have the same name?" Maria said, as if half the women of Europe weren't called a variation of Mary. But I didn't contradict her. In truth, I could barely speak.

Since we'd returned from the baiting, my every breath was sour and polluted. The cries of the animals and the raucous cheers of the crowd echoed in my head, so that everything appeared foreign, even myself.

After I untied her hands and rubbed fresh salve over the open sores on her wrists, she insisted we rehearse each scene of The Ultimate Act one final time. Of course, Maria located new opportunities to increase dramatic tension. As tired and raw from the day as I was, I was grateful for the routine from our life back home, which in the short time we'd been away seemed so very distant. Every few minutes, Maria interrupted our rehearsal to quote a piece of the queen's praise. Finally she said, "I think we are ready, Pieter."

I prepared her for bed, unfastening the jewels and pins from her hair, unwinding each coiled chignon, and brushing out her locks. I took my time. *This is Maria's hair. The hair I brush every night*, I repeated with each stroke in the hopes of regaining some inner balance. Over the years her lustrous hair had thinned, and although brittle from age, it was now simpler to manage. As I worked the brush, my mind drifted from the stadium's horrors to the queen's fingers as she'd touched Maria's signature and I thought how it was me who'd painted the still life, me who'd carefully painted each letter of Maria's name. "Yes," I said, "I believe we are."

FROM THE CONSTANT SCURRY and motion in the castle, it appeared to me that the queen's lady had been correct, and, despite every effort, the staff wouldn't be able to ready the Banqueting House in time. I recalled my long days, even weeks, of preparation for Maria's salons years before. Now more than thirty servants worked just to provide illumination, lowering the chandeliers, then polishing the cut glass, fitting the candles, and then pulling them back up. How many candles filled the hall I couldn't even begin to guess, though it was common knowledge—or fable—that at the birth of a French royal child, 175,000 candles had been lit to celebrate the heir. Now, carpets were unrolled, drapery hung. In the center of the hall a stage was constructed for our performance, the dinner tables set in rows flanking the stage.

Miraculously, by evening, every sign of labor was gone and the room gleamed with the light of thousands of beeswax candles flickering overhead. The polished silverware and gold-rimmed plates sparkled under the table candelabras. The height of each candelabra was perfectly measured so that the pale ladies of the court were not made to look older by the cast of any shadow.

Maria was invited to enter the hall in procession with the king and queen and was placed at the left of the queen to dine, though she informed the queen she never ate before a performance. Maria told me later that the queen replied, "Then watch me eat," and between bursts of laughter, quipped to Maria, "You're in good company. Some of these silly ladies want to please me so badly they starve, claiming that the satisfaction of my hunger fills their bellies."

"Oh, I hardly think about pleasing anyone but myself," Maria told me she'd retorted. "I'd rather feast on the sapphires and diamonds stitched on the neckline above your pretty young breasts, than any fine dish your kitchens could prepare." Indeed, even from where I stood, a serving maid's distance from the table, it was hard to look away from the queen's gown. The queen said she'd chosen the bejeweled dress embroidered with flowers, each sleeve threaded with fruit garlands to pay homage to Maria. "It's as if I'm a walking Van Oosterwijck painting," she told Maria.

"Well, if you're a walking Van Oosterwijck, then I'd like to claim these," Maria said, nodding toward one of the jeweled bouquet brooches that fastened the queen's sleeves to her bodice.

According to Maria, the more outrageous her comments, the happier the queen. "At one point I caused her to laugh so violently, she spit forth her wine and stained her ermine mantle," Maria reported.

Truly the two women appeared to be the coziest and dearest of confidantes, leaning so close they were practically rubbing noses. I knew Maria was playing for the whole room, enjoying becoming a spectacle and relishing the jealousy smeared on the chalked faces of all the queen's ladies. Even the king could not contain himself, and at one point reached across his wife and, taking her ostrich feather fan, wisped it across Maria's face. From the bursts of jabber in the hall, I was evidently not the only one to notice and try to decipher the gesture. But later, when I asked Maria what had transpired, she demurred, saying, "In the end, a king has much in common with any other pitiful man."

While the hall seethed at the friendship between the queen and Maria, I was mostly annoyed that Maria prolonged the fifteen-course dinner. Despite all our practice, I was nervous. What if my boast that I'd win the competition against their best painter was an empty one? If I failed, Maria would lose her money. There'd be no commission. We'd be tossed from the court straight into the home of Jacobus. Finally, Maria nodded in my direction. I hastened forward to pull out her chair.

"Your Highness, I'll take my leave to prepare for our extravaganza."

"I refuse to let you go," the queen said, her face suddenly crimped and severe. Then she broke into a wide, girlish smile. "Not until you call me Maria!"

"Here is Pieter," Maria narrated from her high-backed chair as I stepped from behind the heavy brocade curtain and strolled onto the stage in the center of the crowded hall wearing the cap and threadbare trousers of a servant boy. As we'd rehearsed, I acted out my daily chores with the chickens, rabbits, and the old family milk cow, while Maria described with every embellishment how I came to her family home as a thin-boned child. From the start it was going better than we'd practiced. Maria's voice was confident—emboldened, no doubt, by the rapport she'd established with the queen. I felt no stage fright, though more than a thousand nobles watched. As I pretended to churn butter and split wood, I felt steady. Finally, I was no longer at sea, or in the chaos of the Beargarden. Finally, I was no longer listening to nobles nattering on about the antics of the king's latest mistress. As much as I hated the tired old narrative of my transformation, I was comforted by knowing the arc of the story. I was so relaxed that I added my own flourishes—pretending to drop the heavy axe on my foot, hopping about in pain, my leg hoisted in the air, which brought whoops of laughter that echoed through the hall.

"Then there was word that little Pieter's mother had died," Maria said, my cue to clasp hands, scuff feet, and walk about forlorn and lonesome. But when Maria said it, a sadness so abrupt, profound, and unrehearsed tore through me that I doubled over. I tried to right myself. To concentrate on playacting the sad child. *This is nothing new, this is nothing new*, I counseled myself. *I've heard these same words every time we've rehearsed*. But as I tried to right myself from the blow of her words, I tumbled within.

My mother is dead. Even to speak of it now, the momentum is vertiginous—a collapse not of my body onto the hall's marble floor but of time, the intervening years gone, and I am that child hiding under straw. *My mother is dead*. The loss acute, like a terrible illness, or the shattering of bones from a high fall. I am secreted in the shed. *How is it possible that I will never see my mother again?* Every time I try to shake off my sadness, invent a new movement of tossing my grief away and up to the rafters, it rains down on me till I am soaked in her death. I bed myself in straw and when I come forth, brushing stalks from my pants, Maria leans against the doorjamb, coldly drawing a grieving boy.

"Mother!" I cry out.

"My goodness," Maria says from her chair in the great hall. She's surprised. This is not how we had rehearsed it. She's supposed to be the only one of us to speak.

I try to orient myself.

London. I am in London.

I am in the royal court.

This is pantomime.

But the damp hall fills with the smell of dirt. The petrichor lingers on my mother's palms as she comes in from the summer garden.

"Mother!" I say again.

"Poor servant boy." Maria hurries the narration. "All too soon he loses both his father and sisters, too."

Pain shoots through my head, my limbs. *My father! My sister and the sweetest baby! They are dead.* The milk pail bangs against my leg. *They are dead. They are dead. I haven't had a chance to rock my baby sister's wicker cradle. I'll never again be tossed in the air and caught in my father's arms.* I sob. Not the rehearsed hands to face. Here's the sting of real tears—*they're dead*—nasty ugly gulping sobs. The pail bangs and bangs against my leg as I weep.

"Yes, so very, very sad," Maria responds. She's happy that my performance has elevated. It's better than she expected. Real tears. I'm holding nothing back.

"Shall we comfort the child?" she asks the audience.

The courtiers roused to participate, shout in mocking tones, "Poor little boy!" They rub their eyes. "Boo-hoo, boo-hoo."

"How I pitied this orphan." Maria's voice vibrates with tenderness. "All alone in the world. What could I do for this pitiable child? I set out to advance his life. To change him from nothing into a man able to sit among distinguished men and women. Hours spent teaching him his letters till he could read the great poets, though how much he understood was always in question."

"Give us a gobble of Dante!" a man hollers. This strikes the other nobles as hilarious. The idiot peasant orphan reciting works of great art.

"I'd prefer a recitation of our Marvell."

"Or Donne."

Maria allows a barrage of quips before she quiets the crowd. "Then I began the very first transformation, a most practical one—turning the boy from our family servant into my workshop apprentice." She details teaching the rudiments of ink preparation. I force myself back to the simple gestures we've planned, pulling walnuts from my pockets, while Maria gives instruction for soaking, boiling, and sieving. "So, imagine my surprise." Maria allows three dramatic beats of silence. "Imagine my surprise, when one day it was revealed Pieter was not a boy at all." Another beat. And another. "But a budding young woman in disguise."

The moment for me to untie the belt strap and step out of my ragged trousers is now. And I do so, smoothing my linen skirts and replacing my cap with a well-starched bonnet. As if on cue, the audience gasps.

"Oooh, she's more than budding!" a man sneers. Shame itches up my legs.

"Better the pretty girl than the pretty boy," another answers.

Over the increasing lewd commentary, Maria declares her commitment to continue my training despite the revelation that her apprentice has, as one courtier shouts, "a fine woolen kitty and not a bag of hairy whirligigs."

"Nay," she says. "That she was a mere girl was better, her training a truer challenge. It made for a more improbable transformation."

"Give me an hour with her," a man hoots. "That'll be ample training."

In my skirts, I am to skip about the stage, a girlish sway to my hips. But as I take a first step, my foot buckles and I'm unable to budge, to will my foot forward. It's fastened. Tacked in place. The room begins to wobble, then spin, and I am stuck, spiraling through some thick molasses of time until I'm not acting at all but truly a child again at the minister's supper table, my wretched girlhood revealed. The neighbor's donkey whinnies, warning that I'll be thrown to the streets.

"I'll take a chunk of her," someone brays. Others volley for their own bits of me.

The room spins and shakes and I'm naked, holding the kitchen chair, the sunlight slashing through the room while Maria draws my figure for the first time. "Pass her on." Hands paw at air. The hall careens toward my violation, the harsh press of him against me.

"But I am undeterred." Maria shouts, determined to regain control of her audience and knock me back from wherever she sees I've strayed. "It is simply a greater challenge to take this girl and make her my workshop assistant, preparing the finest paints in Europe."

I close my eyes. Touch my skirt. *I am this girl.*

"But I have a fuller vision. I will accomplish what all others say is impossible—to teach this simple maid to paint."

I open my eyes. She will make me into whatever she wants. *"Yes or no,"* the minister asks. I have only ever said yes. I hobble forward. Do as we have practiced. Bring out paint. Bring out brushes. Easel. Prepared panel. I fumble with the paintbrush, a detail we have rehearsed over and over. But this time the tremble, the vibration is real. I can barely hold the brush. The colors mix, run a muddy brown.

"What patience I must have for all of her ineptitude," Maria says. "You see how slow her progress will be. Many consider this a waste of my time. A maid cannot be trained to paint. What do you think?"

The lords and ladies, with their terrible foul stench, their squatting to empty themselves in the palace stairways, all bark my worthlessness.

"Often I feared it was impossible," Maria confides, turning to address the king and queen directly. "It is one thing to grind pigment, a skill of an entirely different variety to paint. But I persist. I have a deep faith." Maria keeps her pacing measured over the raucous comments. "I persist, and slowly, under my strict instruction, she becomes an assistant worthy of underpainting. But my vision is greater still. To teach the maid not only to paint a flower still life. But to paint one as well as any man."

This is the cue for me to change into my fancy dress and bring forth the flower arrangement, but I disregard the costume change, managing only to set the vase upon the table despite my trembling. This is the final section of The Ultimate Act. If I can just steady myself enough to paint the flowers, the vase, this humiliation will be over and Maria can propose the competition. This is the part where I best know what to do. Where I am most myself. The noise of the room dims. I barely hear Maria explain how she has taught me, step by step. The people fade. The ruddy drunk mockery, their banging mugs fall silent. All that endures is my hand and the brush. Shape and color. The ruffle of a carnation. Light from the left on a tulip's curve.

With each flower, each blade of grass, the palace is farther from me. I live again every good afternoon Maria and I have spent in the workshop. All our quiet hours. Our irreverence. Days in the medical gardens drawing specimens. With each stroke, every bloom, every dragonfly, every bending stalk, I live all the hours mulling pigment, rendering paint worthy of the workshop of Maria van Oosterwijck. The light slants through the workshop. The blue light of late afternoons. This is all I want. Smoke from clay pipes. Her bright laughter. Arm in arm down canal streets. To touch the arch of her foot with the toes of mine.

Somewhere far away, Maria's voice: "She's trained to follow my every instruction."

Maria saying, "My nephew wants to be painted . . ."

Maria saying, "You will have to take care of it."

The floor drops, the great hall tips sideways. Anger rises, lathers my mouth. How have I not seen that I am the elephant, La Bella? Hauled across Europe, forced to kneel at my master's command, to pretend I am too clumsy to step onto a dainty stool and teeter on one leg?

Maria is saying, "See how she works the ridges of the nasturtium when I tell her to." I am only ever the clever trick to her. Her spectacle. She cavorts with Jan Six, Huygens, and the other men, while I stand behind them. "Look at what I have wrought," she says, and twirls me about in a dress that matches hers. When the door closes, the others out of earshot, she asks, "Butterfly, what do you think?" My answer only matters to her when we're alone.

"But she is terribly clumsy," Maria explains to the court. "It takes constant attention and scolding to refine her hand."

All my devotion has come this. To stand before them in shame and fury. *No. No.* A wave swells, breaks. I am rough waters. Vortex and maelstrom. I am bear and dog and the storm's turbulent waves. I keep myself from running across the reed-strewn floors to where she sits. Keep myself from cutting the straps that bind her arms to her dress. From lifting her useless hands and shouting, "Look, you pathetic leeches. The painting that hangs in the queen's dining room is not Maria's. It's *mine*."

Maria says, "Now she will use a fine brush to stipple, building the leaf's tonal gradation."

She. She. She. Maria has not even spoken my name. In this hall I am anonymous, even less than La Bella. I am only *she*.

I lift my hand but the brush does not touch the canvas.

Maria saying, "She will do this stippling."

My brush slashes at the canvas.

"Gentler," she commands. "Gentler," she repeats. Confusion vibrates in her voice. I am not behaving. "She does not always take the master's instruction," Maria jokes. Listen, hear how her voice quakes.

My brush rears up, disobedient. I ignite. "Who is the master?" The question blurts out of my mouth before I realize that I have shouted aloud. "Whose canvas will be chosen for the king?" I shout even louder. Maria recoils as if I have struck her. The old game. Which singular great painting will be brought for the Emperor of Mughal, for the Ottoman Sultan? Wherever the empire, the answer has always been her canvas, her name. Now what can she say?

"See what an insolent, peasant temperament I have had to tame!" Maria addresses the king and queen directly as if they have shared a similar plight ruling laborers and lords.

There is no taming me. I am the paintbrush thrown down. I am the bear. I am beyond the bear, gnawing till I hobble free, my chewed foot abandoned at the stake. I hold my hands out as I stumble toward where she sits. I wave my arms. I breathe fire and the room thickens with smoke. We will all burn in the great blaze where she set flame to my paintings. Where she throws in canvas after canvas. Nothing will be salvaged.

"Maria van Oosterwijck. Who exactly is the painter, Maria van Oosterwijck?" My voice, resolute. The dog faces of the whiskered lords and ladies lean in, salivating, eager for what will be tossed into the pit next. "Who is Maria van Oosterwijck?" I shout and they chorus back, "Who is Maria van Oosterwijck!" They turned from my demise to hers. Haven't they wanted her shredded, this new fancy of the queen's, this latest royal pet, this impudent holy painter who will not deign to join the court artists when they draw in the gardens?

"Who is Gerta Pieters?" I stand above her. Maria looks stricken. I am unreconcilable. I cannot be controlled. She shrinks back. Her strapped arms useless. "Who is Gerta Pieters?" My voice is sonorous, louder than I have ever dared speak. I turn in a circle. "See me. I am mineral and raw earth. Stone chipped from earth. Iron and glass, a shatter of boy, bosom of maid, scatter of leaf, of stem. Rock, rock, crush to green to blue. I am bugs ground to red. Dirt sieved to red. Urine in jars. Poisonous yellow. Purple iris and forget-me-not. I will be forgotten. Far seas I have sailed over to become her Aleppo. Wing and salt air, sealed pail of manure, I'm change and change and changed again."

I rip the linen that binds her hands. I turn circles. Will whirl, whirl, never stop. Become tornado. Become beast.

I turn to the king and queen. The king leans forward, his ungloved hands spread wide over his knees. The night is no longer whatever he expected. No, this is gay and unruly, a tournament, a jousting. Look at the stomp of this woman, she is the horse rearing and unseating her master. There will be a winner. If he had known, he would have put money down.

Oh, but the poor queen, her jeweled shoulders have sagged inward. Nose to nose over dinner she'd whispered to Maria, "I've heard rumors of your bound hands. They are sacred. Two angels. I'll feed you as I would have fed all of my babies that refused to live."

In the next breath what will I say? *Look at this woman with her infirm, palsied hands, her spastic arms. There is no God, only illness in these hands. Let Maria van Oosterwijck and Gerta Pieters both take a brush to this painting and sign Maria's name.* And when the paintbrush wiggles and falls from her grasp, as it will, then it will be known. I am her. The great painter with a treasured still life hung in the queen's dining room.

"Gerta." Maria's voice is small. "Please." She cowers. She looks so slight. Already broken. I stop. I say nothing. Because I am only what I've ever been, an orphan servant. When Maria's father asked, "Yes or no? What will you choose?" what fool was I to think in the stillness, in the balance of full spoons of pea stew, that anyone awaited my answer. That it was ever me who was choosing. That there was any future in which I wasn't handed from the father to the daughter. Handed to Jacobus.

I drop her arms and walk back to the unfinished panel. Do the only thing I can. Return to the banquet hall. Return to our scripted act. I groom my brushstrokes back to a smooth steadiness, then take care working the shadows. I provide for the thickness of each overlapping petal. Maria rights herself, not so much unfurling as springing back, each vertebra restacked as she assumes her rightful place in the world, the timbre of her voice confident as she commands the audience to marvel at what she has made from nothing. She is not cowering anymore, as if my standing above her had been an extra flourish in her scripted performance.

Then Maria is standing, walking toward me, rejoicing, "Here, before the king and queen, is my creation." *My creation.* I lift the painting from the easel. There is furious stomping and applause. The men and women press forward, fevered. This cannot be a painting by the idiot maid. Impossible. It's too masterful for this simple girl. What is the trick, the sleight of hand? They crowd close. I'm handled. A woman lifts my hand, inspects then counts my fingers. But I feel untouched, outside the body they pet, looking for what—a concealed seam where a true artist is hiding? I thought I'd perform a simple story for the king and queen, instead I blasted like an iron cannonball into the deep center of my own existence.

When the clamor finally subsides, Maria intones, "You don't believe this possible? Well, you who love your games and your gambling, here is my challenge to England. Select any painter of the royal court to compete against my genius." She motions for me to curtsy. I sink into a deep one, numb, exhausted, uncertain that I have the strength to press back up. Again, the noise is deafening, as though she has promised a match of gladiators and not two artists in smocks, standing before easels and painting floral arrangements.

LATE THAT NIGHT, after the dancing horses, after the dancing courtesans, after the bards sang bawdy madrigals in celebration of Maria, after my hands were lifted and inspected, after I was regarded like the wild panther and tiger in their cages, ragged with exhaustion, we climbed into the bedstead. Maria curled close. "Pieter, do you think . . ." she began, but before finishing her question, she was asleep.

Exhausted, I lay very still beside her and waited for sleep to claim me. The torment, the anger, the sadness that had so unexpectedly ricocheted through me during The Ultimate Act was gone. Instead, my body ached as though I had been exposed to the extremities, pelted by ice, knocked by bracing winds, as if I had traversed glacial mountain passes and crossed arid deserts. I turned toward Maria. Her skin glowed from the taper. "Maria." I hoped she would wake. A pucker of breath rippled from her mouth. She settled deeper into sleep. Then her body jerked, her eyes flashed open.

"Maria," I said, "here's what I think—"

But she interrupted, "It was a grand spectacle, better than I could have imagined. You were a bit dramatic, Pieter. It certainly created tension, but a little extreme. Still, that can be fixed. We've drawn attention now." Her eyes fluttered closed. "And soon more commissions. More palaces to perform in. We are a spectacle." And then she was again asleep.

I wanted to shake her. Have her say anything else. Wanted her to insist that she wanted to—needed to—know what I was thinking. To ask what happened to me during The Ultimate Act. But her sleep was quiet, even her arms and hands relaxed and quiet. I lay beside her. Sleep smoothed years from her face. She looked like a girl and not a woman near fifty. Still, we were no longer young. Together we had navigated a life. I touched the thinned skin beneath her eyes, the fan of creases on her cheeks. I outlined the narrowed ridge of her lips. How I had loved this face.

My mind at last stilled, clear as the air after a downpour. I slipped from bed and wrapped Maria's crane shawl about my night dress. There was one thing left to complete The Ultimate Act. At the narrow oak writing desk, I composed two letters. Before Maria woke, they had been handed to palace couriers and were on their way.

OBVIOUSLY, when it came to the competition, I won. Was there another option?

I was called the Little Maria. I wore a pale red gown and Maria wore crimson. Maria was celebrated, the queen's painter. We were both commended for the extraordinary tension in our performance. Some hailed it a masterpiece of theater. Per the wager, a second painting was commissioned, with an offer of a sum far greater than for the first. For the companion painting, the queen requested particular blossoms. Roses, of course, but would Maria include ranunculus and carnation? And while the queen loved the two butterflies in the painting that hung in her dining room, could this companion canvas include other insects? Perhaps a bee or a dragonfly? Or both.

Half of the commission was awarded in advance to Maria. The rest upon delivery. Then, despite an elaborate offer that Maria become a royal painter with an esteemed studio and apartment at the palace, I packed all our trunks, and we boarded a return ship to Amsterdam. I did not pressure her to stay.

TWENTY

How great was Maria's surprise when she saw Jacobus waiting at the docks when we arrived.

"Jacobus!" she called from the ship's deck. "Jacobus!" she shouted as if his name were a revelation. He waved to her. Nodded tersely in my direction. "This was your idea, Pieter?" she asked, clasping my arm. "You knew, knew how much happiness this would bring me."

"I'll hope only for your happiness," I said, guiding her down the steep, warped ramp. It wasn't a lie. When it came to her, bitterness and love were so knotted in me, I couldn't untie them. But wanting her happiness was a strand that never frayed.

I watched as she embraced her nephew and, in a flurry, began recounting to him the highlights of her London extravaganza. Then, in the bustle of coming ashore, the unloading and hefting of Maria's many trunks onto the carriage, I completed my final scene in The Ultimate Act.

It must have taken some time before my presence was missed.

TWENTY-ONE

1700, Delft

I'VE WAITED ALL THESE YEARS to speak of this. I would have waited whatever length of time necessary to be certain Maria would never see these words. None of it has been easy, then or now, but I'm determined to see it through.

HISTORY MAY ASK what monster I'd become that I, who devoted my life to her care, who loved her as servant, apprentice, and lover, who was her committed, good wife, would, without warning, slip away? How could I abandon her? Leave her to that nephew? How could I trust that such a selfish man, who expected his every urge and need be attended to, would attend to Maria in her illness?

Let history make of me what it will—perhaps my head's too big and I'll actually be scoured from her biography—yet I'll not reproduce for you the entirety of my blunt words I inked in the first letter that night in our room in the palace. Only that my letter ensured that Jacobus would be dutifully waiting for his aunt when we returned and said that if I were ever to learn that Maria wasn't well cared for in his house, given proper medicine and attended to by a personal maid, I would publicly declare his and my various crimes, happily watch his ruin, even if it included my own. I went further. I let him know that all the events of our sordid past were excruciatingly detailed in a second letter, held by a most trusted apothecary in Amsterdam. And if I were to die, this apothecary understood that a belated scandal would be not only a terrible blemish on Jacobus's good name in the community but put in question the claim to his inheritance.

Though it hurt to admit the depth of my errors to Luyc, I knew he'd remain a steadfast friend. I sent him the money from the painting I'd sold to Huygens and pledged to continue sending money so that he could travel three times a year to see Maria to administer and supply new medicines.

I'll again say I had no trust in Jacobus. But I also didn't trust Maria or myself. My care for her had become both our suffering, even if Maria didn't realize it. If we continued, it would only worsen. Living with me, Maria would never be willing to turn down a commission. And as she became increasingly debilitated, my beloved would only agonize and twist with anger at herself and me. Furious and bitter, I'd paint her paintings for wealthy patrons and great courts across Europe signing her name.

And if she were to end the Van Oosterwijck workshop? Then I'd be merely her servant once more, with no place left for me as a painter. This, I understood, was no longer possible. Long ago, Maria had pointed to where the grass and sky stitched at the horizon and asked me, "What do you see?" Now I see that what was mine and what was hers wasn't easy to unstitch. I was for a time servant, maid, and apprentice to the greatest flower painter in Europe. It was all I thought I needed. It turned out there was much more. This is life. Once it was hers. Then it was ours. Now it is mine. I hear Maria laugh. "Is it really that simple, Pieter?"

Let me try again: Who among us comes through this life without regret? Without apology? How often do we create the fire we must step into and hopefully through? And if we are lucky to emerge charred, we must then survive coarsely scarred and patched. And still longing. That's love. Difficult to reckon that something so burnt and crusted with anger and hurt can still be called love.

EACH DAY, apart from her, I am unsteady. More than once I've gone to the shops and, before I catch myself, I've bought two fish fillets and her favorite cake. We've been apart for fourteen years, my Maria dead now more than seven. How impossible it is to imagine the world absent her curious smile. Without the force of her imagination. Is it strange to say that I often speak aloud to her and would swear I hear her quick reply?

It hurt to receive the letter from Jacobus detailing the misery of her last days. He made a point of telling me that she'd repeatedly asked for him to send for someone named "Pieter." That she'd insisted only this Pieter would know how to ease her passage. "But," he wrote, "when I understood this Pieter was you, Gerta Pieters, you'll understand I could not befoul our home, nor end her redeemed life in shame."

Still, she'd asked for me. In the end, she'd asked for me. Were there nights when, like me, she curled around the shape of us sleeping in her bed? Or when, waking before dawn, she reached to hug my hands between hers to settle back to sleep? Even now she is never far. Always in my head. I see her upturned face, how her wide gray-green eyes wrinkled just before she delivered some unexpected thought. How she could surprise me.

. . .

IN 1689, four years before I received word from Jacobus, I finished the painting *Still Life with Flowers, Insects, and a Shell*, the Van Oosterwijck workshop's final commissioned piece, and signed Maria's name for the last time. As Maria had anticipated, it was sent to the court of a new queen. In advance of wrapping and shipping it, I sat on the window ledge of my small workshop, smoking a pipe, and looked at the painting. As requested, alongside the butterfly, I'd included a bee and a dragonfly.

"Pieter," I heard her say. "That marigold is just right, the orange so good, isn't it?"

"Yes, Maria," I said. "It's just right."

"But Pieter, that was clever."

"What?" Though I knew what she would say.

"Did you think I wouldn't notice it's you, Butterfly, who's landed on the uppermost flower?"

Oh, how I missed her.

The painting was sent to the royal court, the remaining money delivered to Maria under Jacobus's roof. I thought I might hear from her then. I did not. And, I suppose, that was for the best.

I CAN NO longer manage the clean curves of a rose, let alone my signature. The canvases I work now are short thick marks of pure color. Still there are days when someone knocks at the door to inquire, "Is this the home of the painter Gerta Pieters?" Without even looking up from where my brush turns roughly in a mound of blue, I say, "Yes, I am the painter Gerta Pieters." There are those days. And they are good.

ACKNOWLEDGMENTS

In addition to imagining the hearts, minds, and souls of other humans, one of the truest pleasures of writing fiction is learning about worlds and fields of study new to me. In preparing to write *I Am You*, I attended workshops in paint-making from minerals and plants and gobbled books about painting, pigment, trade, war, medicine, plagues, botanical art, artists, abortions, games in the 1600s, and then tried to forget most of it to hopefully create a lived world. That said, if you're interested, there is great reading to explore. I read widely on the Dutch Golden Age, but both Simon Schama's *Rembrandt's Eyes* and *The Embarrassment of Riches* were particularly rich reads, as were Svetlana Alpers's *The Art of Describing* and Russell Shorto's *Amsterdam*.

I've wanted to write about paint and pigment for more than twenty years and, for years, read widely about color, color theory, and the fascinating, storied history of the global pigment trade. I've learned to make paint from spinach, iris flowers, azurite, and eggshells. Here are just a few of the books on color and paint that I've loved: *Color*, Victoria Finlay; *Colors: The Story of Dyes and Pigments*,

Bernard Guineau and François Delamare; *The Materials of the Artist and Their Use in Painting*, Max Doerner; *The Artist's Assistant*, Leslie Carlyle; *Botanical Art Techniques*, Carol Woodin and Robin A. Jess; and *Historical Painting Techniques, Materials, and Studio Practice* from the Getty Conservation Institute virtual library.

As I mentioned at the front of the book, there is little information on the life and work of Maria van Oosterwijck and Gerta Pieters. The website https://mariavanoosterwijck.nl/ is the most comprehensive place to see the known body of Maria van Oosterwijck's paintings and to learn a bit about her life and practice. A cursory read of the website will quickly let you know how freely I veered from some of the assumed facts to shape this novel.

GIVING PROPER ACKNOWLEDGMENT and thanks for the help I've received while writing this book is both the easiest and hardest part of these pages because my appreciation is manifold and hard to rein in. So without naming every rock, river, and tree that's been a gift, I'll thank the miles of trails (on foot and horse) where I worked out story, scenes, and character concerns that eluded me at the desk. And a special hallelujah to the backcountry flower fields where nature's paintbrush brought me to my knees.

A book is composed alone but is brought forth with the help of many people, and for their attention, care, and love, I'm deeply indebted.

I would not be half the writer I am without the consistent brilliance, encouragement, and generous attention to my work by Bill Clegg, exceptional agent and human! All thanks to his encouragement after seeing those first thirty pages, and for insight and patience as I grew a novel from what sometimes seemed as compressed as a poem.

ACKNOWLEDGMENTS

All thanks and appreciation to the mighty team at the Clegg Agency.

A tremendous thank-you to Sarah Jessica Parker, for her excitement and passion, yes, for *I Am You*, but also for heralding the importance of novels and the life of the imagination.

Thank you, thank you to Erin Wicks for the laser-sharp editorial tenacity, care, and consideration she's given to every word, scene, and idea in this novel. Thank you to Katie Burdett, Sam Mitchell, Zoey Cole, Nathalie Ramirez, Stefanie Chow, Christopher King, Marina Padakis, Kayla White, and Ash Tsai—the team at SJP Lit and Zando for their manifold skills in shepherding *I Am You* into the world. Thank you, Joy Hoppenot and Sarah Schneider, for cleaning up my mistakes. A deep bow and whoop of thanks to Jaya Miceli for her gorgeous book cover.

Concurrent with my writing about a still-life flower painter, my sister, Jessica Redel, became a certified botanical artist. Watching her work in watercolor, pen, and graphite was a mini tutorial on the precision and close observation required in botanical art. This has been a profound sister pleasure to share.

For generous and insightful reading of early and later drafts or for listening to weekly installments, thank you to Hillary Jordan, Rebecca Frankel, Tracey Rogers, Maria Basescu, Bruce Van Dusen, Jessica Redel, and Honor Moore; the Friday Writing Group: Marie Howe, Donna Masini, Ricky Ian Gordon, Nick Flynn, Pádraig Ó Tuama, Sophie Cabot Black, Michael Klein, Martin Moran, Vievee Francis, and Mark Conway; and to the Adirondack gang. Along with these dear readers and friends, a shout of love to Sonya, Fran, Melinda, Marisela, Michael, Gaye, Roger, John, Michael, and Martine for listening to me ramble or go quiet while I was writing this book.

My thanks to the late great artist Varujan Boghosian, who, with his sly humor, nudged me to write and not paint.

ACKNOWLEDGMENTS

I had the good fortune to have grown up in a ballet household, where the possibility of an artist's life was never questioned, only encouraged. Both my parents modeled discipline, determination, and passion, and in this, I still strive to make them proud.

Thank you again and again, Gabriel, Jonah, and Hannah—your love and encouragement is my heart and anchor. And to the joy baby, Eden, my exuberant welcome. To the other wild rascals: Sydney, Ellis, Sky, and Falcon, thank you for the hugs you give. And gratitude to the motley gang—Wynn, Shea, Dara, Magnus, Ellen, and Zane—for putting up with me.

And, finally, for Bruce, who makes every day not just possible but a whole lot better, thank you doesn't do it justice. This book wouldn't exist if you hadn't suggested we live in Amsterdam above the flower shop that spring.

An independent publisher with authors at its heart

Join our Friends of Firefinch quarterly newsletter to discover more captivating reads:

Follow us @firefinchbooks
firefinchpublishing.com